Travel Arrangements
Diane Drake

Copyright © 2016, Diane Drake

All rights reserved. This book or any portion thereof may not be reproduced or used in any manner whatsoever without the express written permission of the publisher except for the use of brief quotations in a book review.

ISBN-13: 978-1541005631
ISBN-10: 1541005635

Travel Arrangements is a work of fiction and though references are made to real places and people, I have manipulated some of the facts to fit the story.

Cover image by Reece Alan Photography. Printed in the United States of America.

CHAPTER 1

With the tips of her fingers, Gina Downing touched her forehead. Nothing. Knowing it was a lost cause, she tried again, this time with the inside of her wrist. *Cool as a cucumber.* At least that's what her mother would say.

"Darn it."

Half the comforter was bunched between her arms and the sheet was missing. Her feet were ice cold. Gina lay on her back to stare at the ceiling. She'd hardly slept and decided that the blame should rest squarely on the shoulders of the Dallas Independent School District and her mother's vigilante garden club.

"I don't want to go," Gina said.

"Uh huh," a muffled voice answered from inside a perfect cocoon of sheet and comforter that extended the full length of their bed.

From somewhere on the floor, Gina heard Sarge licking himself. The dog's wet strokes went on and on until she couldn't stand it anymore and finally threw her pillow hard in his direction. The groveling sounds shifted into high gear.

"Sargent! Stop!"

He did, but only for a second.

Gina untangled herself from the comforter and slid her feet into her moccasins. Grabbing a thick sweatshirt off the floor, she hurried inside it. October mornings in Dallas were chilly but it was still too soon to turn on the heat. It'd be hot by noon. Gina left her husband Blake to get a few more minutes of sleep but still let her heels clack loudly on the wood floors. The old dog, a mottled grey Keeshond, stayed close behind her.

Standing in the kitchen, Gina surveyed last night's dinner dishes still piled in the sink. She plugged in the coffee then filled the sink with soapy water, picked up the junk mail, hamburger wrappers and ketchup packets and started compiling supplies for a small backpack.

When the ads had first started appearing for the 2003 Texas State Fair, Gina had made an executive decision. That meant she made it by herself and without discussing it with Blake. She didn't want to bother him. She decided that it would be perfectly fine to let the Fair just pass the Downing family by. *Fly right over my doorpost, like the Angel of Death passing over the children of Israel,* she'd thought to herself. Besides, she'd continued the debate, her daughter's fourth birthday was coming up and she'd already planned the perfect party. They'd throw up a few strands of crepe paper, blow up some balloons, her mother would make the cake, they'd have everything at the condo.... Or something like that. Nice and simple and since she and Blake both worked full-time, she as a cop, he as an artist, *simple* was important.

Gina wasn't exactly sure why she dreaded the Fair so much but she had a pretty good idea. First, there was nothing simple about it. It was big and crowded and she could never seem to get her bearings. Instead, she stayed perpetually lost. Maps didn't help and peoples' directions were hopelessly wrong. "Head past the Midway and the exhibition halls. You can't miss it," they'd always say, but then she always did. Miss it.

After a few hours of wandering, lost, her feet hurting, Sammy grumpy and sunburned, Gina inevitably would turn on Blake and blame him for letting her spend twice what they'd agreed upon. All for the Fair experience of a few rides, a couple of corny dogs and a funnel cake. Maybe this year, if she just stayed quiet, the Fair would come and go and no one would ever know the difference.

But thanks to the school district, that's not what happened. Two weeks ago, she'd walked in the door of their condo after a stressful day trying to find evidence on a Dallas comptroller who'd been skimming profits when a streak of lightening ran toward her and attached itself to her legs. The little girl was waving something in the air like her soul was on fire.

"Mamma, Mamma, look what my teacher gave me! It's a ticket to the Fair and everyone got one!"

"Oh my goodness," Gina said, getting down on one knee with her precious child looking like she'd just discovered gold. "Let me see, Sammy."

"Can we go for my birthday, can we go for my birthday?"

"Oh, my! Well, that's a great idea!" Gina said. What she'd really meant to say was, 'Damn you, school board'.

"Why does my kitchen look like this?" Gina asked the empty room. Sarge slunk to his bed beneath the kitchen table and began licking himself. Gina funneled crumbs into her hand, frowned at a hardened mound of jelly, then noticed a stack of Sammy's coloring books that needed to go into the den because they belonged in a basket by the couch, not in the kitchen. Again, the dog followed.

"Okay, gang, from where I'm standing, I count six, that's SIX pairs of shoes! And if you're going to ignore the rule that we all agreed upon about NOT letting Sarge get up on the couch, then everyone needs to help keep these cushions rolled. There's dog hair everywhere." Hearing his name in that tone of voice, Sarge ambled stiffly back to the bedroom.

Gina ran the sticky roller over the cushions then went back into the kitchen, looking longingly at the coffee pot. First, she'd make a quick trip to the bathroom. The bed was empty, so Blake had left with the dog for Sarge's morning walk to the small green space behind the high-rise.

A few seconds later, Gina yelled, "Is there a law that says 'Only women can change the toilet paper?'"

She struggled to reach another roll, then heard her husband's happy whistle, followed by the sound of the front door closing. She and Blake were a perfect example that opposites attract. Even if he'd heard her complaining, her gentle husband would have smiled and asked what he could do to help. Just like the waded up comforter and perfect cocoon scene in the bedroom, Gina created storms while Blake remained a calm breeze. As her mother often reminded her, he made her look good. With this in mind, she replaced the empty roll.

Pouring two cups of coffee, Gina set one in front of Blake and then ripped open a blueberry Pop Tart. Crumbs fell from the corners of her mouth as she crammed one more glass into the dishwasher. She dutifully began spreading sunscreen on Sammy's arms, who by now had appeared fully clothed in Strawberry Patch regalia. This included the hat, the T-shirt, sunglasses, socks and a pink plastic watch.

"Are you mad, Mommy?" Sammy asked, her pale blue eyes looking worried while her arms were outstretched, trying to keep her balance.

Gina slowed down. Once everyone had had their breakfast and were loaded down with waters and hats, the family left for the Fair.

Blake drove while humming to the radio. Sammy seemed content to look at books in the back seat. Gina used the time to think. There were several possible scenarios ahead and she wanted to be prepared for them all. She glanced again at her backpack in the seat next to Sammy. Satisfied, she began massaging Blake's neck while watching the road ahead. Suddenly, the car erupted.

"The Texas Star!" Gina said, bolting upright and pointing at the Ferris wheel. "And look over there, Sammy, you can see the Cotton Bowl!"

"Where?" cried the little girl, straining against her seatbelt in the back. The women kept watch as Blake maneuvered them down the slope of the highway, then back up and when it crested, mother and daughter swiveled in their seats to get a better view. Gina reached over and took her daughter's hand. It was hard to tell, of the two, which one was more excited.

Blake took the next exit and right away there were flag-waving people lining both sides of the street, each one fighting for their attention. The Downing's car passed dozens until they were within a quarter-mile of the fairgrounds when Gina recognized a heavy set woman in a huge red T-shirt and shorts waving a giant Texas flag. Blake saw her, too, and pulled the SUV into a rut-filled front yard where a child not much older than Sammy guided them between two other cars with only inches to spare. Blake handed over a twenty dollar bill.

The Downings merged into a stream of people that stretched from sidewalk to sidewalk. Gina and Blake smiled at each other seeing the excitement in their daughter's eyes. It was pure joy and they felt it, too, the magic of the Fair as the family walked alongside complete strangers who smiled and moved over to include them.

Blake and Gina swung Sammy between them. The Strawberry Patch sneakers reached into the October sky and the skinny, double-jointed arms went crooked. The second she came back down, she made another running start, looking like a new-born giraffe, to do it all over again. Tall for her age, Samantha, Sammy to everyone except her grandmother, looked just like her father.

Blake, who had just moved to Dallas when Gina first spotted him, was huddled in a corner booth at Jackson's Bar with a beautiful woman who, she learned later, was his agent. He was a painter.

From the beginning, Gina felt like she could drown in his grey eyes and even after five years, she still had the irresistible urge to reach over and fix an untamable cowlick. She'd taken him on a tour of Dallas and discovered they were neighbors, and then, terrified, she'd let him meet her mother and the rest of her mother's garden club. Everyone liked him, but mostly they were happy that Gina had finally met someone.

Within a year, Gina and Blake got married, then pregnant, and were still living in Gina's old condo on the twelfth floor of a high-rise in downtown Dallas. It was only a few blocks from police headquarters where Gina worked, within walking distance to Sammy's pre-school and about fifteen minutes from her mother's house. Recently, Gina had been toying with the idea of trying to buy a house, but for now, life was good and the young thing they swung between them was the product of their yin and yang.

"Again!" Sammy demanded, pulling on their arms. Shocks of yellow hair - hers a stroke of watercolor, his like darkening sand on a cloudy day - fell across their faces where the one-sided dimple of both deepened.

"If we keep doing this we're never going to get there," Blake grunted.

"Last time, Monkey, then we pretend to be like normal people," Gina insisted, lifting and throwing in one swinging motion to send her daughter as high as she could possibly go.

Seconds later, Sammy shouted, "We're here, we're here!" and then she dropped her parents' hands and raced toward the ticket booths.

That's when Gina saw what she'd been looking for. She reached inside her small backpack and pulled out a child-size wrist guard and slid it over her left hand, wriggling her fingers into the black netted holes. She then twisted the guard so that the rigid metal was snuggly pressed over the ball of her hand. Blake noticed and rolled his eyes.

"You know those are for rollerblading, right?"

"I have a sore thumb."

"Sure you do."

"Wait a minute," Gina said, stopping at the entrance to the small parking lot tucked between storage buildings marked *Handicapped Parking Only*. A *Lot Full* sign hung on the chain-link fence.

"I need to do some research. You guys go on. I'll catch up with you in a minute."

"Oh, come on, Gina," Blake whined. "Here?"

"I told you, the Garden Club has a bee in their bonnets and the Captain has made it very clear that it is now my bee. I'll try to keep it short." Something about her smile told him what they both knew. It would take as long as it needed to take.

Blake, the man who could still make his wife go weak in the knees by just brushing back a stubborn cowlick, knew he was powerless to change her mind when it came to work, especially if it involved her mother's garden club. He swung Sammy up and onto his shoulders, holding on to her feet.

"Okay, but be careful. We'll wait for you at the base of Big Tex and if you're not there in half an hour, I'm calling the police."

Gina ignored the inside joke and took hold of her daughter's rubber shoes. She raised up on her tiptoes and still he had to meet her part way so that she could give him a kiss.

"I'll be careful," she promised, then backed up to look at Sammy.

"Bye, birthday girl. I love you. Have fun and I'll be right there."

Gina watched as father and daughter merged with the crowd, then turned her attention toward the lot. She stretched her neck muscles and loosened her shoulders. An ominous feeling came over her as she took in the parking lot's cracked concrete and pot holes. Dark Fair memories of strange ride operators and getting lost on the Midway and confusing maps and smashed corny dogs stirred somewhere inside her. Gina took a deep breath and walked into the lot.

CHAPTER 2

Gina felt it before she saw it. A dark car came up on her right side a third of the way into the lot. She kept her eyes straight. The car kept going, ignoring her as well as the sign at the entrance. At the end of the lot, it turned around and started back her way. As it passed her a second time, Gina lifted her brace-less hand and waved. Even though the dark tinted windows made it impossible to see inside, there was clearly a handicapped card hanging from the rearview mirror. Gina was pretty sure no one was waving back.

An ugly blackbird landed a few feet in front of her, cackling over a smashed corny dog. Its rounded beak looked like a piece of black ice and Gina tried not to break eye-contact as she walked in a wide arc around him.

By now, the sun had warmed up the morning and a breeze picked up a thin plastic bag, pulling it from beneath a car before flattening it against the side of an orange 280Z. Gina peered inside the sports car and spotted the handicapped card. She stood up and squinted against the sun.

Something wasn't right. There were way too many Mustangs and pumped up Chevy trucks in a lot meant for people unable to walk far. Something was definitely wrong.

Another car pulled into the lot. This one looked like it belonged.

"Doesn't anybody read," Gina muttered to herself.

The olive green car moved slowly but not suspiciously, bouncing like a pogo stick every time it hit a pothole. When it reached Gina, the car stopped and the window cranked down, revealing a smooth round face with Oriental eyes and silver-grey hair.

"Excuse me, but are ya' leavin'?" the woman asked in a strong accent.

"No, Ma'am, I'm sorry, I'm just passing through."

"Oh dear," said the old woman. "Do ya' know if there's another handicapped lot? I'm in a wheelchair and I'm too heavy for him to push me too far." Gina looked across at the driver. His hands were massaging the steering wheel at ten and two and he refused to look at her. It was obvious he didn't approve of his wife's asking for help.

Gina relaxed and let her right hand, the one without the wrist guard, lower from the small revolver nestled in an inside holster. "No ma'am, I don't."

"Darn it," the old woman said, using it like a cuss word. "I'm sorry. We tried ta' come yesterday but the lot was full then, too, so we thought we'd wait and try it today. We thought it mighta' been the weekend and then I thought sure to God it wouldn't be like that today since it's a Monday." She craned her neck and looked around. "Not one empty spot and it's not even a football game. It sure wasn't like this last year."

"My mother's been complaining a lot about the same thing, only not here. She says it's worse at the grocery store."

The woman's eyes lit up. "Her, too? And the mall! Those places are impossible."

"That's what my mother says."

"I guess we're all going to have to start using cabs but that's so expensive. Dallas must be getting old."

They shared a few more complaints and then the window went back up and the car bounced out of the lot.

Gina started thinking. So maybe it wasn't a coincidence. Maybe the garden club was right. Gina hadn't thought so two weeks ago when her mother had first come to her, complaining about how all of a sudden, handicapped parking stickers were everywhere.

"Everyone's mad," Claire Sessions had said to her daughter, the detective who would know that *everyone* meant all the members of the Hillcrest Heights Garden Club, "and the police need to do something about it."

"Like what, Mom, arrest disabled people?"

"No, Gina, those people aren't disabled! Mona and I parked outside the Albertson's on Friday and we watched several cars park in our handicapped spaces and they were definitely not handicapped. SueBee and Charlotte parked outside of WinLee's and they saw the exact same thing."

WinLee had been doing her mother's hair, as well as most of the other women in the garden club, for almost fifty years. The beauty shop was in the middle of their favorite shopping center in town. Unless you had a handicapped sticker, parking was a problem. A glut of handicapped stickers would be a travesty.

Gina tried not to sound bored.

"Mom, just report it to the grocery store. They can call it in. That's really not my department."

The garden club waited two days before they decided to take matters into their own hands. Claire, SueBee, Mona and Charlotte, who also happened to be founding members of the garden club, cancelled that month's program entitled *Cooking with Curry* and instead, met to come up with a plan.

Claire was assigned City Hall. She called her political friends who'd retired long ago but still had connections. Mona, the most powerful one of the bunch, called her next door neighbors. One was a retired U.S. Congressman and the other a Texas Senator, and since Charlotte and SueBee were the two most tactful ones of the bunch and already lived at The Village Retirement Center, they went after the Mayor's mother, also a resident.

Bingo! After a nice meal and a short nap, the mayor's mother called her son, who promised to contact the Chief of Police.

That had been on a Thursday. On Friday, as Gina was just about to leave for the weekend, the Captain tapped on her door and entered with a file.

"Your mother's garden club is up to something, Downing. The Chief said his mother got," then he stopped to read, "'an inside tip'." He tossed the yellow folder onto her desk. It slid within millimeters of the edge. "What do you know about this?"

Gina didn't reach for the folder, thinking that if she'd only left five minutes earlier she'd already be in her car and on her way home.

"Actually, my mother did mention something about that a few days ago. I guess they decided to look into it themselves. Obviously."

"Well, now the Mayor knows and he's concerned about the lack of *handicapped parking*. If your mother and her friends have gotten into some kind of trouble like last time...." Gina interrupted him.

"No, Sir, I'm sure there's a simple answer. I'll talk to Mom."

"Too late. You're going to investigate. In the meantime, tell them they can carpool to church."

Gina hesitated. "Sir, this sounds like the City Manager's problem to me. I'll call City Hall and tell Transportation they obviously need to reserve more spots."

Her boss smiled. "Again, the mod squad already thought of that. According to the Mayor's mother, her sources have learned that the City does not think it's their problem. In fact, they said they've issued fewer stickers than ever. They told her the spots that are out there should be more than enough."

"So is someone making fake stickers?"

The Captain shrugged. "Good question."

Gina tried one more time. "I know it's my mom, but shouldn't this go to someone downstairs?"

"What are you working on now?"

"A skimming job and some robocalls."

"Well, the Mayor's *mother* isn't having a problem with robocalls. I don't even think she can hear. It also doesn't matter that she doesn't drive but she claims that if we don't investigate, the city must be discriminating against the elderly. We don't discriminate, do we Sessions?"

"No Sir, we don't." He'd used her maiden name so she knew the subject was closed.

Gina picked up the folder. "Okay. But don't forget, I'm off Monday. Blake and I are taking Sammy to the Fair for her birthday."

The Captain's face immediately softened.

"It's Sammy's birthday? Of course, take the day," he said, then added, "but do some research while you're there."

Gina stood in the middle of the handicapped parking lot, looking lost. The morning breeze had disappeared. She wiped her damp forehead and reset her ball cap then fanned her T-shirt against her chest and headed for a strip of shade beneath a horror movie trunk of a tree. She figured she had about ten more minutes before Blake and Sammy would start missing her. Thankfully, she didn't have to wait long.

They were coming from the direction of the Fair - two couples, sauntering down the middle of the parking lot. The men walked like they were full of beer and she caught a glint of sun reflecting off of a steel-tipped boot. Their shirts flapped open, showing off white muscle shirts. The women walked between them, giggling and stumbling in their high heels, their arms full of stuffed animals. One held onto a giant Tweety Bird. No one walked with a limp.

The couples stopped at a metallic red firebird with spinners and a license plate that read JAILBRD. When one of the men put his hand on the car door, Gina emerged from the shade.

"Excuse me, but are any of you handicapped?"

The question startled them.

The taller one recovered first. He puffed up a bit and then he drew in his arms to make sure she saw the sleeve tattoos. For a moment, Gina marveled at his thick black hair, slicked back and stiff.

"What?" His eyes looked angrily over her body.

Gina let them. Normally, she wore navy suits and hose but today she had on her favorite orange Bermuda shorts and a ball cap. Blake had told her she looked like a zoo keeper but she thought it made her look younger than her thirty-eight years. Not knowing how to dress had its advantages.

Gina waited patiently while the guy measured her small frame and skinny white legs.

His face broke into a smile.

"I'm not asking for me," Gina blurted out, keeping her voice shaky. "My boss told me to bring him one of those handicapped sticker thingies, or he'll…" She didn't finish the sentence, but nodded toward the front of the car. "He says I should figure out where to get them. I mean, you got one and you aren't handicapped, right?"

"Who says I don't have a condition?" stammered the other guy. "You want one, you go get your own. Or get some blue cardboard and some scissors."

The girls thought that was funny.

"Sure, sure," said Gina. "But I'll give you fifty dollars for it."

"Seriously?" said one of the girls.

"Get outta' here," growled the stiff-haired guy.

The other girlfriend shifted Tweety Bird to her hip and pushed around him. "Cash?"

"Forget it, Della, I'm not selling my sticker."

"But fifty bucks? That's a ton more than what you paid for it. You can get another one."

"Shut up!"

Gina said, "I'll give you fifty for just a name. Forget the sticker. I just need a name and I'll go get my own."

"Boy, you are stupid," said the man. "I'm not talking about this. Get in the car." He pushed his girl toward the car door but she jerked her arm away.

"Hey, don't do that. Tell her where you got it, Felix. She wants a sticker. What's wrong with making a little money?"

"Shut-up," Felix said. "I don't know her."

Gina pulled out a wad of cash from her back pocket and held it toward the girl. "I'll give you a hundred for the card and a name."

"Whoa," said the other woman, her eyes widening.

Gina noted a green snake tattoo covering tall guy's forearm as he suddenly grabbed the money.

"Thanks, now leave," he said with a satisfied grin.

Without breaking eye contact, Gina centered her core over both feet, raised her right arm, dropped her left, then twisted slightly to her left and focused on channeling every ounce of her small frame into the hand that was coming around in a wide swing. The centrifugal force took care of the rest. The metal wrist guard landed at the base of his jaw. With her other hand, she grabbed his wrist and flipped him over like a pancake, pressing him against the car. At the same time, she pushed aside her backpack to give the others a peek at her badge.

"Okay, no more chit-chat. It's my daughter's birthday and she's waiting for me to take her on the Ferris wheel so give me a name and that handicapped sticker and maybe I'll let you keep the money."

Tweety Bird girl started talking. "His name is Xavier."

"Write it down." Gina handed her a small notebook with a tiny pencil.

"Now give me the sticker."

The other girl reached in and grabbed the handicapped sticker and handed it to her. Gina got off the guy. He stumbled to the side, rubbing his jaw.

"On behalf of the Dallas PD, thank you for your help in this matter." Gina waved the card and moved backward to a safe distance.

"And don't take up any more handicapped spots. My mother is sick and tired of not having a place to park." Then she reached over and while the guy was still rubbing his jaw, she took back the cash.

"On second thought, I think I'll keep the money. You have no idea how expensive it is to bring a kid to the Fair."

The car's tires sent up a spray of broken gravel as it fishtailed out of the lot, its spinners blazing in the sun's reflection. Gina waited a few minutes to make sure they hadn't had second thoughts about running her over. She put the wrist guard, handicapped sticker and notepad back in the backpack and started sprinting toward **Big Tex**. As she ran, she turned over her hand and stretched out the fingers. Her palm was a little sweaty but nothing hurt, not even a little.

CHAPTER 3

"We're going to be late," said Claire.

"We're not going to be late. I told them we'd be there between eleven and eleven-thirty," said Mona. "It's only eleven now."

"Are you taking Northwest Highway the whole way?"

"I thought I would."

"Did you know that at Rawlings you can take that side-street and miss the light?"

"Yes, I know."

"Just making sure."

Once they'd covered the directions, an awkward silence descended over best friends Claire Sessions and Mona Johnson. Both were close to eighty, Mona just shy, and Claire a little bit past.

"Where are we going again?" Claire asked.

"The Lakewood Independent Living Forum."

The Lakewood Forum could be seen from miles around. It was a four-star facility with a beautiful view of a man-made lake that shimmered in the distance. It would have made a lovely backdrop for a TV commercial. There was usually a nice breeze and often a flock of egrets could be seen floating over the high grasses. Also, there was a narrow bike trail that wound its way along the water's edge. The brochures described it as pastoral. It was the perfect setting for a retirement home.

Based on their body language, the women were like two slow-burning embers. Beginning with tiny facial movements under powdered skin, Claire tended toward sighing while Mona adjusted her white-knuckled grip of the steering wheel. Claire cleared her throat and Mona responded with a sniff before looking left and right.

Claire blamed herself. She'd accepted Mona's invitation to lunch even though she didn't want to, but Mona didn't take no for an answer. When she made up her mind about something, that was the way it had to be and somehow, she was always able to wrangle Claire into agreeing. To be honest, Mona usually had pretty good ideas, and yes, they usually were better ideas than anyone else's, but then Mona had ideas about everything, especially once she got wind of a problem. It didn't even have to be a big problem. One time Claire mentioned that she didn't know what she was going to do with her leftovers. It was hardly even a problem, but Mona spent thirty minutes telling her three different ways to handle leftovers.

"I don't know why you scheduled me for another lunch," Claire erupted. "I could have gone to the Fair with Samantha. And just in case you hadn't noticed, I'm tired of visiting old folks' homes."

"What a surprise," said Mona.

"I told you, I like living by myself. I like my own little house. Gina doesn't think I need to move."

"That's because Gina doesn't know how many times you've fallen and if you don't stop arguing with me, Claire, I'm going to tell her. Try to think of it as a free lunch."

"One time."

"Three."

"Three? You can't count that time I fell off the chair. I just misjudged where it was." Mona was probably right about the other two.

"Three."

"Hummpf," said Claire, crossing her arms.

In a smooth move, Mona picked up speed and passed a creeping Buick. Claire didn't drive much these days and hardly ever at night. Little things had been happening. Things like trouble backing up and mini-panic attacks on crowded freeways. She looked at her friend, so completely confident. She was only a few years younger than Claire. Mona wasn't finished.

"Your house is too far from me and if you ever had an emergency, who knows how long it would take me to get there. I know it's at least twenty minutes from Gina and Blake's. She's got crazy hours and Sammy's getting older so you can't expect Gina to be able to check on you." Mona stopped to take a breath before adding, "and you never know when the next fall might be and you know what they say happens to people our age. You fall, you die."

Claire was appalled. "That's the last time I tell you I've fallen, especially if you're going to use it against me."

The two friends went back to having this conversation in their heads.

Claire hated the word *Independent*. *Independent Living*. It sounded like a platitude. Who were they trying to kid? She'd seen enough to know that someone was always telling you what you could and could not do. The food at the Lakewood was alright and one ordered from a menu, but it still was like all the other places. She'd never feel at home at The Lakewood, even if it was *Independent*.

"If you could just pick one, Claire, we wouldn't have to do this," Mona said, interrupting her thoughts. "I still don't know why you don't want to be at The Village with SueBee and Charlotte. You'd have so much fun."

"Then you move there. Have you seen the rooms? They're tiny little cracker boxes and if you turn around in place, you've seen everything. And the bathrooms! They don't even come with a tub. I'm used to soaking my feet every once in a while."

"Being able to soak your feet is not what you base a decision on, Claire, and no matter where you end up, you're going to have to downsize. The whole point is to find a simpler and safer place. I'm sorry, honey, but it's our turn to get old. You might as well do it while you've still got your marbles."

"I don't see you *downsizing*," mumbled Claire. *Downsizing*. Another buzz word she didn't like.

They drove the rest of the way in silence. Mona parked in a handicapped spot and came around to help Claire. She held out a hand but Claire waved her away. Mona kept her ground to make her point and Claire made hers by refusing to bring her cane. She didn't care what Mona said, she was going to leave it in the car.

The front doors opened and closed automatically after them. The ladies stood for a moment, gazing up at the high ceilings of the Forum. There were several couches and floral decorations in fall colors dotted the coffee tables. Claire counted two fireplaces and even though it was warm outside, the gas flames were a nice touch.

By now, their entrance had attracted some attention. Their audience had stopped what they were doing to stare at the two visitors. Claire immediately lifted her chin, raised her eyebrows and walked straight to the front desk. Mona had to hurry to keep up.

The receptionist greeted them warmly. She made a quick phone call and a beautiful, middle-aged woman appeared from around the corner.

"Hello, ladies, I'm Susan, so nice to have you here today." The marketing director had a beautiful smile with big white teeth and dark red lipstick. Claire liked her right away but tried not to show it. She wasn't too young to be trusted and stayed a comfortable distance in front of them as they walked along a wide breezeway decorated with artwork toward the dining room. Her voice was pleasing to the ear, but more importantly, she talked loud enough for Claire to hear.

"Three please, Lisa," Susan said to the hostess.

Lisa led them to a table by a window that overlooked the lake. While waiting for their food, they talked about the view and Claire guessed in her head if it would be curly fries, sweet potato fries, crinkle-cut fries, French fries or polenta that tasted like French fries.
    "Most of our rooms have a view," Susan offered, "with a slight premium, of course."
    "Of course," Mona repeated.
    After lunch, Susan suggested they go look at a room.
    "Is this the largest apartment you have?" asked Claire, referring to the model.
    "I know what you're thinking, Mrs. Sessions, 'Where in the world am I going to put all my pretty things?' Trust me, everyone feels the exact same way but it always works out. And don't forget, the most important thing is who do you want to live with, and I can promise you that we have the most wonderful people living at The Forum. Several have already been asking about you and they're all hoping you decide to live here."
    "Umph," Claire responded.
    Susan continued to read her mind. "I know you're probably thinking about your house, aren't you? It's probably one that you've been in for many, many years?"
    Claire nodded.
    "And you have a lot of memories and feelings for that house, am I right?"
    Claire shrugged.
    "Well, I understand. But moving to the Forum doesn't mean you'll lose those memories, Mrs. Sessions. You'll always have them. You'll just be making new ones. The Lakewood Forum will be a place where you can make those new memories. And don't forget, Mrs. Sessions, you do get your own personal storage closet in the basement."
    "She's good," Claire whispered into Mona's ear.
    "As of right now," Susan continued, indicating the apartment they were in, "I'm not sure how many rooms of this size are still available, but if you'd like, you can put down a deposit and we can hold it for you while you're trying to decide."
    Claire walked to the window. "I think I'd like to sleep on it. Besides, I believe I left my checkbook at home."
    "How convenient," said Mona.
    Back in the car, Mona put on her seatbelt with a heavy click. She waited while Claire put on hers.
    "Nice lunch," said Claire pleasantly.
    Mona was in no mood to be pleasant.

"What's it going to take to get you out of that house?" Mona asked. "A broken hip? In that case, it'll be me and Charlotte and SueBee who'll have to take turns sitting with you in that hospital. There'll be six weeks of rehab and then you'll probably have to go *back* into the hospital because everyone gets pneumonia when they're our age. Then more rehab and that's when you'll probably die and then *I'll* have to plan your funeral and do the reception. Please don't make me do that." Mona was fuming.

"For pity's sake, Mona."

Claire stared out her window. They might as well just put her down like an old dog. She'd tried to imagine her life without a garden or her yellow shed out back with all her tools and flower pots, but she couldn't. There wouldn't be room for her cedar chest that held her mother's quilts and Gina's baby clothes. She'd been saving them for Gina because she didn't have room for the chest, either. Just because a person got old, were they suddenly supposed to be able to fit their life into a storage closet in the basement?

Claire realized they were already back in her neighborhood. A young mother pushed a baby stroller and the little boy named Kenny was being lifted into a swing by his mother. That's when it came to her.

"Mona?" Claire said softly, her voice ending on a high note.

"What?"

"Can I move in with you?" Her heart was pounding.

"Claire?"

"Yes?"

"Absolutely not."

"But why not? You have such a big house. It's gargantuan. It should be illegal for just one person to live in a house that big. If I lived there, you'd probably never see me. I'd pay you rent and there'd be room for so many of my things so I wouldn't have to get rid of everything. And, and, and, you're no spring chicken, either. We could watch out for each other. I bet Ruby would love taking care of both of us."

Mona refused to look at her.

Claire felt the pressure building behind her eyes and instantly they began to water. She blinked rapidly, trying to stop them. Mona hated tears but her old friend looked so cold and her angular jaw was moving ever so slightly. Claire wished she could be strong but a tear escaped and began tracing down her cheek.

"Please don't take this personally, Claire, you're my dearest friend, but I don't think that's a solution. I think we would positively kill each other."

"Well, according to you, I'm going to die anyway." Claire kept staring. How could she say no? Couldn't she see how hard this was for her? She thought her friend knew her better than anyone else in the world, even better than her own daughter so why was she making this so hard?

Claire looked at the familiar houses. She dabbed at her eyes. They were almost home and now Mona was going to make her decide on the last place she would probably live. She glanced again at Mona's face and there was something sad about it.

"Okay, whatever you think is best," she said, barely above a whisper.

"I'm sorry," said Mona, "but I'm sure it would be I that would get on your nerves, dear, not the other way around. I personally drove Cleeve crazy at times. And oh, seriously, Claire, stop being so sad. I'm not an easy person to live with. And ever since Cleeve's been gone, I'm sure I've gotten worse."

"It's alright," Claire said, "I know you're doing this for me." She buried herself deeper into her seat and dug into her purse for a tissue. Mona's car pulled to a stop. She was home.

In silence, they both looked at the cream-colored brick home where Claire had lived for over twenty-five years. Her fall garden was in full bloom. The small rectangles of grass were a deep blue-green, neatly raked and there were marigolds with golden yellow heads and mountain sage edging the sidewalk. At the door were pots of various sizes that overflowed with translucent potato vine, verbena and Mexican sunflower. The house was welcoming her with open arms. Claire put her hand on the door handle.

"I guess it's time," she said softly.

"I'm sorry," whispered her friend.

The air was thick with longing.

"Oh, alright," Mona sighed loudly. "If that's what it takes to get you to move somewhere safe, then yes, you can come live with me. But don't forget, if you end up hating it, remember, I told you so."

"Really?" Claire cried. "Are you sure?"

"I just said so, didn't I?"

"Oh, thank you, Mona, thank you! I am so happy," Claire beamed. Mona still held tightly to the steering wheel so she knew it wasn't time to give her a hug or anything like that.

"Thank you, sweet friend. I promise, this won't change a thing. We're going to live happily ever after."

CHAPTER 4

It was seven forty-five in the morning and Gina was already at her desk. She barely touched the bridge of her nose and it hurt. Sammy had inherited her father's skin and turned brown like a piece a toast the first day of summer. Gina, however, glowed like a light bulb anytime she was in the sun for more than fifteen minutes.

A box in the bottom left hand corner of her computer screen was blinking, telling her it was still searching. Seconds earlier she'd typed in 'XAVIER', the name she'd gotten from the Tweety bird girl.

No Results.

The phone rang. Because of the hour, Gina already knew who it was.

"Hi, Mom."

"What about the program at the Woman's Club on Thursday?" There were no pleasantries like *'Hello, Gina', or 'Good Morning, Gina, this is your mother speaking'*. Claire Sessions got directly to the point.

"Can you go?"

"I don't know what you're talking about, Mom. I think you forgot to invite me."

"Oh. Well, it's this Thursday. The former Secretary to the former Naval Commander at the Pentagon who was involved in that hostage rescue mission back in '85 is going to be the speaker at the Woman's Club. I have a table and it'll be me, Mona, SueBee and Charlotte and the girls. I was hoping you could come." The pronoun *girls* meant the daughters of the aforementioned friends, the second generation of the four founding members of The Hillcrest Heights Garden Club, a Dallas (some would say sacred) institution.

"I don't think I can go, Mom, but thank you."

"Are you sure? It's going to be such a good program and the other girls will be there."

"Mom, I have work. I can't just take a long lunch whenever there's a good program at the Woman's Club."

"Can't you work it into a stake-out or something? I bet the Captain wouldn't mind if you told him who the speaker was going to be. Oh," she interrupted herself, "there was something else I wanted to talk to you about. Tell me about the Fair. Did Sammy have fun?"

"She had a great time. We both got…"

"Are you sure you can't go?" she asked again. They were now back to the first subject. Gina shifted easily, used to the back and forth of her mother's mind.

"I'm sure."

"Oh, alright. I guess we'll have an empty chair. It's too late to find someone else."

The line was quiet for a second. "What time?" Gina asked.

"Oh, I'm so glad. It's going to be crowded so try to get there by ten forty-five. SueBee and I are going to get there early to save seats but that's against the Club's rules so don't be late. I'm not sure how long we can get away with saving them."

Gina genuinely loved her mother's garden club friends and on some days, she thought she loved them more than her own mother. She'd known them her whole life, but sometimes…, and this was where Gina usually closed her eyes and took several cleansing breaths, *sometimes, sometimes,* she wished they'd slow down. They were all circling eighty and still kept their calendars full.

Just last month, Gina had let the mothers talk her into joining them for their annual 'Shop Til You Drop' bus tour around Dallas. Gina had assumed that meant they'd be done no later than four o'clock and had taken a day of vacation. She'd hoped to get some things done at home, like steam clean her carpets before dinner. But no one ever dropped! They kept going and going, from store to store until finally, when it was getting dark and the bus driver kept looking at his watch, Gina thought, 'Surely, they're ready to drop'. But then someone told the driver to head for a little-known consignment store that stayed open until eight. That's when Gina begged the driver to please let her off at the next gas station so that Blake could come and pick her up.

The Hillcrest Heights Garden Club had begun in 1955 when Claire and her three best friends had graduated from SMU, married their sweethearts-soon to be lawyers, produced at least one child each and decided that they desperately needed something more challenging than bridge to stimulate their minds. They picked gardening because no one knew anything about it. In order to be a real garden club, they borrowed a constitution, elected officers and enlisted SueBee's aunt, a master gardener and drill-sergeant of a mentor, to help them. In short order they'd worked their way up to becoming one of the premier garden clubs in Texas.

This was what the daughters had to deal with. Fast forward to 1998. That's when the daughters finally agreed to follow in their footsteps, which meant carrying on such traditions as the family picnic at Mona's ranch and participating in the annual flower show which included awarding each other large pieces of engraved silver bestowed on them by the elderly club. Who had picked their name was still a subject of controversy, but other than that, the Junior Group of The Hillcrest Heights Garden Club was a source of joy. The mothers made it clear that they were already eyeing their granddaughters as the third generation of gardeners.

Gina stared at the blinking light on her computer, then called the only person she knew who might know how to find Xavier. They arranged to meet for lunch at a Tex-Mex restaurant on the west side of town. Gina was already waiting in a booth when she arrived.

Lucy was a proud woman. She wore a billowing moo-moo covered in modern splashes of flowers of turquoise and green and as soon as she could work herself into the booth, she began dipping chips into a bowl of chunky salsa.

"Hi, Gina."

"Hi, Lucy."

"You ordered?"

"I was waiting for you."

A waitress stopped at their table.

"I'll have a full order of the beef fajitas," said Lucy without looking at a menu, "and don't be shy with the jalapenos."

"Fish tacos, please." Gina waited for the waitress to leave before passing a piece of paper across the table.

"Do you know this guy?"

Lucy chewed as she read the name.

"Hmmm, yep. Steven's been around forever. Both my nephews worked for him, when they weren't doing time. I don't like him."

"Why not?"

"He's that guy that waits until you've turned over the two thousand puzzle pieces and separated all the edges then comes over and puts it together. Steven does what's best for Steven."

"Do you know where I can find him?"

"He used to be at this warehouse over by the fairgrounds. I actually think he owns it, maybe even lives there. He's a good-looking old coot," Lucy wiggled her eyebrows. "He looks just like that 'stay thirsty, my friend' man in the commercials."

"So Xavier is Steven? You sure?"

"Don't ask me why. Adds to the mystique. It's Steven alright."

"How old is he?"

"Late sixties, maybe seventy. What's he done?"

"I'm pretty sure he's making fake handicapped parking stickers. He's seventy?"

Lucy smiled, licking grains of salt from her top lip before answering. "Sounds like Steven. Non-violent but very creative. By the way, how's the kid?"

"Which one?"

"The baby, of course."

Gina's face softened into a motherly glow as she took her first chip, scooping up a full load of salsa. "Sammy's four now. She goes three days a week to a sweet little school near the condo. She loves it," Gina added proudly.

"Does she love blueberries like her Momma?"

"Worse. Kiwis. The one fruit even more expensive than blueberries. She's going to be an artist when she grows up."

"Oh yeah? And you know this how?"

"All she wants to do is draw. She told me her favorite color is 'clear' and the other day I heard her ask Blake, 'if red means stop and green means go, what does brown mean?' Isn't that amazing?"

"Amazing."

The food arrived and Gina began separating her tacos. She put the shredded lettuce into one pile then made a small mound of the chopped tomatoes. The shredded chicken made a third. Per her request, the cheese had been brought on the side. Next, Gina took the taco shell, broke it in half and started piling on a small portion of each of the ingredients.

"Why do you do that? Take it apart and then put it back together?"

"I like it this way."

"Man, I'd say you had a control issue."

When they had finished, Gina paid the bill and the two women walked outside into the sunshine. Lucy's car was parked in a handicapped space. Gina looked longingly at the beautiful blue Cadillac with its white landau top.

"That's a gorgeous car," said Gina.

"Thanks," said Lucy. "She's my baby. I wipe her down every day. No one messes with this car but me."

Lucy got behind the wheel then rolled down her window.

"Thanks for lunch."

"You're welcome. Thanks for the info."

Lucy waved it off. "I didn't tell you anything you wouldn't have found out eventually. Steven can take care of himself."

Gina checked the directions she'd written on a napkin. She called in her location and headed toward the fairgrounds. She passed trendy coffee shops and restaurants, then gradually, the neighborhood became more blue-collar with rising warehouses in uniform grey. It was a familiar part of town.

Gina had been on the force only a couple of years when the Captain finally said he felt like the rookie was ready for undercover. It's what she wanted, he reminded her. She'd spent her first two years on patrol trying to prove how tough she was, a challenging task considering she and her partner spent most of their time writing parking tickets and speaking at neighborhood watch meetings. Gina had let the Captain know she was hungry for more.

Now, she let the SUV coast past the windowless blocks of cement known for cheap manufacturing. At a red light, she rolled down her window and listened to the sounds of the freeway not far away. Her eyes locked on the corner up ahead. It had been the stage where she'd almost played her final role as an undercover cop. Now it was just a bus stop sign, a light pole, and a shuttered bar.

She spent two years undercover, long enough to bury what had become a manageable fear, no longer throwing up before work, dressing in black leather and chains, ready to gyrate with her best moves. Part of her loved the acting, the control, the impending capture. Every second could be electric, talking to scumbags who thought they were about to get lucky until she'd throw them against a car and pull out the cuffs.

But two years was enough and they were going to move her out. No more dressing up like a hooker or sitting in bars or standing on street corners. She would be working in an office and talking to people without pretending to be someone else. But she had one more shift.

They'd been looking for a particularly angry client, a mean John, one who was suspected of kidnapping the ladies and making them disappear. Gina concentrated, as she walked cat-like along the sidewalk and waited at the street corner.

Gina remembered glancing at her partner who was sitting safely in their car. He'd given her the nod that said she wasn't in any danger, then the traffic started to pick up and Gina had begun stretching her long legs toward the Cadillacs and BMWs that appeared out of nowhere. Suddenly, all Hell broke loose and she was on her own.

A car screeched to a stop, jumping the sidewalk until it was only a few feet away and a crazy man jumped out. He was wild from drinking or drugs or both. He waved a gun, screaming at her and anyone else who happened to have wandered out of the bar, and then he started shooting wildly in the air. Gina pulled her own gun from inside a boot and yelled for him to stop and then, she remembered very clearly, they stared at one another and she remembered feeling like she was facing death.

Suddenly, Gina lost her balance. She heard four or five bursts of gunfire all at the same time, and as she hit the ground, there was a searing pain in her shoulder. She remembered the kick of her own gun and seeing the man as he jerked backward. She survived, he didn't.

Gina looked away from the corner and studied the napkin again. Eventually, she found the building. It was a lonely three-storied warehouse, its windows painted over and a black stallion on the door. Parking was behind a chain link fence topped with razor wire but she parked on the street in front. She could feel the heat rising off the concrete as she banged on the door. It echoed inside and then suddenly the door opened and an older man with movie-star good looks stood in front of her.

"Ms. Sessions, I presume?" he asked with the bearing of a Spanish aristocrat.

"It's Downing," she corrected him. "I'm with the Dallas PD, may I come in?"

"I'm sorry, Officer Downing. Lucy called me and I thought she said Sessions and yes, please, come in."

Immediately, she saw that the place was empty.

"What can I do for you?"

"Should I call you Steven or Xavier?"

He laughed. "Please, call me Steven. I just use Xavier when I'm in unknown waters. It has a bit more of a sinister sound, don't you think?"

Gina ignored him. Looking around, it was obvious the cavernous space had been stripped clean of everything except for some tables and a few pieces of paper that now lay scattered on the floor. A few piles of thick electrical cords were still there. Whoever had been there had left in a big hurry.

Steven waited for her to finish her observations, then said, "Please, come this way."

Gina's professional eyes continued to sweep back and forth as she followed him through the cavernous space. Eventually they arrived at a corner office, enclosed in glass and even though they were alone, he closed the door behind them. A single desk of a modern style still sat in the middle. It was without drawers and on it lay a leather briefcase and a small bonsai tree. Steven sat on the edge of the desk while Gina remained standing. There were no chairs.

"Now, what can I do for you, Officer?"

"Detective. Where is everyone?"

"Everyone?"

"The people who work here - from the size of this place, I'd say you had at least fifty, maybe a hundred people working here."

"Possibly. I was never very good at keeping records. But as you can see, there's no one here now. I'm so sorry you've wasted your time. I'm surprised Lucy didn't tell you."

"It must have slipped her mind. What sort of business were you in?"

"Greeting cards."

"Uh huh. Are you leaving, too?"

"Actually, I was on my way out just as you arrived. You know, the economy is so bad. I thought this would be a good time to regroup. I'll miss Dallas very much but I'll keep the building - rent it out to some new age church. I think it's a good investment, don't you agree?"

"Where did you say you were going?"

"I didn't but somewhere further south."

"Mexico?"

He laughed out loud. "Mexico! Oh no, but that's funny. Not that far south." His face became serious. "Now, is there anything else? I'm ready to turn out the lights."

As he spoke, Steven wet his thumb and tenderly wiped the dust off of several of the leaves on the tiny bonsai tree. He surprised her by ceremonially holding it out for her to take.

At first, she didn't take it.

"What do you know about people making fake handicapped parking stickers?"

"What? Absolutely nothing."

"So if I brought in some people and we did a real good search of this place, we wouldn't find anything resembling little blue cards?"

"It's clean as a whistle. Like I said, I'm hoping to find a good tenant."

Gina turned to face him. "So whatever was here is gone for good?"

"Gone for good. Here, Detective, I want you to have this," he said, handing her the plant. This time she took it.

"Take good care of it. Like many things in life, you can ignore it for days but not forever."

Gina followed Steven back outside. He waited for her to get in her car, and waited as she put carefully the plant on the seat beside her.

"I'm sorry I couldn't be more helpful," Steven said, stepping back.

As Gina pulled away, she watched the pasted on smile disappear in her rearview mirror. She began to smile herself, glancing at the bonsai tree. There was a distinct thumb print on one of the waxy leaves, courtesy of Mr. Xavier.

Later that night, after dinner and once Sammy had been tucked in bed, Gina collapsed on the couch and nestled her back into her husband's solid body, covering herself with one of her mother's many crocheted Afghans. Naturally, Blake began massaging her head with strong fingers from one hand while switching channels on the TV with the other.

Sarge nestled his head on the couch next to her and looked up at her with soulful eyes. Next, he put both front legs on the cushion, waiting for any sign of disapproval, then gradually inched the rest of his body on the couch. Sarge circled several times, then plopped down with a sigh, his front paws draped over Gina's covered feet. The final victory came when she laid a hand across his head. As Blake massaged her, she massaged the dog.

Sarge had been named for one of Blake's favorite artists, John Singer Sargent. The dog was like a mind-reader, nestling against Blake after a discouraging art show or waiting patiently by his side while he struggled to finish a painting. When Gina entered his life, Sarge seemed to switch sides and began to follow her around, practically glued to her side.

Now twelve, Sarge had arthritis in his hips and preferred sleeping over playing. Still, he would growl at strangers in guard dog mode, then return to his bed, satisfied that he had done his duty. Blake was convinced he would die for them, Gina not so much.

Gina was just about to tell Blake about her day when he started in on his.

"Sammy's teacher stopped me in car lines today," Blake said, letting his strong painter's fingers rub deep into her scalp. Gina whimpered. "She said she noticed we hadn't signed up yet for the Fall Carnival."

"Rats," Gina moaned, "first the Fair, now the Carnival. Don't these people have a life? I don't care. Sign us up for anything. No, wait, not the photo booth. I can't stand watching teenagers act like idiots in a locker."

Gina wriggled deeper against Blake, barely hearing the drone of the sports guy on TV and wishing she could be carried to bed. She wrapped her arms around herself. Thoughts of Steven had gone. It was too early to go to bed, but she could so go to sleep, right there on the couch, if only she could just lie there for a few more uninterrupted minutes.

"You feel so good," Gina said.

"Are you talking to me or the dog?"

Gina smiled to herself. He was doing it. He knew if he made her laugh, the odds of getting her in the mood doubled.

"You, of course."

"I'm never sure."

Gina giggled and turned her face up to look at him, once again swelling at the pleasure it gave her.

"Well, then, I guess I better make sure you know who I'm talking about."

Blake kissed her deeply. She felt him reaching into her, pulling her into himself. She forgot about anything else. They kissed until Blake let her go.

"Sexy momma," he said, then asked, "and how was your day?"

"It was okay. I followed up on that handicapped parking scam. I found the guy I think is running it, but just barely. He'd already cleared out his warehouse. Mom and her friends aren't going to be happy but now that he's left Dallas, I'm hoping I can close it."

He kissed her again.

"Congratulations, Officer Downing."

"It's Detective Downing to you," she said, wrapping his lips in hers.

CHAPTER 5

Gina arrived at the Woman's Club and took the empty seat between her mother and SueBee who immediately leaned over and squeezed her shoulders. Her mother's friend was wearing a pale blue sweater dress that matched her slightly cloudy eyes. Also at the table were Charlotte and her daughter Brooke, SueBee's daughter Helen, and Mona and her daughter-in-law Sheralyn.

"Late as always. Sorry," said Gina.

"Oh, you're not," said SueBee.

A luncheon plate appeared in front of her and immediately her mother picked up her fork to signal everyone to begin.

Gina unrolled her silverware and draped the champagne colored linen napkin over her lap. She was relieved to see that she was appropriately dressed in a dark A-line dress and flats.

"You cut your hair," her mother said. Gina instinctively reached up where the ends used to be. "I'm sorry you missed the program. Rosemary did a talk on all the Presidents."

Besides being a descendant of a famous family, Rosemary Rothschild was also brilliant and very unlike her sophisticated and very proper audiences. Her grey hair travelled where it wanted and she wore layers of mismatched clothes and jewelry. But everyone loved her and tried to book her at least once a year, not just because her research was legendary but because she had an irreverent sense of humor that no one else was brave enough to admit. After one of her talks, people left with a greater appreciation for whatever subject she spoke on, whether it was art, literature, history, or politics and at least one new off-colored joke. Rosemary was a renaissance woman long before people even knew what that meant.

"What happened to the spy guy?" asked Gina.

Mona answered, correcting her, "he was the Naval officer in charge of the hostage crisis and he contracted that Asian flu. Thank goodness the program committee was able to get Rosemary. She was very funny, though I think I've heard that talk before." SueBee nodded.

"So, girls, how is everything going with preparations for your flower show? It's coming up, isn't it?" Charlotte asked.

Now that the mothers had 'passed the baton' to their daughters' Garden Club, they kept a close eye on how well the girls were doing in carrying on their traditions.

"The flower show is the week after Thanksgiving," said Gina.

"Do you need any help?" asked Claire. "I have a wonderful luncheon menu with pumpkin soup and a crabmeat mousse."

"No thanks, Mom, we're good," said Gina.

"What's your theme?" SueBee asked.

"Fantasy and Fairy Tales," answered Brooke.

Charlotte beamed over a forkful of strawberry salad. "I love that!"

SueBee turned to her daughter. "What's your fairy tale, Helen?"

She laughed. "I have no idea. It's still a few weeks away. I usually wait until the last minute."

"Gina, have you picked yours?"

"No, not yet."

The mothers shared a concerned look. It was obvious they were thinking of what their own preparations for a flower show had been like. Guests lists needed to be made, invitations should be mailed, publicity needed to go out, there were place cards, ribbons and specimen glasses to be found. And that wasn't all. Why, at their flower shows dating back to the sixties, a photographer from The Dallas Morning News had been scheduled weeks in advance, then came early and took pictures of the house and special guests. Members wore long dresses and the resulting photos holding awarded silver pieces and ribbons would appear in Sunday's Garden section. Despite the occasional weather event such as a downpour or tornado, most years had been successful. Now all they could do was shake their heads.

"Who's your Flower Show Chairman?"

"Rachel," answered Gina. "She's a new daughter-in-law."

"Has she ever done a Flower Show?" asked Mona, concerned.

"No, but she'll be fine. Helen's going to help her."

Helen nodded. She'd been the junior group's Flower Show Chair three years in a row, mostly by default.

"I heard she's only gotten ten people to commit to doing an arrangement," said Helen.

Claire's fork stopped midair. "How can that be? You have to be sick or dead not to participate."

Brooke laughed, playfully waving her fork. "Well, we aren't quite so strict."

"We're actually having trouble getting people to come to meetings," Helen volunteered before catching an angry look from Gina. "There's usually a core group of ten, but that's ten or so we're missing."

"But it's in your bylaws," Charlotte said. "Every member has to do an arrangement for the flower show."

Sheralyn laughed. "We don't have bylaws."

"Of course you have bylaws," gasped Mona. "We wrote them and you adopted them."

Gina stared at her plate and picked at her luncheon loaf while the others argued about whether they did or did not have by-laws. It was a three-layered slice of pimiento, tuna and chicken salad, wrapped between thin tiers of crust-less white bread. She knew what was coming next.

"We actually had the same problem," said Mona, "and more than once as a matter of fact. You need to do something about it or it's only going to get worse."

"That's right," said Claire. "One time, we put together a cookbook."

"Oh yes," said SueBee. "That was fun."

"Everyone wanted to have their favorite recipes in there so that really got things going, at least for that year."

"I don't cook," said Brooke.

"I do, but not much," said Sheralyn.

"You don't have to do a cookbook," said Mona. "The point is, you just need to do something."

"Have you thought about a pilgrimage?" asked Claire.

"What's that?" asked Brooke.

"Oh, yes," said Charlotte, "that's a great idea! I loved our trips. We got away from the kids, our husbands, the laundry. Sometimes we let the husbands go, but not too often. One time we went to Tyler to the Rose Festival. Another time we went to Busch Gardens in Florida. I think we went to Puerto Vallarta and Cozumel. Oh, we took some wonderful trips."

"Charlotte was always our tour guide," SueBee informed them.

Claire drew in a sudden breath. "I know. Why don't the mothers and daughters go on a pilgrimage *together*? We could squeeze it in before your flower show and get everyone to go.

Someplace that's not too far, but somewhere fun. And it's always a good idea if it's just a little educational."

"Mom," Gina warned.

"We could go see the Walliburton Gardens right outside of San Antonio," said Charlotte. "That's close. What do you think, Mona?"

"That might not be a bad idea. I wouldn't mind a little trip."

"I got nothin' better to do," drawled Brooke.

"No," said Gina, when the mothers looked at her. "There's no way I could go. I have work."

"But you haven't even looked at your calendar," said her mother.

"There's the Fall Carnival at Sammy's school."

"Which you hate and Blake can handle."

"I can't go either," interjected Helen.

"Oh, Helen, I bet you could get Stuart to let you go," said SueBee.

"It's not up to Stuart, Mom, but weekends are always hard. The twins are fourteen and Benji's ten."

SueBee tilted her head. She'd never approved of letting one's children determine what a parent could and could not do.

"I can go," said Sheralyn.

"Sheralyn can go," repeated Mona.

"Nope, too busy," said Gina.

"Well," Claire began, gazing into space, "you never know when it might be the last time we get to do something together. I'm getting old, you know. It might be my last adventure." Gina rolled her eyes.

"Please," begged Charlotte, focusing on Helen and Gina. "I can't explain it but special things happen when you take a trip together."

Claire turned to Mona. "Don't we know someone who owns a luxury bus company?"

Charlotte pulled out a pen and pocket calendar.

"It needs to be a weekend," said Brooke.

"What about next weekend? It's still two weeks before Halloween," suggested Charlotte, looking at dates.

"That's Sammy's school carnival," said Gina.

"Perfect," said Claire.

"Now, everyone, for this to work," SueBee instructed, "you really must go and the others will follow. You girls are the leaders."

Everyone looked at Gina.

"Fine."

"Oh, good," said Claire. Now that the trip was settled, she asked, "What's going on with our parking case?"

"You should see an improvement pretty soon."

"So you caught the criminals?" asked Charlotte.

"I want to hear all the gory details," said Mona.

"I can't really go into it," said Gina. "Basically, they've moved. They left town."

"You let them get away?" Mona said.

"No, I didn't let them get away."

"Then who was doing it?" asked SueBee.

"I can't really go into it," repeated Gina.

"So what's going to happen to them?" asked Charlotte.

Gina resisted the urge to scream. "I don't know because they left town before I could catch anyone doing anything."

"So how do you know you got them?" asked Claire.

"Mom, I don't. I'm trying to tell you that I think I know who was responsible, but they've already left town, so you should see an improvement, hopefully once the police department is able to weed out the fake handicapped stickers then it'll all go back to the way it used to be. That's it. That's all I know."

"Darn," said Mona. "I wanted to find out who was doing it."

"Sorry. These businesses are like cockroaches. You raise the rug and they scatter."

"At least I can get a good parking spot again," said Charlotte optimistically.

Brooke interrupted her. "Wait a minute, Mom, remember?"

The table went silent. Charlotte paused to think, then frowned.

"Oh, that's right. Brooke has decided that I should stop driving."

"No, *we* decided. I'm not making you do this, remember? You agreed it's the right thing to do."

Gina's mouth dropped open as she turned to face her mother. "I told you I wasn't the only one."

"I can still drive just fine," said Claire.

"I thought I drove okay, too," said Charlotte, "but Brooke's right. It's better to stop too early rather than too late."

"I'm fine," said Claire.

"You told me you were having trouble seeing at night," said Gina.

"Which is why I don't drive at night."

"Sammy says you drive too fast."

"She does?"

"Well, I have an announcement," interrupted SueBee. "I gave up my keys last week."

"Oh dear," said Claire.

Helen shrugged as if it were expected. "Stuart needed a car so we bought Mom's. It just made sense."

Brooke turned to Claire. "How will you know when you are ready? What if you hit something? Or someone?"

"I'm not having any trouble," volunteered Mona, "so Claire, if you ever need a ride, you can call me."

"I've told Mom she could call me anytime. Blake and I are happy to drive her wherever she needs to go. We really don't mind..."

"Would everyone please stop being so helpful? I'll know when it's time," said Claire.

"After you move in with me, it'll be much easier," said Mona.

Gina looked between her mother and Mona.

"What does that mean?"

With great precision, Claire placed her fork diagonally across the top rim of her plate so the server would know she was finished. "Can we *please* stop talking about me?"

"No," said Gina.

"I was going to tell you," she began calmly, "but everything happened so fast, I haven't had the chance. Mona said I could come live with her. I'll be renting. There. That's it. Wasn't that a delicious lunch?"

"But we'll still lead independent lives," Mona informed the table.

As if on cue, a waitress began taking away their dirty plates. Another began pouring coffee. Claire and Gina stared at each other while the rest of the table became distracted by the beauty of a crème Brule with a golden brown glaze.

"What do you think, Gina?" her mother asked.

Gina didn't know what she thought. She didn't see the woman dressed in a starched black dress who stood to her right with the cream. She barely heard someone asking that she pass the sugar. Some detective she was. Gina forced her hand to pick up the cup and put it to her lips. Now she remembered the extra spring in her mother's step and she suddenly saw that her color was slightly rosier. Her mother was still waiting.

"I think that's a great idea, Mom," said Gina. "Mona, I hope you know what you're doing."

The others added their own words of encouragement and jokes about the two friends getting into trouble and when they all began to comment on how good the dessert tasted, Gina looked at her watch and took a final sip of her coffee.

"I need to go. So good to see everyone. And you know what, Mom, your moving in together might work out perfectly because you know, Blake and I have always talked about maybe someday buying your house. The condo's been feeling pretty small and Sammy just keeps getting bigger. Maybe now's the time. I'll talk to Blake and give you a call."

Claire pulled an empty spoon out of her mouth.

"Uh oh."

"What?"

"If you're thinking about my house, I may have already sold it."

The china cup made a loud noise as Gina set it back in the saucer.

"What?"

"That was fast," said Charlotte.

"You've already sold your house?" Brooke asked.

"How'd you do that?" asked Helen.

"It was a miracle! I mentioned it to Betty Rose, she's still a realtor you know, and she told her office and someone said they had a client looking for something exactly like my house so she brought this darling couple over that same night and they made me an offer right then." She was looking directly at Gina. "She offered me the full price and they even said I could take my time moving out, two months if I needed it. It was just so easy, I decided it was meant to be. I'm sorry, Gina, I haven't had a chance to tell you."

"Wow," said several of the ladies.

"Have you signed anything?" Gina asked.

Claire nodded. "It's all done. You were always telling me I need to downsize and to start thinking about selling the house. Now it's done. Oh, did I already say they're giving me plenty of time to pack..." Claire stopped and thought. "That reminds me. Can you come over this week so we can go through the attic? I think there are still some boxes up there that are yours."

Gina nodded and listened to the discussion that now revolved around this new project, while inside she wanted to scream. Her mother's house would have been perfect. She and Blake had talked about it a dozen times. The three of them, living in the cottage-style home with its oversized window-panes and ebony-stained floors. There were shaded sidewalks and a tiny but real garage and the huge old oak in the back yard would have been perfect for Sammy's tree house. Sammy would grow up in a real neighborhood and Blake would turn the small yellow shed into his studio. Gina had wondered what it would be like to actually have a yard and flower beds. Who knows, she might even find her inner gardener.

Gina folded her napkin into a neat square and placed it next to her half-eaten desert. She stood up.

"Thanks, Mom. I should be getting back to work." Their faces were disappointed but understanding.

"Let me know when you'd like to come over to go through the attic," her mother said.

CHAPTER 6

"All aboard! Suitcases over there. No, not there, there!" Claire tried not to shout but shivered in the chilly fifty-four degree morning. "No, where I'm pointing! Just throw them in and then please get on the bus."

It was barely light as the group of sleepy women rolled their suitcases toward the undercarriage of the bus where the driver waited. He insisted they allow him to do the loading. A growing pile of walkers and canes leaned against the side. They would go in last.

Claire spotted a dawdler and stamped her cane then used it to navigate the rough patches of concrete in the Village parking lot to the front of the bus. The sound of the idling engine was loud. She studied her clipboard and took up the pencil attached to it by a thick strand of orange yarn.

The ladies had made it clear they weren't used to having their faces on at such an early hour but Claire, who was in charge of the schedule, had never heard of anyone starting a trip after the sun was up. She'd insisted they meet in the parking lot by six forty-five sharp so they could get on the road by seven. No one dared argue with a woman who had the God-given gift of efficiency.

The sight of the bus rounding the corner of the retirement center's parking lot had been impressive. It was bigger than a city bus and looked so much nicer. It had high ceilings, tinted windows with tiny curtains, polished chrome wheels and a beautiful blue swoosh on the sides that stood out against a white background. It also had wifi, according to the owner. Mona, who had handled all the negotiations, had asked for a discount since none of the mothers knew what that was, but the owner had said no.

Claire checked off the last name on the list. She took hold of the door handle and looked at the first step. It was pretty high. She hesitated.

"Can I help?" the driver asked from his cushioned chair, both arms resting on the steering wheel.

"Of course not, but thank you." Claire grabbed the metal bar and raised her right leg to the first step. One arm wouldn't do it, so she grabbed the bar with both hands and pulled herself up, trying not to make too much noise. She felt victorious, and when she looked at the driver who she knew was watching, her face told him, *And you thought I couldn't do it.*

Gina was seated on the aisle and adjusted so her mother could get by. Claire dropped the clipboard in Gina's lap.

"I thought you might like the window seat," said Gina.

"Thank you. We have twenty-seven going," said Claire. "Seventeen of your group and ten of mine. I think that's pretty darn good, don't you?"

"It is," said Gina.

Claire swiveled her head around to look back. "I see Gwen and Ruthie came. I wish you'd get to know Ruthie better. I don't think she knows many of the girls."

Gina turned briefly to look. Ruthie was a tall, thin woman with soft brown hair. Gina knew that she was married but never had children. They were about the same age, but Ruthie looked older. Her mother Gwen was sitting next to her. She was the severe looking type. Gina turned back around. "She doesn't come much."

"Back in the day, her mother was on several of the museum boards and she's extremely smart when it comes to investments. She used to teach at SMU, but I can't remember. Ruthie seems to be a little shy."

Helen was sitting behind them and spoke between the seats. "Isn't this going to be great? I can't wait to have almost three whole days without a dishwasher."

"Now aren't you glad you came?" said Claire.

A stranger boarded the bus and left two large boxes in one of the forward seats. As soon as he'd set them down and left, the driver put the bus in gear and they started moving. Mona walked to the front and the driver passed her a cordless microphone.

"Welcome everyone! We're off. This bus is bound for the Hotel Minnetonka in Pota, Texas. If that is *not* your destination, then you're on the wrong bus."

Everyone laughed.

"We're going to wait until we clear the city limits and then we'll pull out our usual travelling games. Charlotte has had some special snacks delivered so we won't starve and we'll be stopping in Salado for an early lunch at the Stagecoach Inn and I think we have a movie for this afternoon. *Free Willy*, I think?" The bus driver nodded.

Gina felt her phone vibrating through her purse.

"Hello?" She listened. "It should be in the cabinet."

Claire leaned over.

"Everything okay?"

"Blake's having fun being mommy," then back to the phone, "I'm talking to Mom."

"It's good for him," said Claire.

"What?" Gina said into the phone. "Mom, I can't hear."

"What now?" Claire asked.

"Peanut butter crisis," said Gina, her hand over the phone. "Sorry, Blake, I guess you'll have to make it honey and jelly. She likes that."

Gina ended the conversation and put the phone in the pocket in front of her.

"Did you have to bring that? You're on vacation," Claire said.

"No, but I did."

The phone rang again. Gina answered quickly.

"Really, Blake, Sammy will..." Then she stopped, listening. It obviously wasn't Blake.

"Lucy? What's wrong? Stop screaming."

"What is it?" asked Claire.

Gina shook her head slightly and held up a hand for her mother to wait. "Sorry, Lucy, I'm on vacation. Have you called the police?"

Claire tried again but the hand went up.

"Lucy, stop screaming. You need to call the police. I'm leaving town right this minute. I'm sorry but there's nothing I can do." There was a pause. "Trust me, they'll help you." There was a longer pause, and then Gina said finally, "I'm sorry, Lucy. They'll help you." Out of the phone came what sounded like more screaming, and then Gina repeated herself one more time before hanging up.

This time the phone went in the purse and the purse went under her seat. Claire looked expectantly for an explanation but Gina didn't volunteer one, so she opened up her crossword puzzle book. The bus jerked left and right to dodge some traffic and then everyone was pressed into their cushioned backrests as the engines surged forward.

"Alright, everyone," Mona began again from the front, "we've hit I35 so we are officially on our way. I think we should start the charades. I've already picked the category which will be current events. Ginger, will you please hand out the little paper thingies."

Ginger immediately hopped up with a baggie of white strips of paper and began handing them out. "These are the things you have to act out," continued Mona. "All y'all are Team A, and everyone on this side is Team B." The passengers looked around to assess their chances of winning.

"Ginger, you're up. Sheralyn, you keep time – everyone gets three minutes."

Gina looked behind her where most of the other daughters were sitting. They all had the same deer-in-the-headlights look.

Ginger quickly read her piece of paper. Someone shouted 'Go!' and she began waving her arms like a fountain.

"Ho hum," sighed Gina, ignoring Ginger. "Where exactly are we going? I know it's someplace called Poto?"

"The Hotel Minnetonka. It's just outside of San Antonio. Charlotte made all the arrangements. It's supposed to be a five-star hotel with gourmet food and it's very close to the gardens." She had to talk loudly to be heard over the shouting.

"How far is it?"

"It's on the south side of San Antonio. Maybe five or six hours? The whole town was originally part of the Walliburton family estate. They're the ones who started Sea Island Amusement Parks. We're getting a private tour of their gardens tomorrow morning, and then dinner...."

"Jimmy Hoffa!" SueBee shouted at the front of the bus.

"Herbert Hoover!" shouted Mona.

"Howard Stern," shouted Helen.

They must have been wrong because Young Ginger almost collapsed then went back to waving her hands. Suddenly, she slapped her fingers against her upper forearm. Not everyone understood but it didn't matter because those that did couldn't be heard over everyone else who was still shouting guesses. Ginger shook her head furiously and Sheralyn called out "Time!"

"What was it?" asked Mona.

No one heard the answer because a noise made up of grinding gears and backfiring engines erupted outside the left side of the bus. Those that could, stood up to see what the racket was.

"Well, that's a scary bunch of people," said Claire, looking out the window. A long line of motorcycles was passing the bus. Some were riding by themselves, others had a passenger perched on tiny seats over the rear tire. The bus watched in silence. Gina counted twenty-two bikes.

"I hate motorcycles," mumbled Claire. "I just hate them."

"Oh, Mom," said Gina, "they're just weekend road warriors. Probably going to some convention in Austin. I'm going to go visit with Helen."

Claire went back to her crosswords and Gina flipped around into the seat next to Helen, whose mother had already moved somewhere closer to her charades team. SueBee was extremely competitive, Helen was not.

"Hey," said Gina.

"Hey," said Helen.

"Whatcha' doin'?"

"I'm working on the invite list for the flower show. We need to get the invitations in the mail next week. You've got them, right?"

"At home. Sitting on my kitchen counter. Mom said she'll address them when we're ready. Who do you have so far?"

"The mothers, of course. The Dallas Garden Club. The Greenway Garden Club. A few others. Husbands?"

"Naaa," said Gina. "They don't want to come." Helen agreed.

"I thought we'd let everyone invite up to five friends."

"Sounds good."

"What about help?" asked Gina.

Helen turned a knowing eye. "Nothing's changed. All daughters have been told. Angela and Laney will be there," she said, naming Brooke's two daughters. "I think we have at least five more to pick up dirty dishes, keep the table filled. I told Rebecca to plan on working in the kitchen. She wasn't too happy but she knows it's tradition. Just like we did it for our mothers."

"Helping is good for them," said Gina. "Sammy will be there."

"I told Rebecca that serving at a flower show is part of her passage into adulthood. She wanted to know if it was like menopause."

Gina laughed out loud. "Sammy doesn't even know it's work. I told her she's going to be in charge of keeping the strawberry platter filled. She can't wait."

"That's cute," said Helen, making a few notes.

Gina put her hand lightly over Helen's. "How are you?" she asked.

"Pretty good." said Helen.

"No, really," said Gina. "What's going on with Craig?"

Brooke, who was sitting across the aisle, leaned over.

"Come on, Helen. Catch us up."

"Oh, I don't know. Nothing."

"Yes, there is," said Brooke.

Helen took a deep breath. "Craig's in trouble again but, Gina, I swear, you need to be my friend right now, not a police officer, okay?" Gina nodded. "He can't seem to stay out of trouble."

Gina took her hand. "I know."

"How old are they now?" asked Brooke, referring to the twins.

"They're fourteen."

"Craig's at that age where he's going to push the limits. Just keep reminding yourself that's his job, he's a teenager. It's your job to hold the line," said Brooke.

"I'm trying," said Helen, "but I hope he figures it out before he gets arrested. But how are your kids?" Brooke had four.

"Oh, they're fine. Practically grown and gone. Laney's still a giddy newlywed." Brooke's oldest girl had married while still in college. The garden club had thrown her a shower, of course.

"Angela's getting her masters in Art History. Not dating anyone."

"Nice," said Gina, then she noticed Helen's eyes were still glassy. She patted her arm.

"She wants to work at a museum and you gotta' have that masters degree. So she's living at home, going to SMU."

"Like her grandma," Gina smiled.

"Like her grandma," echoed Brooke.

"And the babies?" Helen asked.

Brooke laughed. "The babies are nineteen and twenty. Rose is at Texas and Bobby's at A & M. It's a lot of fun at our house during football season."

"You finally have some peace and quiet at home," said Gina jealously.

"Yes, and I hate it! So I got a cat. Right now I'm trying to clean out all my closets."

"You're pitiful," said Gina.

"I know. I miss everyone around the table for dinner, all the chaos, the laundry, kids eating me out of house and home. No one needs me anymore. I only have to go to the grocery store once a week. That's it. I used to go every day."

"So enjoy the peace and quiet for me," said Helen.

"I'm trying," said Brooke. "It's that shitty transitional thing, excuse my language."

The game up front was getting intense. Gina gave Helen a hug and went back to her seat. She looked over her mom who was happily working a puzzle and stared at the Texas landscape. The fields were stubble grey, the crops gone. In a few months, they'd be charcoal black, the ground turned and the rich soil waiting for the seed. After that, the fields all the way to the horizon would be tall with wheat and corn.

Gina loved the nothingness landscape of Texas. She loved the cities but there was something breathtaking about being able to see forever. She imagined the families, living in that small house in the distance, isolated, working the land, a world so far removed from hers she wondered how they survived. She wondered how many pre-conceived ideas she had about them were wrong and how many were right? They were people and they had a family, probably friends and children. She wanted to know what kind of people they were and what did they know and how did they survive so far from her world that was crowded by streets and tall buildings, traffic and noise. She knew better than to feel sorry or jealous. They were the same.

Now the land rolling by was in color, greens and browns, with the occasional red-roofed barn, rusted green tractors and black and white cows. Maybe one day she'd drive out into the middle of nowhere and stop and ask perfect strangers about themselves.

Claire, as though waiting for her to finish her thoughts, said, "I'm sorry I didn't tell you about selling the house."

"It's okay, Mom. We probably couldn't afford it anyway."

"When Mona said I could move in with her, it just all happened so fast," her mother explained.

"I'm fine, Mom. Don't worry about it."

Claire relaxed and returned to her crossword puzzle, but Gina watched her mother's pencil hover over the printed page.

"But to be honest, it does bother me a little bit that you kept it to yourself."

"I knew it! You're so busy, Gina. I didn't want to bother you. If I'd had trouble, I would have called you but it all went so smoothly. I'm sure there will be plenty of other things that I'll need you for."

"Like what? There's nothing left. Your funeral arrangements?"

"No, I've got that all planned."

"See? It's like you don't need me unless it's cleaning out the attic."

Her mother was silent for a second.

"When you were seventeen, you walked in to the den and you said to me, in a very mature way, that you were ready to move out. You said that as soon as you finished high school, you were going to get a job and then figure out a way to get an apartment and you'd be fine. You told me that you couldn't wait to be on your own."

Gina nodded, smiling. "I remember."

"You don't know this but right after that, I went in the bathroom and cried my eyes out. Because what I realized, at that moment, was that you were ready. I'd done my job. I'd spent seventeen years teaching you how to be independent, and suddenly, you were there. You really could do fine without me. So I really do understand and I'm sorry."

"Gina," said Claire, "let's promise to stop analyzing ourselves. I'm going to live at Mona's, but I promise to need you."

"Just a little," added Gina.

"As little as possible."

"Okay," said Gina. "I can live with that."

"But if I start losing my mind and I'm put somewhere," continued Claire, "can you please pretend you're keeping everything? Like the andirons from my mother's house and the china plates. I know you don't really care for them but tell me you're saving them for Samantha. Just until I'm gone. Okay?"

"Okay," said Gina. "You know it's conversations like these that keep me on my toes."

Mona, from several rows behind them, pounded on someone's headrest and yelled out a guess.

Gina added, "I hope I can figure this out before Sammy gets older. We'll make those big decisions together."

"Honey, Samantha is a sweet, wonderful child, but it doesn't matter what you want. In about thirteen years, it's going to feel like she's coming at you with both barrels."

Sometime later that morning, Mona gave the word and the ladies broke out the two boxes up front. They were filled with gourmet cheeses, crackers, and bite-size sweets and fruit. At eleven, they pulled into the parking lot of the Stagecoach Inn in Salado where they had what the historical hitching post was known for - chicken-fried steak and hushpuppies.

It was still early afternoon when they arrived at their destination. Gina vaguely remembered hearing *Free Willy* playing in the background, when she looked up from a magazine and saw an old three-story brick building. The windows were open on the upper floors and red-checked curtains fluttered in and out. On the wide front porch, a heavy chain linked six old rocking chairs.

"Is this a Cracker Barrel?"

"It's our hotel. The Hotel Minnetonka," said Charlotte.

"Are you sure?" asked Claire.

Helen's voice came from between the seats, "If that's a five-star hotel, my kitchen is going to be clean when I get home."

CHAPTER 7

In regal style, the ladies descended. They stood looking up at what was to be their home for the next two days, but instead of the five star experience they'd been promised, their road-weary eyes took in a feeble replica of Old Red, the 1800's courthouse in downtown Dallas. Like that historical edifice, it had rusty red pillars made of sandstone with scrolls and fleur-de-lis carved in the reliefs. Over the door was a half moon of stained glass and the front doors were heavily carved oak.

"This is creepy," said Sheralyn, stepping forward with a Louis Vuitton bag.

"It's historical," said Charlotte.

The creak of doors closing caught their attention and they turned and watched the bus pull away, their luggage and walkers still in piles. Squinting into the four o'clock sun, they watched until it had turned a corner and disappeared.

"Well he's in a hurry," said Helen.

"Must have been the conversation. I'm pretty sure he was a liberal," said SueBee.

Gradually, canes and walkers were separated, distinguishable by their colorful duct tape.

"Are you sure we're in the right place?" Claire asked. Mona set a small suitcase upright on its wheels. "I sure hope so because it'll be dark soon and we just lost our ride home." A dust-covered car drove slowly by and both parties stared. Other than that, the street was deserted.

"Well, I'm starving," said Sheralyn. She threw the strap of a bag over her shoulder and handily snapped up the chrome handle of her rolling suitcase. "I hope they have a cocktail hour." It was dark inside. Heavy draperies covered the front windows and there were thick carpets over old plank floors. There was also a tall, wood-paneled counter but with no one to greet them.

Mona rolled around to the front of the group and pounded on the counter.

"The website said the chef uses all fresh vegetables and herbs from their own garden and they raise their own beef and pork," volunteered Charlotte while they waited. "It's supposedly all organic. It said they're completely *off the grid*, whatever that means."

Gina said, "The garden must be out back."

"What does off the grid mean?" asked SueBee.

"It means if the world were to lose power, we'd be fine. It's called a Pioneer Experience," said Brooke.

"Why would anyone want to be *off the grid*?" asked Charlotte.

"You sure this is the right place?" SueBee asked.

"It's a dump," said Mona. She slapped her hand hard on the countertop again.

"I'm here, I'm here." A woman appeared wearing a full apron, flour and a broad smile.

"Howdy! Oh, I'm so sorry, I completely forgot what time it was. Here," she said and rushed to the draperies, flinging them back and sending dust and flour everywhere. Light streamed through the front windows. She hurriedly turned on lamps and flipped on switches, then came back to the counter.

"Now," she said, clasping white hands and much more satisfied with the illuminated room. "What can I do you for? Oh, never mind, what am I saying? You're obviously checking in and you're in luck 'cause we got rooms."

"I'll bet," said Mona.

Charlotte stepped to the counter.

"You should already have us down. We have reservations."

"Oh, you do?" The friendly woman reached under the counter for her records and flipped over a few pages of a legal yellow pad.

"Name?"

"Charlotte...."

"I'm just kiddin'. Here you are. You're the garden club, obviously." She looked over the group. "We used to garden, but not anymore. Too much work."

Charlotte laughed weakly. "Really?"

"We used to a have that lot 'cross the street - my son-in-law used to work it. But the sprinkler broke and everything died and then someone wanted to use it for a Christmas tree lot." She shrugged. "I guess that's progress."

"But your website says you serve gourmet meals with things from your own garden."

The woman looked confused. "Oh, that's on the website," she remembered. "We stopped paying for that a couple years ago but no one knows how to take it off the internet. I hate the internet. I told my husband he needs to fix that. But we still serve really good food. You'll see.

"And anyway," she continued, "we got your rooms all ready. Right up those." She pointed to some stairs with her pencil.

"Where's the elevator?" asked Brooke.

"We got a small one, back behind me and through the dining room. It's a little temperamental, though. I recommend using the stairs. How was your trip?"

"Fine," said Charlotte, "but I'm afraid we were expecting a different kind of hotel."

"Well, we're the only game in town and listen, I promise you'll never sleep or eat better. And it's right down the road from the gardens. That's good, right? And you got my favorite bus driver picking you up at 9 am. You'll love her."

"Your rooms are all on the same floor, another perk I might add, and there's cocktails at six in the parlor, dinner's at seven. And don't be late unless you want to help with dishes 'cause the staff gets off at 8:30 pm sharp. Now, here are all your keys and I'm going to get back to my soufflé. Follow me if you want to find the elevator." Their hostess turned and was gone. A few had no choice but to follow.

The others herded themselves toward the stairs and had just made it up a few of the creaky steps when the front door opened and the lobby area began filling with men and women wearing black leather jackets and heavy boots. A lot of them had fringed chaps strapped to their legs that jingled when they walked and those with bald heads wore the tight bandanas of a motorcycle gang. Those that had hair, male and female, wore it braided down their backs. There was the glint of silver everywhere – on their hands and hanging from their ears. The smell of gasoline permeated the confined room.

A blond giant emerged from the group. He slapped his hand down on the counter, exactly as Mona had, then slowly turned and surveyed his audience. The obvious leader was a Tutonic man with bare, tattooed arms and multiple bands of leather wrapped around both wrists. He relaxed against the counter. His smile told Gina he understood what he was up against as his eyes glided over their faces, many of whom had taken a few steps back in fear.

"Well, will you look at what that woman has in her ear," said Gina's mother too loudly.

"Shhh," Gina said.

Her mother began walking back to the counter.

"Mom! Wait. Where are you going?"

"I forgot my purse." Gina saw her mother's big green bag still on the counter, directly in front of the biker. Her mother worked her way through the crowd until she was eye level to his biceps.

"Is that an angel?" Claire asked the giant, pointing at a tattoo.

"Please, Mom!"

"You know what the Bible says about that?" said Claire, as she tilted her head back to look him in the eye. "It says that when people start mutilating their bodies, that means we're getting near the end times."

"Mom," Gina moaned quietly. Every bare arm in the lobby was tattooed.

"Excuse me?" said the giant.

"Okay, Mom, time to go." By now Gina had gotten to the counter. She grabbed the purse and pulled on her mother's arm.

The Viking drew up a fist and flexed his muscles so that the tattoo came to life. Everyone watched the heavenly form dance then he said, "The Bible also says that we're supposed to live in the world but not of the world."

A challenging smile spread across Claire's face. "Very interesting."

"I'll take that as a compliment," he said.

Claire started to say something else but Gina pulled her back toward the stairs. As she did, her mother caught her foot on the carpet and started to trip. A strong wrinkled hand reached out to steady her. It belonged to one of the older bikers whose snow white hair was swept back into a thin pony tail that reached the middle of his back. In his other hand was a helmet.

"Thank you," said Claire.

"Take care," he offered before letting her go. "I hope you ladies don't mind sharing this hotel with us."

Claire didn't answer.

"Thank you," said Gina, taking her mother's arm and pulling her toward the stairs. "We don't mind at all."

The proprietor popped out just as suddenly as before.

"Welcome! Welcome! Everyone got here at the same time. Who do we have here?"

As the bikers checked in, Gina did her best to hurry her mother up the stairs. Claire kept turning around, looking over her shoulder and, Gina noticed, the older gentleman was still watching her. At the top of the stairs, Gina looked down on the leather-ness of everything and for the first time, she caught a glimpse of the design on the back of the bikers' jackets. It was a large white cross and the words *Road Warriors* written across the top.

On the second floor, Claire and Gina found Room G at the end of the hall. It was small but adequate with two single beds and a small dresser. There was one comfortable-looking chair and a frayed ottoman with a lamp beside it. The only other furniture was a small desk beneath the window that looked out over the street below.

Gina dropped her bag on one of the beds and took out her make-up bag. She looked around.

"Where's the bathroom?"

"Well, that's strange." Claire said, sidestepping to the only other door in the room and opening it.

"Closet."

Gina's phone rang. She put it on speaker and continued to unpack.

"Hi, Gina. It's me, Lucy."

"Hello, Lucy. I've got you on speakerphone. My mom's here with me."

"Okay, so I called the police like you said and they said to call San Antonio because that's where Steve said he was headed and I told them to call you if they spotted it. Gina, Steven's in San Antonio and that car's my baby. You have to help me."

Gina faced the phone. "Lucy, I'm on vacation."

"I know, but you're down there, right?"

"No, I'm not," said Gina.

"Hey, I looked up Poco and you're like five minutes away."

"It's Pota," said Gina.

"Awww, come on. It's like a suburb of San Antonio. They'll only call you if they have to, but I told them you know Steven and my car."

"Fine," Gina said, sitting on the bed, "but I wish you hadn't done that."

"Lucy," her mother interrupted, leaning over until her mouth was only a few inches above the phone, "this is Gina's mother. Don't worry, I'll keep a lookout."

"God bless you, Gina's mother. Thank you so much."

"Call me Claire."

"Thank you so much, Claire."

"Okay," Gina said, staring at the phone. "My mom is now on the case. I hope you're happy. So will you please stop calling me? I'm on vacation!"

"Okay, okay," said Lucy. "Thank you, Claire."

"You're welcome, Lucy. I'll let you know what I find. Can I call you back on this number?"

"Yes, ma'am. Thank you so much."

"You're welcome, dear," said Claire.

Gina closed her phone.

"That's what you get for bringing that thing," said her mother. "So what are we looking for?"

"You, not we. You're looking for a really long blue car with a white, landau top. I'm on vacation."

Gina looked around the room again, then stuck her head into the hall. She yelled, "Is that the bathroom?"

"Yep," came the reply.

"It looks like there's a bathroom at both ends of the hall, Mom, so you better plan ahead."

"I always do." Claire had already stripped down to her slip and was putting things into the small dresser.

"You better hurry up if you're going to change."

"Why do I need to change?"

"Well, I just thought...."

At seven sharp, the ladies were seated in the small dining room. The owners and their teen-aged daughter served the meal.

"Where's the biker gang?" asked Brooke.

"Oh, they left to have dinner on the River Walk," said the teen-aged daughter, referring to the main tourist attraction in San Antonio.

Dinner was surprisingly good. The vegetables were fresh and crisp, they served a delicate crab mousse with a choice of chicken or prime rib.

Gina purposefully sat with some of the daughters she didn't know very well. After all, it was the reason for the trip.

She learned more about Kathleen's job as a speech therapist and she was surprised to discover that Emily had done contract work for a computer company for at least ten years. Kathleen's husband was an attorney and Emily's husband was in sales. Both had a couple of grown kids.

"And how old's your daughter?" Emily asked.

"She's only four. I started a little later than everyone."

"So are you going to have more?"

"No, we're done. Sammy's all we need."

"I hope you're not planning on letting her be an only child," said Gwen, the severe-looking former schoolteacher. She'd been invisible until now. "I was an only child and I always wished I had a brother or sister. I feel sorry for the only child."

"Mother!" said her daughter Ruthie.

"I think they need to learn how to share at home and parents tend to treat them more like adults, rather than children. You'll spoil her, I'm sure. If there's any possible way to have another child, you should do it."

"Mother!" Ruthie could hardly stand it.

Gina was about to reply when her mother kicked her under the table.

"Never mind, Gwen," Claire said, "I can vouch for the wonderful job Gina and Blake are doing with Samantha. You'd never know she was an only child." Gwen lifted her brows in disbelief.

Gina noticed the shame in Ruthie's eyes as Claire continued. "She's turning out to be very normal and the most pleasant four-year old I've ever been around. Now, not to change the subject, Gwen, but did you read about what Senator Forbes got caught doing?"

After dinner, while everyone began moving into the next room where a warm fire burned, Ruthie indicated she wanted to talk with Gina and Claire alone.

"I'm so sorry, Gina," said Ruthie. "Please forgive Mom. I'm so embarrassed."

"It's alright, Ruthie," said Claire. "No harm done."

"Did I miss something?" asked Gina.

"Gwen is not herself these days," Claire explained. "It happens and we all understand, Ruthie. Don't worry about it."

"But it's worse than that. She's arguing with the grocery clerk and questions every bill. She can be so mean sometimes. I never know what she's going to say." Ruthie looked at Gina with pleading eyes. "She would never have talked like that a year ago. It's like she's forgotten that there are some things you shouldn't say out loud, even if you believe them. Sometimes I think I should keep her at home."

"Please don't," said Claire. "Have you taken her to a doctor? It could be chemical. Or maybe her diet? And I know medications can do some crazy things to your brain."

Ruthie looked hopeful.

"Don't worry," said Claire. "And please encourage her to come to the meetings. We've all learned to let her have her say." Claire looked tenderly at Ruthie. "We'll take care of her."

CHAPTER 8

"Everyone, please come on, the bus is almost here," Claire shouted up the stairs. "I don't want to be late for this tour."

At least she hoped the bus was almost there. It was already eight-fifteen and it was supposed to be there at eight-thirty but she wanted it there now! Everything and everybody was getting on her nerves.

Claire checked her clipboard again. She had eighteen signed up for the garden tour and she was really glad to see that all the daughters were going. The less mobile members of the senior group had wisely elected to explore the town on their own.

With her good ear directed at the stairs, Claire listened for sounds of progress, then gave up and went to watch for the bus.

Outside, the street had the same ghost-town feel of the previous day. All that was missing was a tumbleweed hop scotching its way across the dusty road and maybe two talking buzzards clinging to the utility line that stretched between the hotel and the empty Christmas tree lot across the street. It was now 8:19. Claire was tempted to call the bus company but decided to give them five more minutes, but that was it. Then she'd call.

Claire wished she could be the easy-going one, like certain other members of the garden club who were always late but also well-liked. Just this morning, several had been under the impression that they could take their time in the bathroom so Claire had stood outside the door with a running narrative of how many minutes each member was taking.

Just then, a bus made a wide turn onto Main Street and came to a stop in front of the hotel. It was exactly 8:25. The driver bounded off. She was dressed in a green hat and uniform and when she landed on the pavement she arched her back, put a perfectly level right hand to her brow and announced, "Yellow Rose Tours, at your service. The uniform's green, my name is Jean and I'm pleased to be your driver for the day."

Immediately, she reached to cradle one of Claire's arms, the other one being occupied with the clipboard and pencil, and with soothing sounds, steered the older woman toward the bus.

"Come on, dearie, let's take it slow. This first step is a doozy."

"No, I'm not..."

"Don't worry, honey, I've got you," the driver in green said, lifting the arm to guide the foot.

Claire pulled herself out from the woman's clutches.

"Excuse me, but I'm not an invalid, thank you very much. I'm waiting for the others. I have the clipboard!" Claire stepped back as best she could. "Everyone's still inside but hopefully they'll just be a few minutes. I think you better wait on the bus."

"Are you sure? That first step's a doozy."

"Yes, you said that."

Jean remained unruffled. "Yes, Ma'am, not a problem. You're the boss. Let me introduce myself again. I'm Jean, ex-Marine and I'm in no hurry. You just let me know when and where and I'll get you there." She gave Claire another official salute then disappeared inside the bus.

Claire did not like all the attention and she wasn't sure what she thought of a female bus driver who spoke in rhymes. For now, she'd ignore her and yelled even more forcefully than before in the direction of the hotel, "Everyone, the bus is here! It looks like rain so bring your umbrellas! And hurry up!" The sky rumbled while the canopy looked like a thick piece of grey felt.

"God, can we *please* do without the tornado?"

Gina was the first to emerge with a few of the daughters. Gradually, the others came along in ones and twos with the casual, carefree pace of women on vacation. They exclaimed as they exited the hotel at the size of the bus, then looked cheerily at Claire until they caught a whiff of her demeanor.

Some carried umbrellas and raincoats but most were loaded down with bags and sweaters. The daughters wore minimal clothing, fanny packs and running shoes while the mothers were generally dressed in colorful pant suits and Naturalizers.

As soon as Jean saw the crowd, she bounded down the steps again and extended a hand to the first in line. Claire sullenly noticed the help was accepted and concentrated on her checklist, then remembered something very important. She rapped on one of the panes with her cane to get Gina's attention. When the window opened, Claire thrust a large plastic bag into her daughter's hand.

"Tell everyone if they brought 'em, to put their cell phones in here and then take the bag back inside and just put it behind the hotel counter."

"Why?"

"The garden center doesn't allow them."

Claire stayed busy checking off names. "Helen, SueBee, Brooke, thank you, must have been a line for the bathroom, check check. Be sure and give Gina your phones, she's already on the bus."

As soon as Claire had checked everyone off, she looked at her watch and yelled, "Eight forty-five, ladies. Load 'em up, move 'em out."

Suddenly, from around the corner there came a deafening roar and something that looked like a black thundercloud moving in slow motion rounded the side of the hotel. Like parading Shriners, the Road Warriors began doing figure eights in the street and once the whole gang had formed two perfect lines, they began a slow procession toward San Antonio.

Claire was about to board when the last bike slowed in front of her. It was the white-haired gentleman from the night before who had helped her catch her balance. He raised his visor and their eyes met. He grinned with a broad, happy smile, then he nodded once, lowered his visor and sank his heal into his pedal. The engine roared and something stirred in Claire. She didn't protest this time when Jean took a solid grip of her elbow and helped her up the steps.

"Everyone, why don't we all try to sit with someone different," Claire instructed before sitting down.

Some looked up but most ignored her.

"I give up. No one ever listens to me," Claire said, dropping into the aisle seat next to Gina.

"Yes, they do. They just aren't going to do it."

"Hmm."

Someone began distributing songbooks entitled *All Texans Sing*. It had already been decided that there was plenty of time for a group activity.

"What should we sing first?" someone asked.

A voice started singing, "There's a yellow rose in Texas, I'm goin' there to see, no other fellow knows her, nobody only me. You may talk about your dearest friends and sing of Rosalie, but the yellow rose of Texas is the only girl for me."

After that, they sang *Deep in the Heart of Texas*, and then *Texas, Our Texas*, and then finally, *Red River Valley*. There were no shrinking violets in the Hillcrest Heights Garden Club.

"Have you seen anything?" her mother asked. Gina was singing but she was also looking out her window at the dry landscape.

"Just countryside."

"I mean the car. Have you seen Lucy's car?"

"No, Mom, I don't think we're going to see Lucy's car."

"Switch places with me. I'm going to keep a watch out for it. You never know when you're going to get lucky and I'm too old to go to Vegas. That blue car could be just around the next corner."

"I'm on vacation," Gina reminded her. While her mother was glued to the window, she looked up through the bus's skylights at an angry sky. The morning was still in the sixties but the clouds made it seem colder. Many of the ladies had already wrapped their necks in scarves and many put on the sweaters and slickers they'd brought. Their clear voices rose and fell while some added harmony. The vibratos varied but their enthusiasm made her smile.

Slowly, Gina felt herself starting to relax. Her sweatshirt felt warm and comfortable as the bus sailed smoothly along the highway, staying in the far right lane so there was very little jostling. The singing continued and Gina kept watch on the street. She was beginning to see more and more billboards and knew they were getting closer to San Antonio.

"The Space Needle!" Helen cried a few minutes later, spotting the 1968 World's Fair icon. Others called out historical hotels and museums or street names they knew. Of course they all looked when someone yelled, "Alamo!". They caught brief glimpses of the River Walk, the architecture of the San Antonio River that ran below the street level, and Charlotte pointed out the place where they'd be having lunch tomorrow. It was still early so there were only a few tourists strolling along the sidewalks of what looked like perfect shops to explore.

A few minutes later, they had traversed the city. Like Dorothy and friends emerging from the forest into the field of poppies, the bus had crossed from one world and entered into another. Claire even forgot about her search for the blue car. After the urban landscape of stop lights and heavy traffic, they journeyed along a quiet highway, rolling through subdivisions, acres of mobile homes and then several miles of seemingly flat plains that might have lulled a few of them back to sleep except that the bus suddenly turned, tires screeching onto a chalky white road. Just in the nick of time, Jean had spotted the tiny, unassuming signpost that read Walliburton.

A dust cloud up ahead told them they weren't the only ones heading that way, which was a good thing because almost immediately the road was lined on both sides by thirty-foot-tall juniper trees and if it weren't for the sky overhead growing greyer by the minute, they would have thought they were in a tunnel.

There were twists and turns in the road, and they dropped lower and lower as if they were sinking into a canyon, and just when it seemed there would be no end to this very strange driveway, the junipers took sharp right turns in opposite directions and they were in a parking lot already filled with cars and buses.

"I wish we'd gotten here just thirty minutes sooner," said Claire, looking for Lucy's car.

"It's like they don't want us to know where we are," said Ruthie. The others agreed.

Jean steered them into a space between other buses.

Claire stood up. "Gina, let me out. I need to tell everyone what to do."

Once again, the ladies descended like royalty, letting Jean take their hands and help them to the ground. Claire stayed at the door to make sure they didn't stray and another member lined them up and passed out accessories like maps and wipes. Once they were all off the bus, Claire led them through the crowd toward the main entrance via a crushed granite walkway. Along the way, there were matte green wire benches with matching waste baskets and little signs with peoples' names on them. Several of the mothers commented on the navigable walkway but little else because if they fell behind, they were afraid they might end up in the Lost and Found.

"Here we are!" Claire cried out, waving to a very old and small dark-skinned man holding a sign with the club's name on it. Without introduction, he motioned for them to follow. For an old man, he was surprisingly energetic and remained far ahead, leading them first through an opening in the junipers, then hurriedly past much larger groups who were standing in long lines and then finally along a sinister path of even taller trees with thicker trunks and limbs draped in moss.

By now, everyone was wondering who the elderly gentleman was. He wore a quilted green jacket with several pins on his lapel but no nametag. He obviously knew the area very well but several noticed he was also struggling to catch his breath. Claire wondered out loud who would save who if someone had a heart attack.

"My friend on the board at the Arboretum told me about him," Mona wheezed to those around her as they walked. "He grew up here. He's related to the family somehow and we are so lucky I was able to get him." She rubbed her fingers together which indicated a nice donation had been promised. "He said he would tell us all about growing up, playing on the Estate grounds and eating at the dinner table. I'm sure he has some wonderful stories."

Finally, they came to a natural clearing where the green-jacketed gentleman awaited.

"Welcome, everyone. While you catch your breath, let me introduce myself. My name is Gerald Fonteneau Walliburton and I'm one of the great-grandsons of Mr. Gerald F. Walliburton, Sr. You may have noticed the dark skin," he touched his cheek, "because my grandmother was Spanish and I had many, many cousins and siblings, if you know what I mean." He gave them a moment to realize he'd just told them he was illegitimate before continuing.

"However, Mr. Walliburton tried to ensure that we were all treated as one big happy family." He paused, then laughed, "Actually, that's not true. The legitimate children and grandchildren all got to live and eat at the big house, while we worked the fields and ate with our mothers and grandmothers in houses Papa Wally built for us just down the road."

Mona's mouth hung open. The others were wide-eyed.

"It would make a great reality TV show, but I digress. The Estate is approximately one hundred and two thousand acres, and it takes a lot of people to run it. I think old Wally wanted to do the right thing, but it wasn't until the last fifty years or so that the courts ruled in our favor and we got a portion of the inheritance. My grandmother never saw a dime, but again, I digress. The good news is we are now all part owners and filthy rich."

"Close your mouth, Mona," said Claire.

"After we're done with the tour of the gardens, your ticket will get you tea at our outdoor cafe and then a tour of the home."

Helen raised her hand.

"I'm surprised it's so quiet here. We aren't that far from all those people."

"It's because we've just descended fifteen feet from the parking lot and you are actually standing in one of the many channels, or arroyos, that have been worn down by centuries of floods. We're also very close to the San Antonio River. This is one of those hollows that acts as drainage for the river after those heavy rains that happen once every five hundred years or so."

He stopped talking and immediately there was only the wind. His voice lowered. "The Indians were able to use places like this to ambush the many poor unsuspecting explorers and expeditions."

"Indians?" said Charlotte.

"Oh yes, Comanche, Payaya..."

"Payaya?"

He stopped himself, realizing another opportunity.

"I'm assuming you drove from the direction of San Antonio?" They all nodded. "Well, if you drove from the city, you were basically following the San Antonio River. The River Walk? Have you toured it yet?"

"Tomorrow," said Claire.

"Well, when you do, remember, we owe our existence to that water. San Antonio's history revolves around it. This land belonged to the Indians but the first description we have of the river was given by Cabeza de Vaca in 1536. Then, on June 13, 1691, Domingo Teran de los Rios, the first governor of the new Province of Texas was accompanying Father Damian Massanet on their return trip to East Texas. In Father Massanet's words, they camped at a Rancheria of the Payaya Indians on a stream they named The River of San Antonio de Padua because it was Saint Anthony's Day. He described the area as a 'very fine and luxuriant place with high walnuts, poplars, elms, and mulberries watered by a copious spring which rises near the Rancheria of...,' several other tribes which names I am unable to pronounce," their guide interjected. He had obviously given this talk a thousand times before but the women were mesmerized, especially as they looked around at the very same trees he'd just named. Their guide continued.

"The Father recognized then that the spring could support not just a village, but a large city. In the language of the Indians, it is called Yanaguana."

His audience tried saying it themselves. 'Yanaguana'.

"Also, imagine being here on that day. Instead of highways and WalMarts and fast food restaurants, the large plain you just crossed is all Blackland Prairie. It would have been covered in natural grasses and dry, cracked open soil and acres of Black-Eyed Susans that had been carried down by stampeding herds of Buffalo crossing the Red River until they came to rest here. There might have been a sea of the giant, hairy animals which are the largest mammal remaining on the continent."

"Buffalo," the women repeated to themselves.

"Now, imagine a young man, my great-grandfather, who, shortly after the Civil War, was industrious, hard-working and could see an opportunity. He looked at the river," the guide waved in one direction, "the arroyos," and he waved in another, "and, most importantly, he decided that if he drilled deep enough, he could tap into the underground river that flows beneath us now." At this, he pointed directly at his feet.

"The population in Texas at the end of the Civil War was about 700,000 and at least a third of the state belonged to the Indians and the buffaloes. Because of the Civil War, there were at least six million longhorns and most of them were ownerless. Mr. Walliburton had nothing but wealth at his disposal."

"Now, with that bit of history, I think we are ready to begin your tour of the Walliburton Estate. I'll give you a broad brushstroke of how the gardens are laid out and then we'll cover several different 'theatres' which is what the family calls them. After that, I'll leave you at the house with much younger tour guides who aren't related but also don't mind going up and down a few hundred steps."

"As I told Mrs. Johnson over the phone," he nodded at Mona, "the home tour lasts about an hour. Out here, it's about a forty-five minute walk and since I am so old, I ordered some transportation. I hope you don't mind."

On cue, there was a growing hum and three battery-powered golf carts rolled into sight. Rather than being confined to the crushed granite walkway the women had used, they bumped gently over soft grass and wove between the trees until they came to rest next to the ladies. Each cart had three rows of plastic cushioned seats and they were also covered with a striped green and white canopy. A nice addition as several had already felt a few drops of rain.

After boarding the carts, which was like boarding an amusement ride, the battery-powered cars jerked before humming forward. They coasted along while the ladies admired banks of ferns and fronds the size of elephant ears, caladiums and some plants they didn't recognize that rose and fell with the landscape.

The narrow path was only wide enough for the carts. It gradually took them downward, and as they did, the foliage thickened. The crowns of the trees crossed overhead and they could hear the sound of water but they couldn't see where it was coming from. Banks of mottled red caladiums were on either side. The tires made soft crushing sounds in the cool silence. Beyond the walkway were other trails with mysterious destinations but the carts remained on the main path. Gerald's voice could be heard with the help of a sound system that linked the three carts.

"Everyone thinks of this part of the state as being almost desert-like but actually, it's some of the richest soil in the state. But because of our dry conditions, Mr. Walliburton knew that the water supply would be critical which is why he dug deep canals that would crisscross the estate, then put in pumps so that from anywhere on the property, they could access a water source. And here," he pointed as they emerged from a particularly dense area, "is Rebecca's Glade, named for the owner's baby daughter who died of cholera in 1849. It was a horrible epidemic and approximately 500 deaths occurred in San Antonio by May of that year." The story caused everyone to look solemnly around this first theatre.

The Glade was thick with ferns and plants with dark green leaves and pinkish-red blossoms. At the end of the walkway were huge plants with the same elephant-ear sized fronds and giant bushes of leafy ferns. Water bubbled up from a natural spring and very little light was able to penetrate the branches of the small ornamental trees that stood in rows. The ladies felt invisible.

Again the carts moved forward, then slowed at the edge of the glade where there was a raised concrete marker. It read, *Rebecca's Glade, In Memory of Eugenia Rebecca Walliburton, 1848-1849. Dedicated 1949.* The carts continued on, bouncing some which entertained the ladies almost as much as the gardens and in a few minutes they crossed a shallow stream which was another adventure though no one got wet. Once they were across the water, they left the dense glade behind and found themselves in a forest where it was once again level. The carts stopped. It was as though they had just landed on the surface of another planet.

CHAPTER 9

To say it was a most unusual scene would be an understatement.

Gerald twisted in his seat to speak to the ladies behind him. The unusual forest lay ahead.

"The owners laid out the Estate, including their gardens, using the natural elevations and soils to create very different spaces. This area was dedicated to tree sculptures because of what was already here. What you are looking at is a type of willow tree that can grow fifteen to twenty feet very quickly. It also contains a hormone that makes them very easy to root. They obviously love this soil and don't need a lot of nutrients to thrive and they do very well in wet locations. I've never seen anything like it, anywhere else in the world."

The ladies stared in disbelief at a scene that belonged beneath the earth, not above it. Seemingly impossible tree limbs scooped down toward the earth where they were buried, only to emerge several feet away to climb back toward the sky to join a canopy of limbs. Thick branches pointed north and south rather than east and west, and it was impossible to tell where they started and stopped. They created openings and closings and in between were individual enclosures, almost like cages. There were breezeways with limb-created walls, then curved branches that looked like sound waves.

"This is unreal. It's impossible," said Mona, as the carts slowly moved forward.

"Can you imagine playing here as a kid?" Gina said to Brooke.

Gerald enjoyed their reactions and gave them plenty of time to soak it in. The carts hummed as they continued along the designated path. They picked up speed and were soon zipping along. They drove through a fence that was made of intertwining grape vines - a hint of things to come. Gerald explained they were now entering the family's vineyards.

Up ahead the ladies saw steep banks that followed the natural escarpment and they were covered in staked rows of bare vines.

There were also rows and rows of trellis-covered vines that spanned several acres.

"This is our newest theatre," Gerald said into the microphone. "Grape-growing didn't really get started until the seventies in Texas. The estate now produces a very nice wine and also several acres are donated to fresh grapes which we ship to market. Mainly muscadine grapes, I believe. The grapes are harvested in mid-September so this is a pretty quiet area right now. Starting in March, it will be the busiest. Vines require constant pruning, training of the vines, weed control."

"Can we purchase your wine?" asked Mona from another cart.

"Most definitely," he said. "Texas passed a law in 2001 that allows the sale of wine by the taste, bottle or case."

"Oh goodie," said Charlotte.

"We can also ship it to your homes whether they're in "wet" or "dry" areas if orders are placed here."

The carts moved along and since the next theatre was several acres away, Gerald happily filled the time with more history.

"As I mentioned earlier, Wally discovered water below, so he put in an elaborate watering system on the estate. He'd arrived in 1847 in a covered wagon from Tennessee. The story is that his father had actually meant to stop in Waco, which was on the Brazos, but he had a vision that he described as 'beyond words'. The vision told him to continue on another week so he kept coming until eventually he arrived here, alongside the San Antonio where he was able to purchase ten thousand acres from the Spanish. It was there, along the river that he envisioned the gardens, the home, and acreage for whatever he could grow. Today, because of the terrain and the water, Walliburton Farms is able to produce drought-resistant rice, award-wining grapes, and fruit sent around the world."

"The Estate is now approximately one hundred thousand acres, which, compared to the King Ranch, for example, isn't very large."

From their reaction, they all thought it was plenty big.

"Irrigation was revolutionary for the time, as were the pumps," he added.

The carts were now jostling along the path. They made several sharp turns and the drivers gunned the motors to climb a steep grade until they were sitting at the edge of a prairie. Their eyes adjusted to the light because the clouds had burned off and it was now bright sunshine.

"Are we still in Texas?" asked Claire. She was looking at what appeared to be watery rice fields. The close quarters were behind them and far ahead were rows of people wearing wide-coned hats.

"I know," said Gerald. "It feels like you're in Japan, doesn't it? You are now in our rice theatre. Rice farming came to the US in the 1600's, but spread through Texas in the 1880's at the same time Mr. Walliburton arrived. Because he had this water source, he was able to cultivate the seed and over time, he developed a strain that was both drought-tolerant, mold-resistant, and could produce up to 30 bushels per acre as compared to the normally produced 18-20 bushels. He also brought Japanese farmers to Texas who gave him seed from the Emperor of Japan. So in 1891, we saw all of these new things. The first rice irrigation and canal system, you have things like the pumps and modern rice mills, and then there's this sudden influx of immigrants from Louisiana and the Midwest so you have cheap labor, and suddenly Texas becomes responsible for almost seventy per cent of the U.S. production of rice. Eventually, Arkansas and Louisiana surpassed Texas, but the Estate is still a very big supplier."

"What are they doing?" Gina asked, looking at the hats bobbing up and down.

Gerald shielded his eyes. "I'm not quite sure. Growing season starts in the early spring, so maybe they're putting in something else. They'll flood the fields soon, and then keep the water at a third of the height of the stalk until harvest. When the seed is ready, they'll drain the fields. We have our own mill, which was another modern innovation, so rather than having to send everything to Louisiana for processing we do it all here." He was finished with the rice portion of the tour.

"Ladies, we'll be covering more typical gardens on our way back to the house. I don't have a lot to say, you probably know the plants as well as I do. They're all beautiful and you're welcome to come back and just walk through at your leisure. Would anyone like some tea?"

"Oh, yes," said Charlotte. Others agreed. The carts began again, taking them, according to Gerald, past breeding operations and they saw cattle and horses grazing in grasses that were at least two feet tall. If there were fences, they were invisible.

"What kind of grass is that?" asked SueBee.

"That's primarily Indiangrass. It puts out dramatic golden plume-like heads in the Fall. Butterflies love it and it's great cover for turkeys and as you can see, excellent for grazing."

As they drew closer to the main house, the gardens became more traditional. They'd been mulched with thick, dark compost and the beds were already turned in soft shapes around large boulders or small ponds. They saw huge bushes of flowerless azaleas, cornflowers, Delphinium and Gerber Daisies. There was a large garden of antique roses and in a shady area were mounds of mahonias holding heavy bunches of purple fruit, red and yellow columbine, turk's cap and tall spires of purple liatris-filled pottery and rounded bushes of blue hydrangeas that had been perfectly placed.

At the base of a hill and on what looked like a golf course but without the traps, the ladies were delivered to a large covered tent with a temporary floor. A cool breeze blew, reminding them it really was Fall, and after being seated at large round tables they were served tea and scones by proper attendants in starched white uniforms. When it was time to move on to the house, they obediently got back in their carts, buzzing and bumping over hill and dale until they were on a concrete path enabling them to cover the ground more quickly. Soon, they were in sight of the famous Walliburton home.

Surprisingly, it looked small and unimpressive. None had known what to expect and only Charlotte knew anything about the Estate but even she hadn't seen the house. Now that they'd arrived, it was a disappointment. Claire said she'd been expecting something like The Breakers in Rhode Island or Hearst Castle in California.

Instead, the Walliburton family home was a Spanish ranch style and looked like it had stretched itself like a rubber band until someone had finally said *enough*.

Gerald offered no explanation. He refused their offers of a tip, saying with a laugh that he'd enjoyed their company and didn't need the money, then he waved goodbye and boarded a cart. They were all sad to see him go.

"First impressions can be deceiving," said Charlotte, as they walked along a simple breezeway of thick stucco walls. "It isn't a showplace but it certainly is practical."

Freshly painted archways were every few feet, and despite the long and low profile, it had a feeling of openness. Large Saltillo tiles covered the floor and they imagined it would have been cool in the corridors, even on the hottest Texas days. Colors were either white stucco or clay red.

The front door, if that was what it was, had a swinging screen door that squeaked when opened. Inside, they were expected and a young man in a blue shirt and nametag was waiting for them. They were each given a lariat with a tape player and ear-phone kit they could use for later if they liked, but first he wanted to tell them about the main rooms. They were led through a crowded area where others were reading plaques and studying photographs toward the 'back' of the house. That's when they realized that looks had been deceiving and the back was actually the front.

Their guide called the large room the *galleria*. It was an enormous room – an uninterrupted space with a vaulted ceiling and heavy beams and hardware running crown to crown. Table-sized chandeliers hung from the beams and the tile floor echoed with their footsteps. The wall they thought was the back of the property that they now realized was the front was of solid glass. Like an endless pool, it gave the appearance that there was nothing separating them from the valley below. The ladies looked out over the landscape they had just been carted over and saw tiny specks that were the horses and cattle still grazing. The guide told them of presidential visits and foreign dignitaries. Also, he said, the life of the ranch centered around multi-generational family gatherings that were traditionally held in this room. Several of the mothers raised their eyebrows at the mention of the extended family and the daughters were relieved that no one asked questions.

Next, the guide led them into the library and stood next to a mahogany buffet on which there was a large sculpture of an Indian on a horse looking down at two ranchers.

"I'm sure you recognize the style of Frederick Remington," said the guide. "This was one of his last pieces and if you look closely, you'll see a strong resemblance between this cowboy and Mr. Walliburton."

The women drew closer and gasped. It was an obvious likeness.

"This was Mr. Walliburton's favorite room and he often entertained Mr. Remington. It was also where he would ask to meet with his employees, handle business, plan for the future of the estate and thus the Texas economy, etc. The bookshelves are approximately forty feet long and you can see they're full."

An hour later, their guide left them in the gift shop and the ladies spread like drops of oil in water. Claire wandered to a wall of books and flipped through the pages of a colorful cook book using home-grown ingredients. There were lawn ornaments, garden statues, bird-feeders and fountains. There seemed to be very little for someone who didn't have a garden.

A colorful scarf behind the counter caught her eye.

"Ma'am?" she said to the saleswoman who was chatting with another customer. Claire drummed her fingers on the counter when the hairs on the back of her neck stood up and a tattooed arm reached around her and pointed at the same scarf.

"May I see that scarf," the Viking-sized biker said loudly, pointing to the scarf with yellow daisies.

"What are you doing here?" Claire said.

The biker ignored her and let the pretty scarf flow through his large fingers. "How much?"

"Twenty dollars."

"I'll take it," he said, handing it back over the counter.

"Wait a minute. I wanted that scarf. Do you have others?" she asked the saleswoman.

"Sorry, that's my last one."

Claire huffed at the biker. "I was going to get that for my granddaughter."

"Little girls don't want scarves."

"Then what do they want?"

He looked around. "That puppy dog poster over there."

Claire looked at the life size image of a sheepdog snuggling with a cat.

"Okay, maybe, but a gentleman would have offered me the scarf. Are you following me?"

"No, you're following me. Get the poster."

"We are not. I'm in a garden club."

"I am, too. And I actually have a season pass." He noticed the surprised look on Claire's face.

"You didn't know you could get passes? Oh yeah, it's a great discount."

Claire eyed the wrapped package and her lips tightened. "Well, I can't believe you're taking my scarf."

The looming figure held out his hand. "I'm sorry. Heavin Jenkins."

She shook it weakly. "Yes. Your name is Heaven?"

"Heavin with an i."

"Why would your parents intentionally misspell your name?" His smile remained steady.

"I think they'd disagree."

"So you're a Christian gang?"

"We aren't a gang, Mrs...?" He waited.

"Claire Sessions."

"Mrs. Sessions. At least not in the way you are suggesting. We love God and riding motorcycles. We even do church on Sunday."

"Heaven," she said, trying not to smile.

"On earth."

"So you're like a missionary?"

He smiled broadly. "Aren't we all?"

CHAPTER 10

It was a much wearier group of women that boarded the bus in the afternoon. Some immediately went and stood in line for the bathroom. For the third time, Claire was there to count.

"Eighteen, nineteen, come on, everyone, back on the bus. They're holding tea for us at the hotel and we don't want to be late."

Mona climbed aboard, followed by a young man carrying a case of wine. He had on the familiar blue Estate shirt.

"Just put it there, dear," she said, pointing to the front row, before handing him a tip.

Like threading a needle, Jean navigated her precious cargo through the parking lot. Claire's eyes swept the sea of cars, looking for the Cadillac, when she was interrupted by the motorcycle riders standing among their big machines while they pulled on gloves and helmets. They recognized the bus and began waving. When Claire saw Heavin, she gave him a congratulatory wave since he had won the scarf. He saluted her in return.

That's when she saw the older, white-haired biker, standing just behind Heavin', waving back. He must have thought she was waving at him. Claire dropped into her seat.

A quiet descended over the bus as the drone from the engine became like white noise. Heads were paired in quiet conversation or with their eyes closed, resting against their headrests. They were arranged differently, Claire noticed. Ruthie was in the back next to Helen, Sheralyn was up front with SueBee. Gina; however, took the empty seat next to her mother.

The bus sailed along in the direction of San Antonio. Traffic was lighter in the middle of the afternoon and it felt like they were floating on ice compared to the rough ride of the golf carts. Jean found a classical music station and several lowered their window shades and found blankets and pillows in the overhead bins.

"I ran into that giant biker in the gift shop," Claire said.

"Uh huh," mumbled Gina, her eyes closed.

"He's their leader. His name is Heavin with an 'I'."

"That's nice," said Gina.

Claire heard muffled conversations behind her. She'd finished her Sudoku book and was bored so she glanced out her window.

"Gina!" Claire said, hitting Gina's arm.

Gina bolted upright. "What?"

"Gina!" Claire shouted again into the window, "that's Lucy's car!"

"Where?"

"There! It's way ahead now but I'm sure that's gotta' be Lucy's car. That's her car! It must be going a hundred miles an hour."

Gina leaned over her mother and pressed her cheek against the window.

"I think I see it. Are you sure?"

"It was exactly what you described to me. What are the odds there are two? What are we going to do?"

"I'm thinking."

"We have to follow it," said Claire.

Gina cursed, then hurried up the aisle of the moving bus and spoke in Jean's ear.

The driver's head riveted with a steely look of understanding, then she shifted her grip on the steering wheel and settled deeper into her cushioned chair.

"Hold on," she shouted over her shoulder.

Claire grabbed her arm rests and the bus surged forward. Those who were resting or sleeping woke up. Gina held on to a metal pole for balance then shouted to the back, "Everyone, hold on!"

Jean shifted gears and pressed hard on the accelerator. The bus was suddenly passing cars, merging left and right, then veered sharply. Everyone grabbed an arm rest or the headrest in front of them.

"Hey," called Helen from the back, "what's going on?"

"Yeah, what's going on?" asked Sheralyn.

"We're chasing a stolen car," shouted Claire.

"Just stay in your seats. It's okay," Gina bent lower to keep her eyes on the car ahead. They were gaining ground and the Cadillac was now only a few cars in front of them. Suddenly, in a daredevil move, it crossed two lanes and took the next exit. Claire screamed.

"He's getting away!"

Jean didn't hesitate. She threw the wheel right and everyone shrieked as the force threw them left and almost sent the bus onto two wheels.

"I'm right behind you, baby," yelled the wild-eyed bus driver.

"Gina!" Claire shouted from her seat, "For pity's sake, don't let her kill us."

Gina either didn't hear or was ignoring her mother.

The bus driver kept the car in sight until it took a sharp turn at the next corner. By the time they'd coasted to a stop, the blue Cadillac had disappeared.

"I don't think this is a very nice part of town," said Sheralyn looking around.

There were old cars parked in the street and boarded up warehouses. It reminded Gina of the old days. Jean squeezed the huge bus between the cars as everyone held their breath. At the end of the block, Gina guessed and told Jean to turn right. Still, the buildings looked abandoned and the few people that were on the street stared openly. The mothers stared back.

"I don't know if we're getting closer or not," said Jean.

The bus drove slowly along one empty street after another. Twenty plus sets of eyes were glued to the windows, searching the side streets. Occasionally someone thought they saw something, but it didn't matter because the bus couldn't make the narrow turn anyway. There was no real sign of the Cadillac.

"Are we still in San Antonio?" asked Mona.

No one answered.

If they did find the Cadillac, Gina knew there would be no element of surprise. The huge white bus might as well be the circus coming to town.

"We lost them," said Brooke, "and I'm afraid we're going to get lost ourselves if we don't head back."

"Too late," said Jean.

"We should at least turn around. I don't like this neighborhood," said Gwen.

"Do you have a map?" Gina asked Jean.

"There!" SueBee suddenly called out.

Up ahead, parked in front of another faceless warehouse, was the blue Cadillac with the white landau top.

Mona struggled to hold onto headrests as she hurried up the aisle.

"What are we going to do? This isn't a safe area, Gina."

The bus stopped next to the Cadillac.

"Is that it?" asked Claire.

"It looks exactly like it," said Gina.

"It has Texas plates," said Ruthie, wanting to make a contribution.

"Let's get off," said Claire.

"No, Mom!"

"But it might leave! Can you hot wire it?"

Gina looked at her mother. "I don't know how to hot wire a car."

"I do," said Jean.

"No one's going to hot wire the car," Gina said, motioning for Jean to keep moving. "I'm going to call the San Antonio PD." Gina reached for her phone when she remembered she didn't have it. No one did. They were all back at the hotel. She looked at her mother who suddenly realized the same thing.

"I can't believe I let you talk me into leaving my phone at the hotel!"

"I'm sorry. But wasn't it nice until now?"

"Hang on," yelled Jean, "There was a gas station back near the highway. We can call from there."

"That's a great idea. I'll stay here just to keep an eye on things. Let me out." Jean opened the doors.

"I'm staying with you," said Claire, moving up the aisle.

"No, you're not. Everyone stays on the bus and when the San Antonio PD gets here, we'll let them handle it."

"Try to hurry," Gina said to the driver before climbing down the steps.

"Yes ma'am," Jean said, saluting, "I'll be right back."

"Jean, wait," said Claire, already at the door. "I'm going with her. Anyone who doesn't need a walker or a restroom, come on. There's strength in numbers."

Jean had no choice and those that qualified got off. Gina couldn't stop them.

"I'll hurry," said Jean, then she gunned the engine and was gone.

Claire pointed a finger at the oldest of the group.

"You four, get inside that Cadillac. Just plant yourselves in there and don't let anyone tell you to get out until the police come. Hopefully no one's going to drive off with you sittin' there. The rest of you, stay near the street while Gina and I check out the warehouse."

Gina put her hands on her hips. "No, Mom, you stay here. I'm checking out the warehouse." She made sure the ladies understood she was serious and drew an imaginary line on the concrete. "Stay behind this line." Then carefully, she approached the warehouse.

The building was in bad shape. It had tall windows of thick milky glass. Gina tucked the small gun she'd retrieved from her bag into her waistband and gripped the crumbling ledges of the windows with her fingertips. She struggled to pull herself up, fighting for another inch but she scratched her chin on the brick and dropped back down. She dusted off her hands and tried the front door. It was locked.

"You should have let Jean teach you how to pick a lock," someone said from behind the line.

"Alright, everybody, we'll just wait outside until Jean gets back with the police."

Suddenly, the door opened, a hand reached out, and Gina disappeared.

CHAPTER 11

"Where did she go?"

"Oh my Lord, what just happened?" cried Mona.

"She was just there!"

Claire recovered first and rushed to the door. She tried twisting the knob but it was locked. She swung her cane and hit the door.

"Open up!"

Helen took her place and banged loudly with the flat of her hand, "Hey, in there. Open up!"

The others crowded around her.

"Sheralyn, run around to the alley," commanded Mona. "See if there's a back door. Don't go in. Just report back."

Sheralyn sprinted around the corner.

"Hello in there? We've called the police so you better open this door immediately," Mona yelled at the door.

Sheralyn returned, breathless. "The back door's locked, too."

"What should we do?" asked Helen.

Ruthie gave it a good kick. "Gina! Don't worry, we're coming to get you."

Brooke said, "Mom, you and the others need to stay near the street. Jean will be back any minute." She looked at Helen, "we need to find a phone. Maybe we can knock on some of the other doors down the street."

Mona ignored her. "You two," she said, pointing a finger as though it were a dagger at Ginger's young daughters-in-law, "go around to the back. Take some others with you. If they run out the back, follow them. At least we'll know which way they're going."

Then she turned to the group, "Does anyone know how to pick a lock?"

"Oh, I do, I do!" said SueBee. She fished in her bag and removed an ancient coin purse with brass clasps. She pulled out a short stick that looked like something one would use to pick out the meat from a pecan.

The ladies gave way. SueBee carefully inserted the tool into the lock, jiggling and twisting it back and forth until she heard a click. She smiled and gave it one last twist and the bolt slid open.

"Okay, stay close," said Mona, her hand on the knob. Charlotte was close behind her.

"Wait a minute," said Brooke, forcing herself in front. "Let us go in first. At least if we have to run, we can run."

Charlotte patted her face.

"Don't worry, Sweetie, no one's going to shoot an old lady."

Mona tried reaching for the knob but Sheralyn fought her for it, and finally wedged herself between Mona and the door like a human shield, her long slender arms creating a full body 'X' over the door.

"You are *not* going in there, Mona," she commanded. "You absolutely may not go in there because you're too old and I don't want my children growing up without their grandmother. I don't think they're going to ask your age before deciding whether or not it's okay to shoot you. At least we can run faster so just wait out here for help. We'll find Gina."

The daughters, packed together, all nodded in agreement.

It was a stunning act of bravery, until SueBee pushed her aside.

"Sorry, Sheralyn, but you need to get your skinny ass out of the way. We're all going in," and without waiting for anyone to agree, she took Claire by the elbow, opened the door and helped her over the threshold. Holding their canes like pitchforks, the mothers stormed the castle.

With the light from the doorway, they could see they were in a small, but emptied out anteroom. It was like a holding cell. Once everyone was inside, the room went suddenly pitch black.

"Okay, who let the door close?" Mona said.

"Sorry," said a small voice belonging to one of the mothers.

"Well hurry up and find a light switch before we all trip over each other."

Hands stretched in every direction and the ladies took a few steps and collided with one another. Claire was afraid to move, too fearful she would fall and never get up in the darkness but she was caught up in the bundle and shuffled along with them until they'd found an opening. This took them into another room. Claire lifted her nose in the air.

"Hey, there's marijuana in here. Do y'all smell that? I wonder if..."

"Okay, that's it," a male voice commanded and at the same time, someone flipped a switch and a light came on.

Naturally, some screamed.

"I found my flashlight!" SueBee said, holding it up.

A semi-circle of about twenty men and women stared at them from behind tall work tables. Single bulbs dangled above them. Cellophane wrapped bundles lay on the tables and there were heavy power tools connected to thick orange cords that curled up from the floor.

Seeing how young they were, the ladies began to relax. They were used to commanding the younger generation. As their eyes adjusted to the light, Claire got a better look and right away she felt sorry for them. They were all very thin and everything about them was undernourished. Their clothes, their hair, their bodies. The marijuana was heavy, but the smell of body odor was worse.

A particularly dirty man came around the table.

"Stop right there," Claire said, pointing the can of pepper spray she'd retrieved from her purse. At least ten of the other mothers were aiming cans as well.

"No, *you* stop right there," he said, pulling out a long knife. "You're breaking and entering and the law in Texas says I can protect myself."

Claire sprayed but she had the nozzle turned wrong and it went sideways.

"Claire, be careful. Excuse me," said SueBee who had no weapon, only the flashlight, "I'm so sorry if we've surprised you but we're worried about someone. My name is Mrs. Lakes and we're just an old garden club that's come down to see the gardens," she said with a sweeping hand. "That's all. And we've lost one of our members. We have absolutely nothing against marijuana, trust me. But Claire's daughter got sucked inside your office. If you'd just point us in the right direction, or send her out, we'll be out of your way as soon as we can hobble ourselves back over that tall doorstep."

The man laughed, unmoved.

"We've called the police," threatened Mona.

The laughter abruptly stopped. He glared at Mona and like two German Shepherds, Brooke and Sheralyn positioned themselves on either side of her.

"Where is she?" they asked in unison. Mona drew herself up as tall as she could and tucked her arms into the girls'. The man curled his lip, then ran his tongue over his nicotine-stained teeth.

He raised the knife and this time it was Charlotte who pushed in front and sprayed. She also missed. When he reached for her, Sheralyn tried pushing him away but he grabbed hold of Charlotte's arm, hurting her. Claire raised her cane.

"Ladies, ladies," a smooth and elegant voice said from a far corner but was fast approaching. "Lawrence, please let go of the lady. There is no need." The voice had a calming effect on the man and as it got closer, he fell into the light and they could see that it was a very handsome, older gentleman.

Unlike his employees, he looked strong and virile. His manner was the same as someone welcoming friends for lunch.

The thin rail of a man released Charlotte's arm and returned to the group.

"Let's start over. My name is Steven," he said, bowing slightly. "How may I assist you?"

Mona looked him in the eye and spoke with authority. "You should know we've already sent someone to get the police. They'll be here any minute, but right now, we want Claire's daughter back. Where is she?"

They smiled at each other until there was an understanding of their equality then Steven cleared his throat. "There are an awful lot of you. Who are you?"

"We're the Hillcrest Heights Garden Club from Dallas. Our daughters are the Junior Group."

"Emphasis on *junior*," said Brooke, not trying to be funny.

"I see, and how amusing. And you say you think someone came in here?"

"My daughter and she didn't come in here, she was kidnapped," said Claire. She didn't care how handsome he was. "That's ridiculous."

"And she's a police officer. Her name's Gina Sessions. No, I mean Downing. Gina Downing and she's a police officer with the Dallas Police Department."

His face soured.

"Your daughter is Gina Downing?"

Claire nodded.

"How unfortunate." Steven suddenly began moving very quickly. He whispered into the same thin man's ear. The man nodded and left.

Steven asked the larger group, "Anyone see a woman come in here?"

There were a variety of no's.

"I'm so sorry, interesting garden club folk. My friends and I will be leaving this way and we would ask you to do the same that way, out the front or you are welcome to stay to greet the police. Everybody, leave everything where it is," he instructed his people. "It's time to take a coffee break," and then Steven disappeared out the back door.

The women didn't know what to do. The workers suddenly started rushing around. They seemed to be concentrating on a few small things, then focused on getting out the back door. It was like someone had activated the fire alarm. Now that they were being ignored, the women started yelling.

"Gina!" Claire shouted. "Gina!"

There was no answer, only the noise of the workers escaping.

"Everyone," Mona cried, pointing toward the door, "that way. Block the door." The women moved as one. The thin people were unprepared for the confusion. Brooke and Helen pushed several back inside. The mothers sprayed pepper spray in every direction.

Suddenly, there was a burst of noise and Heavin was standing in the open doorway with the sun behind him. More bikers flooded in and quickly began chasing the straggling thin people.

The old biker found Claire.

"Are you all right?"

"I can't find Gina," she said, almost crying.

Suddenly, Gina's voice pierced the air. "Mom!"

Claire, the old man, Heavin and Mona followed the sound of her voice into another room where they found her inside a closet, strapped to a chair with her legs and arms bound with duct tape. She had just managed to work her mouth free.

"Are you alright?" Claire asked as Heavin unwrapped the tape from Gina's ankles.

"I'm okay," Gina said, rubbing her wrists, "but where's Steve?"

"He got away," said Claire.

"My guys are trying to round them up," said Heavin.

The sound of sirens got louder and louder and they all knew Jean had found a phone. It must have been a strange sight for the officers arriving to see first a street crowded with rider-less motorcycles then four elderly women sitting calmly in a stolen Cadillac as though waiting for further instructions. Inside, they discovered twenty excited women holding spent cans of mace and canes as well as tough-looking, tattooed bikers standing guard over a group of sinewy individuals hunched along the warehouse wall.

Knowing they were vital to the investigation, the mothers were thrilled to give statements and with their arms waving, they re-enacted the standoff and gave vivid, possibly exaggerated descriptions, adding that they were sure they'd smelled marijuana. When pressed to explain how they could be so sure, the ladies changed the subject.

Gina identified herself and was corralled by the local detectives. Someone found her purse and her gun and everyone, Gina especially, was disappointed to learn that Steven had escaped, though not in Lucy's car. He'd managed to vanish once again.

When the police learned of Jean's military background, they put her in charge of herding the women back on the bus. Everyone - mothers, daughters, bikers and now handcuffed workers - were expected at police headquarters. There was a lot of paperwork to be done.

"How'd you find us?" Gina asked Heavin.

"Dad spotted your bus at the gas station so we pulled off and the driver said you were in trouble. We got here as quick as we could."

"Thank you."

'Dad', the old biker with the silver ponytail, was standing with her mother.

"That's your dad?"

"Yep."

It was time to introduce herself.

"Gina Downing," she said, holding out a hand.

"Andrew Jenkins." He met her with a steady gaze.

"The gang was a God send, weren't they, Gina?" said her mother, somewhat flustered.

"Please, Claire, don't call us a gang," Andrew reminded her and oddly, she apologized.

"Come on, the police are waiting," called Jean from the door of the bus. Andrew extended his hand to help Claire with the first step and she accepted it without hesitation.

CHAPTER 12

Day Two of the pilgrimage, Gina felt like she'd been gone a lifetime. She woke to the familiar sound of her mother getting ready. Untangling herself from her sheet, she rolled over. It was barely light.

"Come on, Sleepyhead," Claire said, fixing her hair.

Gina moaned.

"I slept like a baby last night. How'd you sleep?"

"I can't remember. Can't we just stay at the hotel and relax?"

"Gina! Don't forget, the purpose of this pilgrimage is to do things together. As a group."

"Okay, so let's rest together. I've had enough bonding."

"Yesterday was just a foretaste of things to come." Claire threw the curtains open and raised the window.

"Really, Mom," said Gina, laying back down and pulling the covers over her head.

The sound of motorcycles roared from outside. Gina jerked the sheet off her face and looked at her mother.

"Did you plan that?"

"No, but can you smell that?"

Gina sniffed. She caught a whiff of bacon and maple syrup. Her mouth started to water. She had no choice but to struggle out of bed then slipped into her moccasins. On her way to the bathroom, Gina passed Brooke but neither spoke.

A few minutes later, Gina returned and climbed back into the bed. "No one's in line for the bathroom, Mom, if you want to get down there. I'll wait."

"I already did. Didn't have to wait a minute. You know, when I was young, there were four kids and only one bathroom. Never was a problem. Now come on, it's our last day."

"Aren't you tired?" She watched as her mother put final touches on her make-up. "Why can't I just stay here and relax? If I don't, I'm going to be exhausted when I get back from my vacation."

"Awww, poor thing. Come on. It won't be as much fun without you," then added, "Oh, come on. We'll take it slow. If you need it, I can try to see if someone has an extra wheelchair."

"Ha ha," said Gina.

Downstairs, a buffet breakfast was waiting for them in the dining room with platters of bacon, pancakes, cinnamon rolls and eggs. The owner was clearing off tables as fast as people left them.

"Get you a plate, honey," said their hostess on her way out.

Gina picked out a fat cinnamon roll with icing dripping off its sides, a blueberry pancake and three strips of bacon. She got especially excited when she saw a bowl of blueberries and put a spoonful on top of the pancake.

Brooke, Helen and Sheralyn were already at the table. They looked as tired as she felt.

"Morning."

"Morning," they all mumbled, their faces buried in a coffee mug.

"Almost didn't make it."

"Me neither," said Brooke. "Mom made me come."

"Good morning, girls," sang Claire sitting down. "Is everyone ready for another adventure?"

Sounds of moaning and grumbling echoed inside the mugs.

Gina took a bite of the cinnamon roll. Liquid sugar dripped off her fingers.

"That looks like a thousand calories," said Charlotte, pulling out a chair to sit down.

"I sure hope so," said Gina.

"So what's the plan for today?" asked Sheralyn.

"Oh, we have a wonderful day planned," said Claire.

"I didn't know we'd planned anything," said Gina.

Claire started to laugh. "You've never been on one of our pilgrimages."

"Give us a hint," said Brooke.

"Please say Spa Day, please say Spa Day," said Helen.

"Yes, we're going to start with the Spa, but then after that a cruise and then shopping on The River Walk," said Claire.

"Yes!" said Helen victoriously.

SueBee and Mona joined them at the table.

"Helen wanted to sleep in. Can you believe that?" SueBee said.

"Gina did, too."

"Wimps," said Mona.

Claire hurried everyone to eat up, then ushered them back to their rooms with strict instructions to be at the bus in thirty minutes.

At exactly nine o'clock, she stood ready with her clipboard and checked off names as people boarded the bus. Once all were onboard, the motor roared and the bus pulled out, headed for the city.

"I had a dream last night," said Helen to Gina, leaning across the aisle.

"What?"

"I dreamed we were driving along in this bus and someone shouted, 'Hey, look, there's Sandra Bullock! We must have been near the mall because she was running alongside our bus and she was wearing this beautiful dress, as if she'd just come out of Neiman Marcus or something."

"Our bus?" asked Gina.

Helen nodded. "It was this gorgeous, glittery pink thing covered in sequins and she had on a white mink shawl draped over her shoulders. She was running and I leaned out of the window and I said, "Hey, Sandra, I love your movies!"

"She looked up at me while she's running and she smiles that cute, perky smile and she said, 'Thanks', and then I said, 'Hey, do you need a ride?' And she said, 'Sure'. So then she dropped a shoe, you know, like something quirky that she always does in her movies and gives that snorty laugh, but she got it back on and then she caught up with us and we helped her get on the bus.'"

"What happened after that?" asked Brooke.

"I woke up. She was so nice and looked so beautiful in that pink sequined dress."

"I love Sandra Bullock," said Mona from the back of the bus. "I loved her in Pulp Fiction."

Gina turned in her seat.

"You liked Pulp Fiction?"

"Sure. Especially Mia."

"That was Sandra Bullock?" asked Brooke.

"That was Uma Thurman," said Helen.

"You liked Pulp Fiction, too?" asked Gina.

"Uma's a true blond," said Sheralyn. "Sandra's a brunette. Couldn't have been her."

"Are you sure that wasn't Sandra?" asked Mona.

Helen was. "I'm sure. It was Uma. She wore a wig."

"But what does the dream mean?" asked Mona.

"I have no idea, except that maybe someday, Sandra and I are going to become really good friends."

"Wouldn't that be nice," said SueBee who had been listening from behind.

The bus rocked slightly and settled back down amid the San Antonio traffic. Eventually they were in the city again and came alongside the River Walk where flat-bottomed boats waited in line to load their tourists. It was still early, but there were already small groups strolling along the wide stone sidewalks, admiring store fronts and workers sweeping up patios and up-righting chairs in preparation for the day.

Jean parked the bus and from there they could look across the square and see the Alamo.

"It looks so small," said Sheralyn as they walked toward it.

"The movies do that," said Mona.

Trees older than any living person marked the corners of the grassy area the city had managed to preserve, and there were chalky white walls and gates at entrances and exits so that visitors would know what might be hallowed ground because Jim Bowie or Davie Crockett had once sat down for a smoke on this very spot. There was a growing crowd in front of the entrance to the fort. The Garden Club however, was headed for the hotel, just across the street.

Once inside, they were immediately struck by the natural light that flooded the lobby. It had beautiful Spanish tile floors and everywhere they looked there were inlaid frescos in the floors and on the walls and even going up the steps of a wide staircase that curved around to the second floor. Each scene was a work of art. Water shot from a fountain in the middle of the lobby. When it came down, it spilled into three levels of colorful tiled basins before filling the bottom bowl.

"And why aren't we staying here?" asked Mona, looking wishfully toward the ceiling which was another work of art. "It's like the Sistine Chapel."

"I told you, every hotel in San Antonio was completely booked. We only decided on this trip a few days ago. I did the best I could."

"You did fine, Charlotte," said SueBee.

With help from the concierge, the Garden Club found their way to the spa located toward the back of the hotel. It didn't look like much, just a small waiting room barely big enough for them to stand, but they weren't there long before someone came to usher them to private changing rooms where each was given a big cushy bathrobe, a soft headband and slippers with pillowed soles.

The rest of the morning consisted of facials and then the ladies had the choice of either a massage or a manicure. Afterward, all were wrapped in hot towels and moisturized. For lunch they were given mimosas and a delicious trio-salad plate, complements of Mona's contact at the hotel. Finally, they emerged, camera-ready.

"Follow me!" Walking in pairs, Mona led them toward the stone stairs that curved down to the river where two boats, with guides, were already waiting. They divided themselves between the rocking boats. Those hard of hearing sat toward the front near the guide and the daughters stayed near the back.

As they floated along the dark water, the guide launched into a history of San Antonio and at several places, the ladies looked at each other knowingly because they'd heard it the day before. Rounding a crook in the river, they heard the sharp sounds of a steel guitar and came upon a crowd gathered around a small amphitheatre. The boat slowed to watch.

There was a swirl of color as a woman twirled at dizzying speeds. Her shirt was cut low and the flaring skirt had stripes of bright reds, blues and greens. She was dancing on a small wooden platform with her hands raised over her head, clicking castanets while a guitar player sat in a small chair on the corner of the platform. Another, older women clapped her hands to the beat of the heels on the hard floor.

The garden club watched until the end of the song and then clapped furiously.

The boat pulled away and the guide explained, "you were very lucky. You got to see one of our city's finest flamenco dancers."

"Is it flamingo dancing?" asked Sheralyn.

"No ma'am, it's *flamenco* and this is not salsa dancing. It's a fine art, studied for years. They perform throughout the year, but primarily in the summer. I don't usually see them in the Fall. You were very lucky."

"I'm glad we didn't stay in the room," said Gina.

"Me, too," said Helen, then asked quietly, "Is your mom really moving in with Mona?"

"Yes. She's pretty excited."

"What do you think?" asked Sheralyn.

"I'm a little sad about losing the house but happy for her."

"Well," started Helen, shifting a little because the wooden seats had grown hard, "there's a house down the street from me for sale. I know there are other little kids on the block that look like they're about Sammy's age and there's the park down the street."

"Thanks, Helen, but I don't think we can afford your neighborhood."

"What about Blake's art. Any prospects?" asked Brooke.

"It's slow."

"I don't get it," said Helen. "His charcoals are so amazing."

"It's hard to find a gallery. They want artists who have a following, but how do you get a following without an exhibition?" No one knew.

"So be honest, Helen, how is Craig doing? You made the comment yesterday that you hoped he'd figure things out before he got arrested. You were kidding, right?" She kept her voice down so that only the four of them could hear.

"Oh, he's fine."

No one believed her.

"Stuart and I have gotten a few calls from school. His teachers say they know he's smart, but he doesn't seem to be trying as much as he used to. He's starting to hang around with kids that have a reputation for getting into trouble. That's not the way we raised him."

"He's a teenager, Helen," said Sheralyn.

"I have this feeling he's this close to doing things he knows is wrong. I don't have proof yet, but I keep praying God lets me find out, whatever it is."

Brooke nodded as though she'd felt the same way with her kids. "What does Stuart say about all this?" she asked.

Helen hesitated.

"Stuart thinks I'm too easy on him. He wants to know where he is every minute, and I think we should give him a little freedom. You've got to give them some freedom. See if you can trust them. But it's so hard."

Gina was about to add her thoughts when the guide interrupted.

"And here we are, ladies, back at the beginning. I hope you've enjoyed the tour. Please have a wonderful time in our city, and if you enjoyed the tour, don't miss the tip jar at the top of the steps."

Once everyone was back on dry land, Gina asked, "does anyone else need to stop for a restroom break before we get back on the bus? I know I do."

"Back on the bus?" said Charlotte. "But we haven't even shopped yet!"

"Don't tell me you girls are tired?" said Mona.

Without waiting for an answer, the mothers headed off in the general direction of the shops they'd been floating by. At first, the daughters didn't follow, then Claire looked back. "Moving too fast for you?"

Sunday morning, the bus for home showed up, though sadly without Jean. Their favorite Marine had been hired by the hotel while the bus to and from Dallas was Mona's connection. Still, they'd learned a few things and before the new driver got off they'd already started folding up their walkers and stowing them in nice order underneath the bus.

Looking like a postcard, the proprietors stood on the porch beneath the Hotel Minnetonka sign exactly half way between the six chained rockers to wave goodbye. From the bus, the ladies took pictures and waved back enthusiastically, promising to return next year.

"I wonder how many unsuspecting guests arrive at the Hotel Minnetonka thinking it's a five-star hotel?" said Brooke, smiling and waving back at the happy couple.

Gina gave them two thumbs up, adding, "and that was a great line, 'we don't know how to update our website,'" she mimicked. "And they probably have a steady stream."

Ruthie, who had changed before their eyes over the weekend and now talked constantly, "but it really wasn't that bad, once you got used to going down the hall."

"All part of the adventure," said Charlotte.

"I told you it would be an adventure," Claire said in Gina's ear once they were settled in their seats.

"It was way more than an adventure, Mom. I'm glad we all lived to tell about it. I wasn't so sure that was going to happen."

"You're exaggerating, Gina. I didn't feel like I was ever in any danger."

"I'm talking about the shopping, Mom. I thought I was going to die. My feet were killing me. I don't know how you all do it."

Claire laughed, surprised. "Practice," she said, then changing the subject, asked, "Do you think you'll get a finder's fee for Lucy's car?"

"No, Mom. The police don't give out finder's fees. They feel like it's part of my job."

"Well, they should do something for you."

"I'll be happy if they don't arrest me. By the way, how do you always seem to be getting into something that might get me arrested?"

Claire didn't find that funny and sat back with a humph. "At least our old business is a legitimate one now," she said, referring to the garden club's former marijuana-growing business of a few years ago.

"Only because you sold it to the boys in Colorado."

"Lucky for us."

"Lucky for them."

"Anyway, you and the other mothers are the real heroes. You spotted the car and rescued me. And, thank God, no one was hurt. It could have turned out a whole lot different."

"Exactly. And speaking of which, I've had an idea, but I don't want you to answer. Just think about it. What if you became a private detective? You'd have gotten paid a lot of money for finding the car."

Gina didn't say so, but the idea had actually crossed her mind.

"I don't know. I don't think we could afford to do something like that right now. At least not until Blake starts selling some art."

Gina's phone rang. It was the Captain.

"You go on vacation and solve a case? This is going to look good in your file, Downing."

"Thank you, Sir. I didn't expect it, either."

"I heard your Mom and a bunch of her friends got into it with Steven. I'm looking forward to hearing how that happened. Lucky you were kidnapped before they stormed the castle – if not, you'd all be in a lot of trouble."

"Lucky for me, Sir, but it's a long story."

"You couldn't make them stay on the bus?"

"Not this group."

"Well, the SAPD is going to send us the fingerprints and hopefully we can put some of those workers away. Too bad Steven got away. I just hope he doesn't come back to Dallas. Oh, by the way, are you driving that car back?"

"Sir?"

"The car that belongs to...," he read, "Lucy. Somebody's got to drive it here."

"Actually, Sir, I'm already on the bus with my garden club."

"I hear it's a pretty sweet car. Wouldn't you rather drive it than ride on the bus with your mother?"

Gina saw Ruthie across the aisle in a deep conversation with Helen. She eyed her mother. "No, not really. I think I'd rather ride on the bus."

"Okay, I'll find somebody else. I guess we'll see you tomorrow."

"Listen, Captain, since I worked all day Saturday, could I possibly take Monday off?"

"Nope. Your fault for using your vacation. I'll see you tomorrow."

"Well did he tell you you were going to get a medal?" Claire asked when she got off the phone.

"No, Mom."

"What did he say?"

"He said, 'see you on Monday'."

The bus was once again quiet except for the sounds of the engine beneath them. They'd fought off criminals, fear and exhaustion and now they were going home. Some had been only acquaintances on the drive down. Now they were friends with stories that would be told for years to come.

From up front, the stranger at the wheel had no idea who he was talking to when he asked if anybody liked music and did they want him to turn on the radio? Would they like to listen to something quiet so they could nap?

Charlotte dug beneath her seat and pulled out the songbooks. She sent them around and soon everyone, including Gina, was singing at the top of their lungs.

'Oh my darlin', oh my darlin', oh my darlin' Clementine, you are lost and gone forever, heavy sorrow Clementine.'

The bus driver started to say something but was interrupted.

'In a canyon, in a canyon...'

Without distinction among the women or their voices, they sang jubilantly.

CHAPTER 13

Gina picked up the small framed picture from her coffee table. It was a drawing of delicate flowers, the one Blake had given her at the very beginning of their story when she didn't know him at all. He'd suddenly entered her world, first at Jackson's Bar, then at Mona's ranch. She felt her heart swell with a mixture of love and pride as she looked at the detail of his talent that could be seen in each petal.

She put the picture back down, then shouted toward the bedroom, "Hey, come on, Blake. Mom'll be here any minute!"

"Don't rush me. I'm still in my birthday suit!"

"Sheesh," Gina said, picking up a magazine and dropping on the couch next to her daughter. "Men."

"Sheesh," said Sammy, mimicking her mother and in the same way flipping through her favorite picture book, *The Caboose Who Got Loose*.

"Watch your language, young lady," Gina said, giving her a playful tickle.

The front door opened. Tonight's babysitter had arrived bearing gifts. Beneath a long heavy coat, Gina saw her mother's favorite green jogging suit. A boxy purse hung over one arm and a full shopping bag was in each hand. Both looked heavy.

"You and Blake can leave now. Samantha, Miss Four-Year-Old, come over and help me." Claire stopped mid-stride in front of Gina.

"Where's Blake?"

"Preening," said Gina. "Have a seat and relax," she said, not expecting her to. She knew her mother.

"Mimi!" Sammy ran to her grandmother, her eyes on all the bags.

"Let's go see what I brought you."

Sammy skipped after her into the kitchen where the bags dropped with heavy thuds. She watched as Mimi the magician began pulling things out.

"These are for you," she called out. Gina didn't want to but she went to look. There was already a stack of magazines and books on the table.

One by one, her mother pulled out a shoebox, hair combs, several bolts of ribbon then a gallon-sized baggie stuffed with who knew what.

By now, Sammy had climbed up on a stool to get a better view. Her eyes darted back and forth between the shoebox and the baggie and her bottom wiggled in the air. "What's in the box, Mimi?"

"Well, let's see." Claire removed the lid.

"Wow," Sammy said in an airy voice that oozed with amazement. Orange yarn dropped in a pile on the table then Claire's hand dove back in and came out with a pair of old glasses.

"Wow," said Claire with the same voice, setting them on Sammy's nose.

After the glasses there was a toy that looked like it had come from a nineties Happy Meal, some Christmas ornaments and several pieces of costume jewelry. Each time the hand emerged, Sammy wiggled in excitement.

Gina went back to the couch. She flipped pages of the magazine without reading. She knew what was going on. Her mother was cleaning out her drawers for the move to Mona's and didn't want to throw anything away. She was going to bring it all over to her house under the pretense of being for Sammy. Gina licked a finger and flipped another page, almost tearing it.

Blake appeared, looking handsome in a dark sport coat and white collared shirt. Gina forgot about the growing pile of junk in the kitchen.

"Well, come on. Let's get this over with," he said.

"Haha, very funny."

"Good-bye," Claire said. "When you get home, I want to talk to you about my move."

Before Gina could answer, she saw her mother eyeing the stack of flower show invitations on the kitchen counter.

"Mom, don't mess with my invitations."

"I won't, but you know I could help you with those."

"And I want you to but not until I'm ready. Sammy, show Mimi your pictures and there's ice cream in the freezer and she can stay up as late as you say."

"How much ice cream can she have?"

"Whatever you think is best."

"Don't worry, Mimi, I know what's best."

"I'm sure you do, Sweetie."

"I'll talk to you about the move later." At the door, Gina straightened a candle on the side table where they always dropped their keys. For some reason, it always seemed to be tilting about ten degrees no matter how many times she fixed it.

"Gina?"

"Yes, Mom."

"I was thinking; you know that lamp that's in my front bedroom? I think it would look so sweet in Samantha's bedroom. It was Aunt Jessie's, you know. She brought it from the family farm in Pampa."

"We'll talk about it later, Mom, okay?"

Blake opened the door.

"We'll try to be home by eleven."

"No hurry. You doing okay, Blake?"

"Wonderful," he said.

Gina straightened the candlestick again. "Goodnight."

"Have you decided on what you're going to do for the flower show?" They shut the door without answering.

Blake and Gina waited until the elevator doors had closed before laughing and then they kissed until the elevator stopped on four and an older couple got on.

Blake held Gina's hand until they emerged into the parking garage.

"Are you hungry?" Blake looked hungry but not for food.

"I really am," said Gina.

"Darn. Okay, where to?"

"Can we go to the Square? I'd love to get Chinese and then we can walk around before the movie."

"Get in." The SUV door was high so he lifted her up. She had on a tight black leather skirt that stopped mid-thigh.

"Thank you very much, kind sir."

On the way to the restaurant, they talked about work and a few things that needed fixing around the house. They talked fast because once they arrived at the restaurant, the rule was, they had to change the subject. After all, this was supposed to be a date and if there was shop talk, then it wasn't a date.

Blake helped her off with her jacket. Her blouse was a low, V-neck and shimmered in the dim light of the restaurant.

"You look delicious tonight, my dear," he said, nuzzling her neck.

"Why, thank you. I'm feeling pretty tasty myself."

They smiled playfully at each other.

Blake ordered wine and told the waiter they would order later. In the candlelit room, they sipped their drinks and held hands, slowly moving out of their mommy/daddy roles and anything else that had to do with work. Just as the waiter refilled their glasses, the Blake and Gina they used to be managed to find its way to the surface.

"So what else is going on?" Blake asked after they'd ordered.

"Helen mentioned that there's a house for sale down the street from her."

"Nice."

"I told her we weren't in the market right now, but hopefully soon."

Blake nodded.

She waited until he looked up.

"What? Are you pregnant?"

"No! Why would you say that?"

"I don't know. You had that look of wanting to say something but you're afraid how I'm going to react."

"I'm not afraid," said Gina.

"So what is it?"

"Actually, there are a couple of things I would love to talk about. First, can we talk about a house? With Mom moving to Mona's, maybe this is the right time. She's going to have a lot of extra furniture that I know she's going to want me to have. And Sammy's just a couple of years from first grade. We need to decide where we want her to go and find a really good neighborhood with lots of families and kids, and what junior high and high school we want her to go to. I don't want to be moving around for the next twelve years."

"Gina, slow down. Can we stop at elementary school as far as the planning?"

She picked at the small pieces of chicken in her lettuce wraps. "I want her to have consistency in where we live, not changing schools all the time."

"I do, too. And we'll think about all that, when we're ready. But we aren't ready right now. Right?"

"I guess."

"You know you're the main breadwinner right now, Gina, but hopefully it's just a matter of time before I'll be right up there with you. And when both our careers are solid, we'll have a lot more options. I don't want to buy some shack or run down house. I'd rather buy something we love and can live in for a long time."

"I agree."

Blake offered Gina a piece of his sushi.

"Try not to plan everything, Gina."

That hurt. "I don't plan everything. I think ahead. I think I've been patient a long time. Like I said, I just want to talk about it because it's exciting to me and I wish it were exciting to you."

He was silent.

"So what's going on with you?" she asked. "Are you happy?"

"I'd be a lot happier if I could sell some of my stuff."

"You will, I know it."

"Yeah. At least we have your income."

Gina picked at her food again until Blake couldn't stand it anymore.

"Now what."

"This is probably not the right time for this either but you might as well know, I've been thinking about quitting the police force."

Blake dropped his fork. "Great. We'll really be able to afford a house then."

"Blake! That's not what I'm saying."

They ate in silence.

Finally, Gina began, "I need your advice, Blake. Can you please help me think about this? I'm not quitting today, but what do you think about me going out on my own? Not this second, but someday."

"For a date you sure have a lot of baggage." Neither of them laughed. His eyes softened and stared into her eyes. "Gina, I want you to be happy. Is that what you want?"

"I'd like to be in charge of what cases I took. I'd like to get paid for what I did, wherever it was. And if I were a PI, I think I might be able to be home a lot more with Sammy."

"Okay, but what about the money? You've got to get the business first, right? And right now, I'm still trying to get in a gallery so we need your income, Babe. You know that."

"I know. But couldn't we last a few months?"

"It might take a lot longer than that. It's too risky and even if you did get the business, do PIs make that much? I'm imagining Chinatown right now and Jack Nicholson didn't make much. And can we talk about this later?"

"Okay. Sorry. What do you want to talk about?"

Blake pushed his plate back. He motioned the waiter and asked for coffee.

"Anything other than work."

Claire was asleep on the couch when they got home a few hours later. Sammy's toys had vanished and there was the faint smell of bleach coming from the kitchen. Gina also noticed that the two wingbacks that had flanked the patio window were now in front of the couch and her collection of china cottages had been moved from the coffee table. She had no idea where but she knew she'd eventually find them.

Gina gently shook her mother's shoulder.

"Back so soon? How was the movie?" Claire asked, slowly shifting herself to a sitting position. Gina sat down.

"It was good but I don't think you'd like it. It was pretty violent." Hearing their voices, Sarge emerged from the guest bedroom but stayed away from the couch.

"What did you have for dinner?" Claire asked as she stood and retrieved her coat.

"We went to the Square. We had Chinese. It was good. Are you sure you don't want Blake to take you home?"

"I'm fine. It's well lit the whole way. It's almost like daylight. Samantha was as sweet as she could be. She insisted on scooping her own ice cream and then she showed me how to make a face with Cheerios. She insisted on doing mine as well."

"She likes being in control," said Gina.

"Like her mother."

"No, like her grandmother."

"Ladies, I don't want to be rude but I'm going to bed. Thanks, Claire." Blake gave Gina the look on his way to the bedroom.

"Goodnight, Blake. Oh, Gina, what about the sheets?"

"Sheets?"

"I have lots of sets. You need to come see what you'd like and the movers are coming two weeks from today so we don't have much time. I know you're busy, so just come by when you can."

Gina walked her to the door. "Thanks for babysitting. You sure you don't want me or Blake to run you home? It's really no trouble."

Claire ignored the question and Gina closed the door behind her.

Sammy was asleep, dressed in long red underwear and splayed face down on top of her covers. Her hands were tucked beneath her chest like a mummy waiting to be wrapped. Gina picked up a white teddy bear that had fallen off the bed and tucked it by her side, then worked the covers over her and kissed her gently on the head.

Blake was already in bed reading when she got back.

"How's your mother?"

"She's operating on all cylinders. I imagine she's probably getting five hours of sleep a night and spending the other nineteen planning the move."

Gina changed quickly. Instead of a T-shirt, she slipped into a silk champagne-colored nightgown over her head and admired the way it slid over her curves, then brushed her hair until the natural highlights in the dark brown mass glowed. Satisfied, Gina turned out the light and walked back into the darkened bedroom.

"Oh, I see we're in the mood to talk," Blake said, patting her side of the bed.

"Oh yes, I want to discuss Sammy's college fund. Would that be alright?"

"Hmmm," Blake said, stroking her hair as she lay beside him, "that's exactly what I want to talk to you about. But first of all," he said, kissing her lips, "I think we should discuss the rising bond market."

"Oooo, the bond market," Gina said, scooting closer and laying comfortably on her back, letting him work his way over her, "I love talking about the bond market." She couldn't help it and started to giggle.

"Stop it, you financial genius. Tell me what you really think is going to happen with the Yuan and the," Gina arched her back and moaned, "the price of gold."

"Stop talking about the price of gold," he said.

The next hour was intent on finding new ways to please each other, none of which involved laughing.

It was after one when Gina got up to change into her T-shirt. She walked bare-footed into the kitchen and returned with two big glasses of water, but Blake was already wrapped in his cocoon of sheet and comforter and snoring softly.

CHAPTER 14

Monday morning, Gina had been at her desk only a few minutes when the phone rang.

"Hi, Mom," she said without waiting to see who it was.

"When did you say you were coming by to go through closets with me?"

Gina gazed out her window at the fog still sitting on top of the Ambassador Hotel. Sometimes it got like that in Dallas. There'd be moisture in the air, but not enough to rain and the clouds would hang so low that even the cars in front of you looked misty white. She'd forgotten about their talk last Friday.

"I don't think I did. When would you like me to come over?

"Why don't y'all come for dinner on Wednesday." It wasn't a question.

Gina flipped open her calendar. How many closets could there be?

"Okay. And Mom," Gina offered, "I really am excited about you moving in with Mona. I think it's the perfect solution."

"Well, I don't know about that, but I'm sure it will be an adventure."

"Can I bring anything?"

"Oh, no, don't bring a thing! I'm trying to clean out my pantry. I don't even know what we're having. That'll be another adventure, see you then," and the line went dead.

When Wednesday came, Gina tried to get home early. She straightened the candle at the door and headed for her bedroom.

"Sammy?" Gina called but no one answered. The condo was quiet. Too quiet.

Sarge followed her. She passed the door to Blake's studio, then backed up. Blake was sitting in the battered chair from his bachelor days with his arms lying helplessly open. An empty beer bottle was in one hand and things were open and disorganized, as if he'd been in the middle of something, then suddenly decided to sit down.

"Come on, Sweetie, let's go. Chop chop. Mom's expecting us." Gina paused. "What is it?"

"I'm done," he said, staring at an unfinished canvas on the easel.

"What do you mean, 'I'm done?'"

"I can't do this anymore."

Gina went to stand in front of him. "Okay, what?"

He looked up at her with doleful eyes, then took a dry sip from the empty bottle.

Gina pushed back the cowlick and took the longneck out of his hand.

"Blake, what's happened?"

"They want conflict, they want angst. They want violence and dysfunction. Can you believe that?"

"Who? Who wants violence?"

"I got a call back from that gallery owner I talked to last week," he said, and then in a voice that mimicked a child's whining tone, "My stuff isn't marketable because it's not *commercial* enough."

Gina laughed, then almost fell when Blake leapt out of his chair and grabbed an open can of paint, throwing it against the wall. It hit with a loud crack then fell to the floor where a creeping lava flow began to spread. Now there was a green lightning bolt on the wall that had already started dripping down.

"Blake! What is wrong with you?"

"I can't paint like that," he said, his arms waving. "I can't do this anymore. I should get a real job so that you can go be a private detective and Sammy can go to a private school." He slumped back into his chair.

Gina had never seen him this angry before. He was like a dormant volcano whose pressure had finally been more than he could stand.

"Okay, I get it, and I'm sorry, but you've heard that before."

"Thanks."

"You've heard it before because you're doing what you have to do in order to make it, Blake. You are a wonderful painter and you know rejection has nothing to do with your talent." Gina waited, watching before trying again. "It has nothing to do with your talent." Still, he didn't look at her.

"I love your work, Blake. It's beautiful and inspiring and just because a gallery owner doesn't show your style doesn't mean you're not amazing. *I* think you're amazing and so do a lot of people. You just have to keep doing what you were created to do. And I know it gives you joy. It's just a matter of time."

Gina said one more thing and as she said it, she knew she was right. "Just don't keep all that explosive stuff inside. Maybe put some of that on your canvas. Now snap out of it, okay?"

Blake slowly smiled.

"Yeah, whatever," he said, getting up and wrapping her in his arms.

"Thanks," he said.

"You're welcome. Now let me go so I can call Mom and tell her we're going to be late. You need to clean that up."

Dinner at Claire's house was meant to be an adventure. She served cold beets, canned lite peaches, a small tuna and spinach casserole, and some Uncle Ben's white rice.

"I still haven't made a dent in my pantry," said Claire after they'd all commented on the combination. "I've left a sack of cans by the door for you to take home, Gina. Now, Blake, tell me. How are sales going?"

Gina nearly choked.

"Well, I talked to a gallery in the Westwood district. They said I could bring by some pieces and they'd take a look. I'm not sure if it's a good match but it's worth a try."

"That's wonderful!" said Claire. "That's all you can do. You never know where the ripples will take you."

Gina couldn't look up or she'd burst out laughing. He'd lied through his teeth.

"That's right," Gina coughed, "you never know where those ripples are going to go," then Blake kicked her under the table.

After dinner, Claire made everyone follow her back to her bedroom. The hall was lined with boxes stacked high on both sides.

She asked Blake to open a cedar chest that sat at the foot of her bed. It had four claw feet and was almost as tall as the bed. It had rusty hinges and the cedar smell was long gone but Gina remembered it from her childhood. At her mother's direction, she removed several layers of crocheted quilts until there were only cardboard boxes lining the bottom. Claire tapped one with her cane.

"Get that one," she said. "Go ahead, Samantha, open it."

"Can I?" she asked her mother.

"May I," her grandmother corrected, "Of course you may. I just told you to do it and it's my box." Sammy leaned against the bed and lifted the lid. With both hands, she took out a coal black train engine and set it on the floor, then lay down at eye level and began rolling it back and forth on the carpet.

"Gina, get that other box out," Claire said, using her cane again to point.

The second box held neat stacks of metal train tracks stacked according to shape. There were long straight ones, short straight ones and the necessary curved ones. Sammy jumped back up, still holding her train engine.

"I know you never knew him, but this is your Grandfather's gift to you, Samantha. He always said he wanted his grandchild to have it so when we parted ways," she didn't like using the word divorce, "he made me promise that I'd save it for Gina's child. Never sell it, he said, because one day, Gina's gonna' have a baby and that little guy'll want it."

Claire eyeballed Sammy. "I don't think he cared if it was a boy or girl, do you?"

Sammy shook her head quickly.

"That's so cool, Sammy," said Blake.

"How come I never saw this?" asked Gina.

"He put it away. He wanted it to survive him."

Gina and her mother shared a look. Her father had died of cancer several years ago and even though her parents had been divorced, it had been hard for everyone. Claire cleared her throat.

"I just hope you like trains, Samantha. I never really did have much of an interest in the thing. It took up so much room, but he always hoped a grandchild might like it."

"*Might* like," Gina said, watching her daughter. It was like Christmas morning.

"You know, I was thinking," began Claire like it had just occurred to her, "Why don't we set it up at Mona's house when I move over there? I'm pretty sure she has an empty room so maybe we can put the tracks together and then you can come over to play with it."

The girl's eyes flashed and her face was full of tiny white teeth and dimples.

Gina whispered in her mother's ear, "said the spider to the fly. Nice work, Mom."

It was decided. The train was Sammy's but would reside at Mona's.

Eventually, Sammy and Blake went to watch TV. Gina obediently trailed her mother through several closets, then they went to sit with the others. Claire brought up Halloween.

"What are you going to be, Sammy?"

"I'm gonna' be a hobo and don't forget to leave your light on, Mimi. That tells people you're home."

"Oh, I'm not turning on my light. Not this year. Who's giving out candy and who's going with Sammy?"

"We haven't talked about it," said Gina.

"I'll go with Sammy," said Blake. Gina frowned.

"Why don't I come over and then you can both go trick and treating with Samantha."

"Trick-*or*-treating, Mom," said Gina. "Sure. That would be great. I guess that means we both need a costume. And you can stay the night in the guest room."

"I'll bring candy."

"No, Mom, please, I've already got plenty of candy."

"Oh no, I think I saw some bags in the pantry."

CHAPTER 15

Halloween night arrived and Gina was starting to sweat as she stood over the sausage browning in the skillet. She chopped at several bigger chunks of Italian sausage, then turned to the cutting board and began chopping a few cloves of garlic and bell pepper. The front door bell rang and she heard Sammy getting it.

Her mother entered with several bags. Sammy followed like a puppy dog.

"Mom, could you help Sammy get in her costume?"

"Sure, in a minute. Come on, Sammy. I want to show you what I brought." They left for the couch.

The sausage was browning nicely when the phone rang.

"Can someone get that?" Gina yelled over her shoulder.

It stopped ringing. She added the garlic and spices, then the tomato sauce and took a deep smell. It made her hungry.

"Who was it?" she called, stirring. No one answered.

Curious, Gina lowered the heat and put a cover on since it needed to simmer for a few minutes anyway. She wanted to see what treasures her mother had brought.

When she walked into the living room, Sammy was digging into a pile of colorful beads on the floor but her mother was sitting on the couch. Gina's stomach twisted in a knot.

"Who was on the phone, Mom?"

It was bad news, the cop in her on high alert. Her mother's head began shaking slowly, side to side.

"It was Sheralyn. Mona," she said in a voice barely above a whisper. "She's dead."

"What happened?"

That morning, Ruby, Mona's housekeeper for the last twenty-five years, had let herself in at the house like she always did. Right away, she knew something was wrong. There was a bag of bite-sized Milky Way Bars sitting on the table for Halloween but the coffee pot wasn't on and the newspaper wasn't lying open to the Metro Section, just like it always was.

Maybe she'd slept in, Ruby thought. Maybe she'd gone out. Ruby stood listening, and then she started looking.

"Buster?" Buster was Cleeve's old yellow retriever who'd outlived his master. But there was no sign of the dog, either.

"Buster? Mona?" Ruby stood at the bottom of the stairs for a second, listening for something or someone to speak to her, but there were just the sounds of the big house. She took hold of the banister and started up the steps. The old wood creaked under her weight and when she got to the top, she heard a tiny beeping sound.

Mona's door was open. Buster raised his head when she walked in, then lay it gently back down across her lap. The bedside lamp was on and Mona's dark hair was settled around her face as if she'd just lain down for a quick nap. Her eyes were closed and the book she'd been reading had fallen across her chest, her hands still holding it. Ruby turned off the alarm, then touched a shoulder just to make sure.

"I never in a million years thought Mona would go before me," said Claire, her voice cracking. "Poor Ruby."

Gina hurried to get some tissues and a glass of water.

"I can't believe it, either. I'm so sorry, Mom."

Claire suddenly took in a sharp breath. "I've got to call the others. I've got to get the phone tree started."

Gina put a hand on her arm. "Mom, it's okay. Let's sit here for a minute."

"I don't know where my book is. Oh dear, I think I packed it already! Oh, Lord, what am I going to do? I've got to call everybody."

"Mom," Gina said, her voice slightly hard.

"Gina, I can't just sit and cry until I get the phone tree started." Claire was determined and made Gina help her up then she called SueBee which was one of the few numbers she knew by heart. Still, she wiped her cheeks while waiting for someone to answer.

"SueBee, have you heard?" There was a brief pause. "This is Claire, for Heaven's sake. You've already heard? Who called you? No, Sheralyn just called me and I thought I needed to get the phone tree started but I guess not. Does everybody know?"

Gina could tell by her face that they probably did.

"Well, I guess that's understandable. There's no way I can get to my list anyway. I've been packing and I'm at Gina's for the night. I wish they'd called me this morning. Now, who am I supposed to call?" She listened. "I know, but still, I would have liked to have known at least by lunchtime. I could have taken over a casserole. Who's at the house?" Claire listened, then hung up the phone. She relayed all to Gina.

They were only vaguely aware of Sammy who was still on the floor surrounded by odd things from her grandmother's house and was now peering into a plastic ball.

"Sheralyn's already called most everybody. Ruby gave her the Dead file. Thank goodness she remembered to call me. She knows I'm Mona's best friend."

"Mom," Gina warned.

"That's okay. She has a lot on her mind, but I'm her best friend," and then Claire suddenly started to tear up again. She continued to talk, but the occasional word was hard to get out. Gina had never seen her mother like this.

"She was such a beautiful person. Inside and out. What am I going to do without her?"

Gina stroked her mother's arm a couple of time, but it felt awkward, so she folded her hands in her lap while her mother cried and blew her nose several times.

"Where is she now?" Gina asked.

"At the funeral home."

Claire suddenly perked up.

"I wonder where we'll have the reception. Oh my goodness, I have so much to do," then she noticed Sammy. "Oh my goodness, it's Halloween."

"Don't worry, Blake and I will stay home with you."

"Absolutely not! You must take Sammy. I can sit here between trick and treaters and make my lists. Sammy, let's go get your costume on."

"Mom," Gina pleaded.

Sarge got out of the way as Claire worked herself up off the couch. "I want to be by myself and tomorrow, Sheralyn's going to need you girls. SueBee and Charlotte and I will be at Mona's with Ruby. She's got the Dead file."

Gina looked at her watch. "Oh gosh, it's already five-thirty. Blake!" she yelled to wherever he was. She called Brooke and while she was waiting for her to answer, asked her mother, "I hate to ask but what's a Dead file?"

"The *When I'm Dead file*. You should have one. It was one of our programs a few years ago. It makes things so much easier for everyone. I'll let you look at mine someday, now come on, Sammy, you need to get dressed so you can go trick and treatin'."

"It's trick-*or*-treating, Mimi."

Back in the kitchen, Gina felt numb as she drained the spaghetti. Just as she was about to put a mound of noodles on a plate, she remembered something that made her nearly drop everything. Holding the pan and spoon, Gina hurried into Sammy's room.

"Mom, have you thought about..." She couldn't say it.

"About what?"

Gina didn't move. They stared at each other, and then Claire knew.

"Oh, dear. What am I going to do? The movers are coming next week and the house is sold.

"I know," said Gina. It was another executive decision. "It's not a problem. You'll just move in with us."

"Who's moving?" asked Blake, walking in wearing a sheet.

"Are you sure?" said Claire.

"What?" Blake repeated.

Gina put a hand on his chest, "Honey, I'll tell you later, but Mom needs to move in with us for a little while, now the spaghetti's ready, everybody just help yourselves because I've got to go get my costume on."

CHAPTER 16

Blake followed Gina back into the bedroom. His sheet costume kept getting caught between his legs.

"What's going on?" He sat on the bed next to Gina.

"Mona passed away this morning so Mom's going to stay here. Is that okay?"

"Mona? What happened?"

"We don't know yet, really, but she went to bed and never woke up. I know, it's so sad. I can't believe it."

Blake held her. "What about tonight?"

"Mom insists we still take Sammy."

They were silent together.

"I want Mom to live with us for now."

"You sure?"

"Everything's already packed at her house, it's so depressing. I don't want her to be alone. If Ruby hadn't shown up, we wouldn't have found out for days." Her voice quivered as she spoke. "That would have been so horrible. She'll just have to move in here with us until we figure things out."

"What about all those places she's visited?"

Gina looked at him with narrowed eyes. "Really, Blake? She hates them all. When things calm down, we can go back to the retirement home thing but not now. And knowing her, she probably won't last a week here."

Blake hugged Gina and she held him tight. "Okay," he whispered. Her head nodded.

"She's going to be okay," Blake said, patting her shoulder. "I'm sure she'll be fine. She has the garden club."

Gina felt better right away. "I need to get ready."

As she stood in front of her mirror, Gina pulled her hair into a tight ponytail then used a black eye pencil to draw a thick line along her lashes. Her costume lay like a dead shadow on the bed and her nights as an undercover cop came to mind.

"Just put it on, Trinity," Blake called from the other room as if hearing her thoughts.

"I'm workin' on it, Nero."

Gina pointed a foot into the leather pant leg and struggled to get it on. She repeated the process, then lay on the floor while she zippered up. Gina rolled over and stood stiffly up.

The doorbell rang. She could hear her mother grilling the trick-or-treaters when her cell phone rang.

It was the Captain.

She would have sat down if it weren't for the tight pants. It was more bad news.

"I can't believe it. He escaped? I didn't think he was that smart." She listened. "Well that makes sense. Do they know where he went?" Gina started to laugh, then stopped and looked at Blake who had come back in the room. "Okay, if you think that's what we should do."

Gina hung up.

"I'm starting to hate Halloween. Frankenstein escaped from prison."

"Who's Frankenstein?"

"He's a crazy man I helped put away a few years ago. It was a long time before I met you, maybe eight years ago? They were transporting some prisoners in a van back to the Huntsville unit when there was an accident and somehow, Frank got away. That guy was always so lucky but still, I can't believe it."

"So why are they calling you?"

"Because the last thing he said before they hauled him off to prison was that if he ever got the chance, he was going to come after me." She shivered. "You know, when you look in someone's eyes and your flesh crawls? Frank has those eyes."

Blake sat down next to her.

"What did he do?"

"He tortured his wife and daughter and you don't want to know how."

"So now you're supposed to go after him?"

She chuckled. "No, it's worse than that. The Captain wants all of us to go into hiding."

"Tonight?"

"Tonight. Right now."

Sarge, who had followed Blake into the room, sensed something was wrong and tried to work his way between them and when that didn't work, he lay at Gina's feet.

"Why do you call him Frankenstein?"

Gina chuckled into his shirt. "Frankenstein Frier," she said, almost to herself. "I called him that in front of the press and boy did they run with it. I heard they even started calling him that in prison. He was such a wimp. The man sold John Deere tractors, for Pete's sake. He thought he had everyone fooled but he's bad and he scares me."

Blake held her tighter.

"Do I know how to make friends, or what?" Gina leaned away from Blake and slowly started pulling on a pair of leather gloves with the fingers cut out.

"What happened to the wife?" Blake asked.

"She divorced him the second he went away, then she and her daughter moved out of state. I think she's in New Mexico. We lost touch."

Blake went to the closet and pulled out a couple of suitcases. "I've heard enough."

"I have, too," said Claire who'd been standing in the doorway. "It won't take me a minute and I'll get Sammy's suitcase together."

"Are you going to be okay?"

"As long as I'm with you."

"The Captain says he'll have a car parked outside in about thirty minutes."

The doorbell rang again.

"Don't answer that!" yelled Gina.

"I'll get it," Sammy yelled from the other room.

"Wait, Sammy! Gina rushed by Blake to get the door before her daughter.

It was two little butterflies and a fairy princess.

"Y'all look so cute," Gina said, then she and Sammy both dropped a handful of candy into each of their buckets. The parents protested but Gina assured them it was alright then threw in another handful. She set the bowl of candy outside the door before closing and locking it.

"Blake, you need to call and get us a hotel."

Claire stuck her head outside of Sammy's room. "I've already called SueBee. She said we can all stay at The Village. They have guest rooms and we can eat there, too. She said they'll be expecting Sammy to do her trick and treating there. Won't that be cute?"

"This just keeps getting weirder, doesn't it," Gina said quietly to Blake.

Before leaving, Blake got a neighbor's promise to walk Sarge but also left him plenty of water and food in case they were gone longer. Right before turning out the lights in the kitchen, Gina noticed her stack of invitations for the garden club's flower show still sitting on the counter. She almost grabbed them, then decided against it. They'd have plenty of time later.

On the way to The Village, Sammy pouted in the back seat. Gina and her mom sat silently in their own worlds. Gina pictured Mona. Always statuesque, usually hidden behind her expensive dark glasses, with her beautiful skin and words that were always sharp and to the point. She and her mother had been an odd couple, but that's what made it so special. And now her mother's future crossed her mind, making Gina's eyes brim again with tears. She brushed them away, hoping her mother didn't notice.

Driving through the neighborhoods, tiny voices seemed to come from everywhere. The family could make out shadowed groups of children running between the houses as the light from their flashlights danced like fireflies over the lawns. Parents followed in the street, forcing Blake to go slowly. This made it even easier to watch as the front doors opened and light poured out over the children as they shouted 'Trick-or-treat!'

"Don't worry, Sammy, Mimi's friends at the Village can't wait for you to come trick-or-treating. There's going to be so much candy and it's all for you. And Daddy and I both get to go with you."

"I know," Sammy said without heart, keeping her nose pressed to the window. They all felt her disappointment so nothing more was said. Gina glanced at her side mirror and looked for the detail assigned to them by the department. She was grateful the Captain had insisted.

There were only a few flickering lamps to light the parking lot of The Village. The residents didn't get out at night very much. At first, the four figures that emerged from the black SUV were hidden in the shadows but then gradually came into focus. They walked side by side and the sound effects from the rolling suitcases rumbled behind them. Because of Claire, the little one and Gina's high heels, they appeared to be moving in slow motion. If this had been a movie, this would be the poster.

On the left, dressed in black with her hair slicked back, luminous skin and dark eyes, Gina embodied Trinity, the sinister female lead from The Matrix. Next to her walked Blake as Obi Wan Kenobi in a bald cap and a belted sheet that continued to tangle between his legs. Sammy was dressed as a hobo. She wore torn overalls and her grandmother had helped her with a blacked out tooth. In one arm, she held onto a limp white teddy bear and a knapsack on a stick was over her shoulder. She was also pulling her child-size Strawberry Patch suitcase. The last of the four looked exactly like Claire.

Gina knew her fellow officers were watching The Village and the condo, but it wasn't until the sliding doors had closed behind them that she felt like she could begin to relax. The Village felt more like a home than a retirement place. There were heavy rugs covering the tiled floors and several couches were arranged around the large open room and each one was draped with brightly colored Afghans that looked homemade. It had been cold outside so there was a small fire in the fireplace.

"It smells," said Sammy, wrinkling her nose.

"It does smell a little bit like baby powder," said Gina. Charcoal smudges of hobo dirt covered Sammy's cheeks and more had smeared nicely to her hands and arms where she'd wiped her nose. Her grip on an empty pumpkin bucket tightened.

"Don't worry. You're going trick-or-treating just as soon as we get our rooms," said Claire. "You'll see, Sammy, it's going to be great."

An elderly gentleman wearing a cowboy hat was waiting for them at the front desk. Pieces of candy were strewn as decoration along the counter.

"Howdy, Robert," Claire said. They were familiar friends.

"Hi, Claire. I heard you and your posse were coming over tonight."

"This is Robert, everyone. He's always here in the evenings."

"Howdy, folks, and Happy Halloween! I've got you in Rooms A and B down the hall. Here are your keys." He leaned over the counter to get a better look at Sammy.

"Say, listen, I'm sorry but The Village doesn't allow hobos. We have our standards you know." Sammy's eyes opened wide.

"What?" said Claire. "You can't mean that. This is a really nice hobo."

"Hmmm," said the cowboy, rubbing his chin. "Well, if your grandmother says you're alright, I guess we can make an exception. But you got to promise me that you'll brush your teeth real good before bed. Is it a deal?"

Sammy nodded.

"And don't tell your folks but there are a lot of people hoping you'll knock on their door and yell 'Trick-or-Treat' at them. I hear they got really good candy."

"Really?"

"Yep."

"Thank you," said Gina, taking the keys. "Let's go put our stuff in our rooms and start knockin'."

The apartments consisted of a bedroom, a small living area, a kitchenette and a bathroom. By the time they'd unpacked and were ready to start, a small crowd was waiting for them in the hallway, clearly expecting to accompany the trick-or-treater. Every time Sammy knocked on a door, cried trick-or-treat and held up her pumpkin, the followers, some stooped, others riding in wheel chairs, clapped and had something to say about her performance.

Sammy was asked about school a dozen times. They wanted to know what her favorite Disney movie was and would she like to come over for tea during her stay? Some shared stories of their own Halloweens and for those who didn't have a bag of candy, which was to be expected considering they'd only just learned they'd be having guests, the residents had done their best to find a replacement. Sammy saw all kinds of things going into her bucket. There were pretty papers, bridge pencils and napkin rings and when there was no more room in her bucket, someone supplied her with a beautiful woven basket. When that was full, Gina put her foot down and insisted that Halloween was now over.

It was like working with a limp rag when Gina started wiping off the little girl's face and arms before gently putting her into her pajamas. The eyes were already closed as she pulled the covers up around her and then kissed her forehead and turned out the light.

"Don't worry about anything in the morning. I'll take care of her and we'll see you at breakfast," said Claire, walking Gina to the door. "I want to get to Mona's house early."

"Thanks," Gina yawned as she kicked at Sammy's Halloween haul spread over the carpet. "I'll probably get something on the way to work."

"Tomorrow's Saturday, Gina, and I hear that their Saturday breakfasts are really nice."

"Oh yeah, Saturday. In that case, I'm sleeping in." Gina yawned again. "If you can handle Sammy, that would be great."

"I wish you'd brought those invitations. I could start working on them while we're here."

"Goodnight," said Gina. "Are you sure you're okay?"

"Goodnight," her mother said before slowly closing the door.

Gina and Blake unpacked their small suitcases and got into twin beds close enough to touch fingertips.

"So what's the plan?" his voice said in the dark.

"Sleep in, don't go to the condo…" Gina said, drifting. She thought of the agent who was sitting outside in a dark car.

"Poor guy," she added.

"I mean, what's your plan for tomorrow?"

"Sleep in, go to Sheralyn's, don't go to the condo."

"I'll go check on Sarge."

"You need to ask the Captain."

"You're going to Sheralyn's."

"Frank doesn't know Sheralyn, but you're right. I'll check with the Captain." She was too tired to think and something about the blanket made her feel so warm and cozy. She made a mental note to check the brand.

"I guess Sammy should stay here. Do you think your mom should keep her inside?"

"I don't know, Blake. Let's talk about it tomorrow," she said, rolling over.

"What is there for a little girl to do at The Village all day? We have the whole weekend to kill."

"Mom'll be in charge of the Village by noon. She'll have something going on and now can we please go to sleep?"

"Aren't you worried?"

"No. Frank's going to do something stupid and then they'll catch him."

"I don't want to let you out of my sight."

Gina smiled and snuggled deeper into her covers. "I know. I'll be okay."

She heard Blake pull his arm out of his covers and instinctively, she did the same thing. Their fingertips met between the beds.

"You're so far away. Don't you want to come over here?"

"I'm too tired and your bed is too small."

"There's plenty of room. Come on over."

"You come over here."

"I asked you first."

"Yeah, but I like my covers better."

She heard the springs squeak. Seconds later his body was layered against hers.

"I'm going to protect you," he said in her ear.

"That does not feel like protection," she said, laughing.

CHAPTER 17

Gina woke lazily to the yapping sounds of a small dog outside her door. She snuggled deeper into the covers, then forced herself to roll over which turned out to be extremely difficult. Her muscles didn't want to do what she wanted them to do. She forced her eyelids open and suddenly she was awake. It was nine-fifteen. Gina hadn't slept this late in decades. She dressed and grabbed her phone, then left Blake wrapped like a cocoon in his own bed. At Room B, she knocked softly. There was no answer. She tried the door. It was locked.

On her way downstairs, she called Brooke first, then Sheralyn.

"Hi Sheralyn, this is Gina. I'm so sorry. How are you?"

She listened, then asked a few more questions.

"Okay. That'll give me time to go for a quick run. I'll see you and the others soon."

In the dining room, Gina saw a crowd, some in wheel chairs and some with aides, standing around one of the tables. She worked her way inside where Sammy was holding a handful of cards. SueBee, her mother, Charlotte and Mr. Jones were also holding a hand. A little lady in a wheelchair with a green blanket over her lap was dealing. Gina was surprised, but not really, to see that Minnie was just as active as ever.

"Straight poker, Jacks wild," the wheelchair-bound resident said, dealing the last card.

"Hi, SueBee. Hi, Charlotte. Mr. Jones, Minnie."

Everyone looked up, genuinely happy to see her. Mr. Jones and Minnie had both been involved in the marijuana incident a few years ago and the tiny woman with the mischievous smile had been the ring leader. Both had been notoriously unhelpful, but things had turned out well for everyone and whenever she'd come to visit with her mother, they'd welcomed her like old friends.

"Your daughter is quite a poker player," Mr. Jones said with a sly grin.

"You're teaching Sammy poker?" Gina gave the old man a helpless look. The ladies called him the Casanova of The Village and he looked dapper in a turtleneck and vest.

"Good Morning, lazy bones," her mother said. "Pull up a chair. I bet there's some orange juice over there on the counter. We need to get you some breakfast."

"I had a pancake," smiled Sammy.

"No thanks."

"I'm playing poker," announced Sammy. Her cards weren't quite straight and the books in front of her were face up but she had a huge pile of broken Q-tips. The others had only a few.

Gina noticed Sammy's hair was coming out of her ponytail and started to fix it. The child jerked her head away. "Stop, Mommy."

"She's cleaning me out," said Mr. Jones.

"Did you sleep well?" her mother asked.

"I did. Thank you." She watched as they made their bets.

"You look like you're about to go on a run. It's a little chilly," Claire said. "You can take my sweater."

"No thanks. Sammy, ask them to teach you Go Fish, okay? That's a lot more fun."

Minnie rolled her eyes.

"Thanks a lot, everyone. I really appreciate all you're doing for my four-year-old."

"You're welcome," they said, waving her away.

Before leaving the building, Gina studied the parking lot. The dark car was there and she headed over to say something to the poor man stuck there all night. It was a beautiful morning and she wondered if Frankenstein knew what a fuss they were making. He was probably a million miles away. She did a slow jog to the car and waited while the window lowered. She continued to jog in place and felt her muscles warming, gradually loosening.

Gina recognized the officer.

"Hey," she said, "good morning, Phil."

"Good morning." He was eating off a plate of eggs and bacon. There was a thermos and a sack, probably lunch, on the seat beside him.

"Where'd you get that?"

"Some little old ladies brought it out to me. Wasn't that nice?"

"So much for stealth. I'm going for a quick run. That okay?"

The officer put down the plate and started up the car.

"Sure."

"Do you really need to follow me? I don't think Frank even knows we're here."

"Captain says to follow you."

"Okay," said Gina, "but don't tell anyone what a lousy runner I am."

The window rolled back up.

Her arms pumped in short strokes and the ground was smooth and easy to follow. She was thankful for the twists and turns that made it interesting. Gina waved at a man raking leaves in his front yard. After the deep sleep and now the beautiful fall day, she felt her mood lifting and it was easy to list the things she was thankful for. Her health, her family, even her job. The cloud from Mona's death and Frank was only temporary. Her mother was right. This was another adventure.

Gina quickly got over that place in her run where it was hard to breath and things hurt. She wasn't feeling anything, just the air and sunshine on her face. She picked up speed. The houses were charming and made her think of having her own and as she rounded a corner onto a long narrow street, the branches thick in autumn colors touched overhead. It felt good to be alone, until she remembered the dark car following her.

Gina suddenly sprinted across a park. She looked over her shoulder at the car. She leapt over some bushes, then whipped around a wall. At the other end of the park, Gina darted down another street, turned a corner, then up an alley. She whooped and pumped her fist in the air. She'd lost the car and slowed to a jog. Her lungs were burning and despite the cold air, she was sweating through her shirt. Playtime was over and she needed to let the car find her.

A sudden sound made Gina instinctively jump to the curb and as she did, a dark red car roared past her, so close she felt its drag. She partly fell, partly threw herself to the sidewalk, landing on her hip, her hands skidding along the concrete. The car raced down the street, too far away for her to see a license plate.

"Hey!" Gina yelled after it. She couldn't believe someone would do that! The street was deserted. Gina got up and brushed herself off and inspected the tiny red skid marks on the palms of her hands. Her hip was going to have a nice bruise, too, but other than that, she was okay. Slowly, Gina started jogging again, back toward The Village.

The unmarked car was parked at the door, its driver leaning against the hood, drinking coffee. He was not happy. The morning high was gone.

"What was that all about?"

"Sorry."

"Where'd you go?"

"I zigzagged a few streets. No big deal."

"Yeah, it was a big deal. Don't do that again. Are you going to tell the Captain I lost you?"

"No, of course not. Sorry, my mistake." Gina started for the door.

"Okay. But don't do that again."

"I'm sorry, Phil. Come on, I've never been in hiding before. I just wanted to have a little fun."

"We're going to catch that guy but no more fooling around, okay?"

Gina nodded. As soon as she walked through the doors, Mr. Crawley the Village's Administrator caught her by the arm and led her to a corner.

"Officer Downing?"

"Hi, Mr. Crawley."

"Do you have a minute to talk about the 'um, the 'um, circumstances that bring you here?"

"Sure."

"Your mother has been saying things that are worrying the residents."

"Like what?"

"'There's a killer on the loose,'"

Gina shook her head.

"I talked with the police officer outside and he said that we shouldn't be worried, that this criminal may be long gone, and they're going to protect us. But really, Ms. Downing, can you stop her from talking like that? It's scaring some of the folks around here and some of them have heart conditions."

"I'm sorry, Mr. Crawley. I'll try to get her to stop."

He still looked worried.

"How about this?" Gina said. "Tell everyone The Village now has twenty-four hour police protection. The guy outside and me inside. Is there anything else?"

He brightened. "That's right, you're both here protecting us. Well, if there is anything else you think I should know, please come to me, anytime. If I had it my way…"

"Do you happen to know where my husband is?"

"Oh yes, he left a little while ago. I called him a cab. He said you might need the car."

CHAPTER 18

Gina and Sammy were standing outside and just about to ring Sheralyn's doorbell when a van hopped the curb before angling back into the street. The door opened and Helen clambered out in a giant hooded poncho. Her purse caught on the door handle and turned upside down. Everything spilled out and Helen barked a hearty laugh at herself, then shouted something to Gina about 'I'll be right there' before planting her feet hip width to collect it all. Once that was done, she leaned back inside the van and came out with a white cake box.

Sheralyn let them in. She made a fuss over Sammy and sent her to another room where the boys were watching cartoons. Gina and Helen followed Sheralyn down a long hall. It would have been impossible not to notice the photographs of family hung on the walls as they walked toward the back of the house. They were in identical black frames, like stepping stones. A picture of a laughing Bryan, Bryan with the boys when they were toddlers, Bryan and Cleeve looking like twins in hunting gear, father and son, Cleeve and Mona in a tux and ball gown, and finally, when they got to the den, over the fireplace there was a large portrait of the extended Johnson family, as if no tragedy had touched them. And yet, there had been a tragedy, now five years ago when Cleeve and Bryan had died in a plane crash.

Now Mona was gone, too. It felt like the family had been cut in half, then cut in half again.

Brooke was already there, seated comfortably on the couch in front of a stainless carafe and cups. Helen set the cake box in front of them and immediately poured herself a cup of coffee.

"I brought muffins," she said, choosing one for herself.

"Are you alright?" Gina asked Sheralyn who gave a slight shrug.

"Did you get any sleep?" asked Brooke.

"Not really. We got home from trick-or-treating about nine, and then the boys wanted to go through everything. I made them give me most of it, but they had plenty of sugar. Last night was hard to say no."

"After that, I tried to listen to the phone messages and started looking through some of Mona's papers. That was a mistake. I think I went to bed about two?" Sheralyn rubbed at her eyes, "I can't believe she's gone and the worst part is..."

They waited. Gina noticed a slight twitch in Sheralyn's left eye. The pale lid looked slightly lower than the other one, and self-consciously she rubbed it as if trying to wipe it away.

"When I get tired, my eye does this. The doctor says it's stress."

Helen pretended to be busy with a muffin. Sheralyn took a deep breath before continuing.

"I know I shouldn't feel alone but awww heck, I am alone. I'm still trying to get used to missing Bryan *and* Cleeve and now I don't have Mona to talk to about them. At least we could talk to each other about how we felt without tiptoeing around the accident. We could let the other one go on and on about something without feeling guilty or having to worry if it was okay. Sometimes we just cried together, but it was always a good cry. Sometimes, it's just real hard keeping it together around the boys and now I have to explain to them that God decided that He needed to take their father, their grandfather and now their grandmother. They're only eleven and thirteen."

"Are you sure you don't want a muffin?" offered Helen. No one wanted a muffin. Brooke brought out a legal pad but let Sheralyn continue.

"I was so worried that it was going to be me that had to make her stop driving. It was going to be this big power struggle and I'd have to figure out a way to make her move into an assisted living place when she got too old." Sheralyn laughed at herself. "I was actually looking forward to it because finally she was going to need me. I was going to visit her and help her get dressed and do her hair. Can you imagine? It's crazy, but for once, she was going to need me." Her voice shook.

"I think Mona only tolerated me sometimes," she added.

"You married her son," said Brooke. "Mothers-in-law never think the women who marry their sons are good enough. But I know she loved you so much."

"I know. But it took a lot of work. I tried so hard and then, when we started the garden club, it seemed like things started to change. I didn't have to work so hard at pleasing her."

"You nailed those arrangements," said Gina. "She had to respect that."

"I guess. And then after Bryan died, we spent a lot of time together and talked a lot. She started asking me to come with her to things. Sometimes I even thought she was showing me off."

"I can't believe she's gone," Sheralyn cried suddenly, burying her face in her hands. Helen put down her cup and began rubbing her back, making motherly noises. Sheralyn quickly composed herself.

"I can still hear her in my head, 'Now, Sheralyn, let's think about this,' and then she'd listen to me, and then I'd ask her what she thought, and then boy, would she tell me exactly what she thought."

Tears continued to roll down her cheeks. "I'm going to miss that. I love my mother but to be honest, she's not that smart. She's just a sweet Southern lady who raised a daughter to be a beauty queen." Sheralyn stopped to blow her nose. "Please don't tell her I said that. She's a wonderful mother but she doesn't know the things Mona knew."

Everyone was misty-eyed, being quiet.

"But now I guess I'm it."

"You can do this," said Gina, "and we're all here to help you. All of us."

Helen found a box of tissues and passed out several.

Brooke looked at the pad she'd been holding. "What do you need us to do?"

The doorbell rang and they heard voices. Gina could tell it was one of the other daughters and soon she walked in carrying a voluminous flower arrangement.

"That's pretty," said Sheralyn, accepting the card.

"Kappa Kappa Gamma," she read. "That was Mona's sorority at SMU. Thank you, Louise. Just put it some place."

Louise turned in a circle. "All the 'some places' are taken."

"Just double up," said Helen. "We'll be taking some to the funeral home on Thursday."

"You wouldn't believe the casseroles the mothers have been bringing by," said Sheralyn, looking weary. "And the boys don't even eat casseroles."

"Put everything in the refrigerator," said Gina. "We'll take it over to the church for the reception. And we'll pick out the best arrangements for the funeral. Don't worry about it."

Sheralyn nodded.

Gina turned to Brooke. "So, is someone answering the phone and the door for the next few days?"

Brooke made a note of it and nodded.

"The mothers said they would handle the reception and Mona's house," explained Sheralyn. "I think that's good, right?"

"Definitely," said Helen. "Mom said her Dead file was really thorough, so you might as well let them deal with the details. I'm sure they'll ask you about anything if it's not clear."

Evidently, they'd all heard of the Dead file.

Billy, Sheralyn's fourteen-year-old, ran into the room.

"Mom, where are my soccer cleats? I've got a game. Are you taking me?"

"They're in your closet. I put them there myself this morning. And yes, I'm taking you. But you'll need a sweatshirt. It's chilly out there."

He ran off and she dragged herself off the couch.

"Y'all help yourselves to anything. I gotta' go."

"Let me take him," said Brooke.

She shook her head. "No. I want to try and do something normal."

"Well, don't worry about the house. Someone will be here all day to answer the door and the phone," said Gina.

Sheralyn slid the palm of her hand across those of Gina, Helen and Brooke as she walked by them, and then she was gone. Seconds later, she walked back in.

"Does anyone know who that man is sitting out front in a black car?"

Gina raised her hand and explained the new developments.

When Sheralyn got back from taking Billy, Gina left Sammy watching cartoons and together they drove to the Davis Funeral Home. It was near Sheralyn's in Hillcrest Heights and was fast becoming the Garden Club's funeral home of choice.

Mr. Davis, III, a quiet man in a grey business suit, greeted them warmly at the front desk and led them to a room that conveyed peace and tranquility. There were pastoral scenes on the walls, soothing music played in the background and a pitcher of ice water and glasses were waiting for them on the table. A nice vase of fresh flowers and cool lighting added to the room's ambiance.

Mr. Davis crossed his hands over an important looking folder and glanced tenderly between them.

"Mrs. Johnson, how are you?"

"Fine, thank you."

"Would you like some water?"

"No, thank you."

"Alright, let's begin." He opened the leather folder. "Mona, Mrs. Johnson, your mother-in-law, was very thorough. I mean, *very* thorough with her instructions." He looked over the pages. "She basically decided everything when she was here for her husband's funeral a few years ago."

Sheralyn ducked her face.

Gina spoke up. "We know, we were there. It was Sheralyn's husband's funeral as well."

He cleared his throat. "Oh, I'm so sorry, yes, I see it here. It was a double, oh, I'm so sorry, I knew that. Well," he said, starting again, "your mother-in-law came in right after that and we went through everything. I believe she made almost every decision. It's a very thoughtful thing for someone to do that for their family members."

"That would be Mona," said Sheralyn.

"She selected the black ebony casket with silver handles. Very elegant," he emphasized, "and she was very specific about the dress. She wants the black opera dress. No jewelry except for her dark glasses and she wants Dolores to do her hair." He found the contact information in his notes before adding, "I think we've already called Dolores."

"She wants to wear her dark glasses in the casket?" repeated Gina.

He looked again. "That's what she wants. Really, it's not that strange. You wouldn't believe what some people want buried with them." He looked eagerly at them. Sheralyn started to cry softly.

"So is that it? Are we done here?" Gina asked as he placed a small box of tissues and placed it on the table.

"Almost. There are a few things she didn't mention. Like thank you notes. She didn't order any. They come pre-printed with your name and we can even pre-print the message. Here," he said, sliding over a large picture book of samples.

Sheralyn looked to Gina. Her left eye twitched. "I don't know, what do you think?"

"It might make it easier on you."

"Okay," she said, looking through a few pages and picking one. "I'll take these."

"You might need two boxes. Your mother-in-law was so connected in Dallas."

"She just wants one box," said Gina.

He made a note.

"That's fine. Then there's the stone. Your mother-in-law left instructions to simply add the date to the granite that's already at the gravesite. If you'd like, we can add some decorative things. There's a nice set of praying hands. Or a cross?" He pushed over another picture book.

Sheralyn didn't even open it. "No. I definitely don't want to mess with that."

"I agree," said Gina, pushing the book back.

"Okay, no problem. I guess the only other thing to talk about is if you'd like us to come pick up the flower arrangements from your home for the memorial service. We can send over a van that morning and take whatever arrangements you want to use."

Gina and Sheralyn shared a look.

"Yes, please. And whatever you do, make sure the arrangements cover the casket. Write that down, the flowers have to cover the casket."

He did as they asked, then confirmed the address and time.

"Then I guess we're done." He handed Sheralyn his card. "Please call me if you have any questions."

"Oh, Mrs. Johnson, one more question. Did you want it to be open casket? Your mother-in-law didn't say."

Sheralyn decided quickly.

"Open."

"Really? Are you sure?" Gina asked.

"Open," Sheralyn said again, with absolute certainty in her voice.

"Open," said Gina to Mr. Davis.

He nodded. "Open it is."

CHAPTER 19

Gina dropped Sheralyn off at her house and picked up Sammy then drove to the condo to pick up Blake. The black car followed.

"Hi, Sarge."

The furry animal walked stiffly toward her for a rub. She righted the leaning candlestick at the door, then leaned over to tousle his head. It was good to be home.

Sammy wrapped her arms around Sarge's neck then ran straight to her room.

Gina found Blake in his studio working on a charcoal.

"Pretty," she said.

He didn't answer.

"Good day?"

"I guess."

"What's wrong?"

"Same thing. I heard back from a couple of galleries in Fort Worth. No one's interested. I'm getting nowhere, Gina. And now we're having to pay for The Village on top of the condo."

"No, we're not, Honey, the department is covering it. It was their idea for us to move out."

Blake looked slightly relieved.

Gina knelt next to the old chair so she could look into his face.

"Hey, come on. It's going to happen, Blake, I know it is. You are so talented. If money gets tight, we'll figure it out. One day at a time. Okay?"

He nodded but she could see the worry in his eyes.

"Let me know when you're ready to go. I'm going to pack some more stuff."

Gina went in the kitchen. "Blake, have you seen the invitations? I left them here on the counter."

"Nope," Blake called.

"Sammy, did you take some pretty cards that Mommy left in the kitchen?"

"No," her daughter called back from her room.

"That's weird," Gina said, walking around, opening cabinets, looking in drawers. There were no cards anywhere.

The phone rang and Gina answered it.

"Hi, Captain. Yeah, we dropped by to get some things." She sat in a chair and began rubbing Sarge's belly with her foot. Sammy came skipping in with a sack of things and dropped it as soon as she saw the dog on the floor. She took over the rubbing.

"Did you miss us, Boy?"

Blake walked in freshly scrubbed. "He's fine. He sleeps all day anyway. I took him for a couple of nice walks."

"Shush," said Gina, trying to listen. In a few moments, she hung up.

"What did he say?" Blake asked.

"Well, first he asked how Sammy was doing and I told him she was doing great." Sammy smiled. "Then he yelled at me for acting like there wasn't an escaped convict running around."

"Have they caught him?" Blake wanted to know.

"No. But the Captain doesn't want to take any chances. He says to plan on staying at The Village until further notice. And I told him we'd make sure to always let someone know where we're going and we wouldn't stray too far from The Village. He's okay with you coming here and me going to work but that's it."

They left the condo and went down the elevator. When they reached the lobby, Gina remembered something and stepped over to the concierge desk.

"How's everything, Mrs. Downing?" asked the young guard, looking up from his paperwork. He was aware of the situation and Gina could see that he had two TV screens monitoring the parking garage and lobby area.

"Hi, Cliff. Pretty good. It's not easy trying to live somewhere else. Hopefully it won't be for too much longer."

"Hope not. Some of the other tenants noticed that car out front. I told them someone famous is in town but I'm not sure they're buying it."

"Sorry about that."

"Well, main thing is you keep your family safe."

Gina nodded, studying her fingers as she leaned against the desk. She heard the ding of the elevator. Blake and Sammy were waiting.

"Listen, Cliff, it's okay if this happened but I know you'd tell me. Did you see anyone other than Blake go inside our apartment?"

He sat up stiffly. "No, why?"

"Oh, it's just I could have sworn I left some things on my kitchen counter last night and today they're gone."

"Nobody's gone in there, except for Mr. Downing this morning."

"And you've been here all day?"

"Yes, ma'am."

"At this desk?"

He nodded.

"What about restroom breaks? Lunch?"

"I eat at the desk. And yeah, I left for a few seconds but only a couple of times."

Gina tapped the counter. "Okay. Just must have picked them up. I was pretty distracted." Gina walked back to the elevator where Blake punched the button again. The door opened and they stepped on.

"Mrs. Downing?"

A hand shot out and the door reopened.

"What is it?" Gina asked, leaning out of the elevator.

"I forgot. There was something going on out front around lunchtime. A big van had a blow out so me and that officer helped get it moved over to the side of the street. It was blocking traffic. Took maybe five or ten minutes?"

"Thank you, Cliff," said Gina, and then the door closed.

CHAPTER 20

Gina checked everywhere for the flower show invitations. They weren't at The Village, they weren't in her mother's room or in Sammy's bags or in the car. Gina and her mother were at a loss and both assumed the cards would show up because if they didn't, Gina would have to buy more. Until then, there would be no talk of the flower show. There was too much to do for Mona's funeral.

At Mona's house, Claire and the other mothers followed every detail in the 'Dead' file. As they quietly moved about the house, they boxed things up for Sheralyn to look at later. Then they called the museums to arrange for pick-ups of the art work and sculptures that had been donated years ago. SueBee and Charlotte packed up closets full of clothes and called Mona's favorite charities to come pick them up. Every once in a while, when Sheralyn came over to check on how things were going, one of the mothers would sit down with her and ask her about some of the finer things. They were gently persuasive and with each pat of the arm, Sheralyn agreed that Mona's things were much finer than her own and she would put them in storage and think about them later.

A handwritten letter, personally addressed to Sheralyn, brought them all to tears. Mona wrote that she wanted Sheralyn to make sure the boys got the first editions and Cleeve's war medals. Her daughter-in-law was to keep whatever jewelry she wanted, but her wedding bands and rings were to be divided between the boys. They felt like they could hear her saying the last sentence. 'My family was the most important thing in this world to me. All the rest - a passing fancy.'

Finally, Mona wrote that she wanted to have both the memorial service and the reception at the Presbyterian Church. She and Cleeve had donated the 350-pipe organ that dominated one end of the sanctuary and this was one way she could get her money's worth.

"Please, Sheralyn, you can have the service at the church but let us have the reception at Charlotte's," the mothers pleaded. "That room they use for receptions is in the basement, Dear. The basement, Honey. Charlotte would love to have it at her house. It would be so much nicer," then SueBee added, "You know it has formica floors and fluorescent lighting down there?"

The all-purpose hall was perfect for families on a budget. It was large and non-descript and most often used for children's birthday parties and bridal showers. The daughters, especially, had vivid memories of running through the underground hallways playing hide and seek, among other things.

Sheralyn listened respectfully, but nothing they said could change her mind. The reception would be at the church, just as Mona wished.

With no other choice, the day before the funeral the ladies began working their magic. They brought in linens and china and of course the Club's silver serving dishes and tea service. Everyone had a hand in making sure the flower arrangements were blue ribbon-worthy. There had still been no sign of Frank so with the Captain's permission, Gina took the day off to help. She was only mildly aware of the dark car following her to and from the church and when there were heavy boxes to lift, the officer was happy to help. As for the weather, it looked liked rain.

The day of the funeral, the hall had been transformed while outside, the rain came down in sheets. It meant volunteers with umbrellas stayed at the door to ferry people to and from their cars. It was as though another Garden Club tradition had been honored.

Mona's casket lay open at the front of church. It was lined in white silk and shimmered under the lights, giving Mona a heavenly glow. Like a seed packet of perennials, mothers and daughters mixed themselves in the rows directly behind the family. Friends stood in line to pay their respects.

"Do you want to go up there?" Gina whispered to Blake. He shook his head no. She leaned forward and touched her mother's shoulder. "Do you want to go up there?" Claire shook her head no.

Gina took a deep breath, squeezed Blake's hand and stepped out of the pew to make her way to the black lacquered casket. Mona looked so elegant. Every hair was in place, her make-up was perfect and she held a white rose in her hands. Even the dark glasses looked natural. If Gina didn't know better, she would say Mona was looking at her even now. Gina rested her hand on the edge of the casket.

"You look so elegant, Mona. Dolores did a wonderful job. She wouldn't even let us pay her. I know you'd appreciate that. We're going to miss you. And don't worry, we'll take good care of Sheralyn and the boys. I'll take care of Mom, too." Just as she felt herself starting to cry, a hand covered hers. Claire had changed her mind and come to say goodbye.

"She looks so beautiful," Claire said. They stood together, their heads almost touching.

The organ began to play with a rush of sound swelling from the pipes as it played one of Mona's favorite hymns. Several minutes later, the organist stopped and the minister who had entered earlier motioned the audience to stand. Looking more beautiful than ever a solemn-faced Sheralyn entered, flanked by the two young boys.

It was a simple, to-the-point ceremony. The minister shared Mona's life, including things many had never known. Evidently, she'd continued to give generously, even after Cleeve was gone, and most often anonymously. She'd given to the church, but also to many other organizations that touched people around the world. It was both humbling and inspiring. And then the organ began again and while the family filed out, the mothers slipped quietly out the side doors. The minister invited everyone to the reception downstairs.

"Really, it's not so bad," said Helen, looking around the reception hall that was now an elegant, shining example of garden club tradition. The others agreed. Gina picked up a piece of Italian Cream Cake and went to sit with the others.

"She's so beautiful," said Brooke, watching their friend.

Sheralyn was smiling. She shook hands while the two young boys dutifully did the same. The line of friends and acquaintances was long. Occasionally, she put an arm around her sons' shoulders and looked at them often. Every once in a while, it must have been someone close because her face immediately softened and she would lean over for a hug. Otherwise, the beautiful smile stayed frozen as she introduced the boys to their grandmother's friends.

Blake left early to go pick up Sammy from a friend's. An hour later, most of the crowd had gone and the granddaughters, nudged by their mothers, began the slow process of cleaning up, starting with gathering empty boxes from beneath the banquet tables.

Sheralyn's boys, now down to their white shirts with rolled up sleeves, had begun playing tag with some of the other teenagers.

"Take that outside," Helen called as if they all belonged to her.

"Gina, can you take this to the church office?" Charlotte asked, holding out a check made out to the church. It was meant to cover the cost of the service and use of the hall.

"Sure." She glanced at the officer assigned to follow her and knew it would just take a minute.

"Shouldn't he go with you?" her mother asked.

"It's okay, Mom. It's just a couple hallways over. I'll be right back."

"I'm coming with you. I need to find the restroom anyway."

Gina and Claire left the bright lights of the reception hall. After a lengthy walk down one hall, there were still no church offices. They took a few turns and found other halls but no offices. Each hall seemed to take them further away from the reception and the light grew dimmer by the minute.

"We must have taken a wrong turn," Gina said.

"I think so," her mother said.

"There's a bathroom, though. I'll wait out here for you." Her mother hurried inside.

Gina leaned against the wall, looking left and right, trying to decide which would be the best direction to take. Both seemed to end in darkness, until someone emerged from the shadows and was walking toward her.

Gina moved into the middle of the hall. "Hey. I'm so glad to see someone. You don't happen to know where the church office is, do you?" She could tell it was a man. He was in a raincoat and hat and an umbrella swung from his arm. The other hand remained in his pocket. It felt childish to yell in church, her voiced echoing off the hard floors. Evidently he didn't want to shout.

She waved. Still, the figure didn't respond.

Gina felt something bad growing in her gut. She remembered she didn't have her purse or phone. She had no idea how far she was from the others, but she knew it was too far to call for help and she couldn't leave her mother in the bathroom. Even if she did, she had no way of knowing if the other direction would lead to another dead end. The figure was getting closer. She strained to see his face.

"Hello," she said, trying to make her voice sound strong.

"Gina?" The man stopped, still far away.

"Yes?"

His hand came out of his pocket, holding something. Gina's heart stopped. He began walking again. Instinctively, Gina disappeared through the bathroom's swinging door. She leaned her body weight to hold it closed and looked around the small dressing area that led into the bathroom where her mother was washing her hands. There was no lock on the door.

"Hi, honey, I'm almost done," her mother called from around the corner. Gina heard the water stop. She noticed a heavy desk with two small chairs, a potted plant and a standing mirror.

Her mother came out, rubbing in some hand lotion.

"What's wrong? I'll wait. Go ahead."

Gina shook her head no. She eyed the standing mirror, then rushed to the desk and began heaving it toward the door.

"What are you doing?" Claire asked.

"Frank," said Gina. Their eyes locked and then Claire struggled to sit on the desk.

"Is there any chance you have your phone with you?"

Claire shook her head no.

"Gina? Is that you?" Frank's voice sounded like he was talking into the crack of the door. He pushed against it but the desk, combined with Gina and Claire's weight, barely moved.

"Come on out, Gina. I know you have your mother with you. You don't want her to get hurt. Just come on out. We'll talk and she can go back to the party. I know the way. I actually grew up in this church."

Gina rolled her eyes. The door lurched forward but held.

"What are we going to do?" whispered Claire.

"Frank, I can't believe you think you can get away with this. I have my own personal bodyguard."

"Yeah, and I saw him upstairs. He's enjoying some cake right now."

Gina silently cursed herself.

"If you don't come out, I'm going to shoot through this door and who knows what I might hit. Don't make me do that."

Claire shook her head violently, telling her a strong 'No'.

"Stop stalling and get out here," he said, his voice hard.

"Okay, okay," said Gina. "But you got to let my mother get down the hall."

"Sure." Then, from somewhere far off, Gina and her mother both heard what sounded like....

"Wooo Hooo," the voices sang out. "Claire, Gina, where are you?"

"That's Charlotte!" said Claire.

"Charlotte! SueBee!" Gina and Claire both screamed. "Help!!"

The 'Wooo Hooo,'s got louder as they continued to call for help.

"In here! We're in here!"

Finally, the voices were outside the bathroom. "Is that door locked?" asked Charlotte.

Gina heaved the desk away and she'd never been happier to see the curious faces of several of the mothers.

"Where have y'all been? Gina, your officer is very upset. We told him we'd help look for you and he didn't like that but we ignored him. Have you taken the check to the office?"

Gina was already racing down the hall but at the mention of the check, she made a quick U-turn and came back and pressed the payment into Charlotte's hand.

Claire called after her. "Where are you going?"

"To find a phone!"

""Well, come on, then," said Charlotte. "Claire, I guess you're coming with us. We still need to find that office. What in the world were y'all doing in the bathroom?"

Miraculously, Gina found her way upstairs. Phil had just returned and his relief at seeing her lasted only a second. Without waiting, she grabbed his phone and called the station. He listened as she relayed the story. Soon, there were police cars and officers all over the church. But there was no sign of Frank. Someone found a church official who led them to a room where the video cameras were controlled. They spotted Frank coming in a side entrance, then disappearing. In every shot, he had his umbrella open, hiding his face. Other than a raincoat, they didn't even know what he was wearing.

The search for clues kept up a flurry of activity and the Captain commanded Gina to stay put at a table. She gratefully accepted a cup of coffee from one of Brooke's daughters, the one getting her masters at SMU. By now, the reception hall had been returned to its former glory and since the rain had stopped, the boxing and packing went quickly. The Captain still had some questions for Gina.

"You are one lucky cop," he said. "And dumb. I can't believe you left Phil up here. He's going to get booted back down to parking tickets thanks to you. I can't believe you did something so stupid!"

Gina felt terrible and for once, she agreed with him.

The Captain continued to pace around her and she suspected he would have been shouting if it hadn't been for all the women in the room.

"This is your fault, Sessions. If you'd stayed with Phil, we might have caught that guy. So from now on, and I mean it, no going anywhere without him. My God, Gina, how hard can it be?"

"I know, Sir. I'm sorry. It won't happen again."

"It better not. I'll kill you myself and apologize to Sammy later."

"Understood."

"You okay?" he asked quickly.

"Sure."

"Okay," said the Captain, believing her. He stormed off and joined the men in coveralls who were still looking for evidence. The mothers continued to offer their observations and advice to the detectives taking notes and someone finally suggested they go home and let the men in coveralls do their job.

Gina was free to leave, but realized she couldn't. She felt dizzy and slightly nauseous. She made herself take long, deep breaths, until her heart gradually slowed. How could she have been so close and lost him? His voice was still in her head. She swallowed and closed her eyes, drowning in a wave of emotion that passed over her. She looked to see if anyone had noticed.

Gina gathered her things, then bounded up the stairs taking two at a time in her heels and when she reached the street she ran all the way to her car, her raincoat and purse flapping against her side. She was suddenly desperate to see her family.

CHAPTER 21

The sound of knocking seeped its way into Gina's consciousness. The clock beside the bed said 6:50. Blake moaned and rolled over. Gina lay on her back, tangled in the blanket. After a week, the room had become depressing. Dark clothes still lay in a mound on the chair from last Saturday's funeral and a pile of dirty clothes had been growing daily on the floor.

Gina grabbed Blake's coat from off the chair. The arms extended long past her hands as she stood there shivering.

"Did I wake you?" Claire was dressed in her forest green jogging suit.

"That's okay. I need to get ready for work."

"Sammy and I are already dressed so we're going downstairs for breakfast. I would have called but I didn't want to wake Blake."

Gina stumbled back to her bed and called the office. The Captain got there early and answered on the first ring.

"Morning, Captain. Did you find anything yet?"

After Frank's appearance at the church, there'd been a thorough search but he'd vanished, as if he'd never been there in the first place. He'd hid inside his umbrella so the security tapes were useless and they hadn't found any clues to tell them if he had a car or if he was on foot. For a dumb crook, he sure had a lot of luck.

There was some good news, though, the Captain said. After a few days of searching, they'd found the wife and daughter in Roswell. A couple of the guys were headed there now and because the search had grown beyond Texas, the FBI was now onboard.

Feeling a little bit better, Gina hung up and saw Blake's grey eyes focused on her. His face was fuller now than when they'd first met five years ago. She wondered if she'd aged just as gracefully. Gina went to sit on the edge of his twin bed and he held out his hand to her.

"No thank you, not before you've brushed your teeth. Captain thinks Frank may be in Roswell. They're watching his wife and daughter."

"Does that mean we can go home?"

"Maybe. Captain did mention it. We'll know more later today."

Blake got up on an elbow. "Is your mother coming with us?"

"Yes. We already talked about this."

Blake looked thoughtful. "Think about it. Now that she's had a chance to see how nice this place is, maybe she'd like to stay."

Gina had to admit it was a possibility.

She dressed quickly in navy pumps, a knee-length skirt and hose. It was the appropriate dress of a detective and work had become the one place she felt normal.

Downstairs, Sammy and Claire sat at a table with the others having pancakes. It was still early and only a few other residents had come down but Minnie was there. Gina fixed herself a bowl of cereal and sat down.

"Good Morning, Family. Good Morning, Minnie. You're up early."

Minnie glowed with the same look of mischief she'd had five years ago when Gina had first met her in the hallway of The Village.

"I'm always up this early. Just don't always come down for breakfast. But I heard this might be your last day and I didn't want to miss seeing Miss Sammy," she said, looking at the bright face. "She's a little doll."

"I'm not a little doll," said Sammy.

Gina was confused. "What do you know? How'd you know we could leave? I just found out myself."

"News travels fast," said Minnie. "The Captain came by The Village yesterday to talk to Mr. Crawley and told him you'd probably get to go home today and I apologize, Sammy, you're a brilliant kindergartener."

"I'm not in kindergarten!"

"What? You should be because you're so smart."

Sammy liked that.

"I hope it's safe. Do you think it's safe?" Claire asked her daughter.

Gina stirred her cereal. "Well, the Captain thinks so. He said we'd talk about it later today, once they've confirmed Frank's in New Mexico."

Her mother seemed satisfied.

"So, Mom, what are you going to do today?"

"After choir practice I think I'll start packing."

"Yeah!" shouted Sammy, clapping.

"Yeah!" Claire mimicked.

Gina took a bite and watched the others over her spoon. "Mom?"

"Yes?"

"I know you've probably already thought about this, but wouldn't it be easier to stay here until you figure out where you want to go? One less move, you know. I mean, we'd love to have you stay with us, as long as you want, but staying here might work out."

Claire looked at her sideways. Gina couldn't tell what she was thinking and quickly added, "Really, Blake and I are planning on you staying at the condo. It's just something to think about, right, Sammy?"

Sammy shook her head quickly up and down. Minnie loved the idea, of her staying at The Village.

"That's a wonderful idea!" said Minnie. "Sure, Claire, why don't you just stay here? We love having you and I know Mr. Crawley loves the way you've pitched in and joined the choir and the food committee. It's only been a few days and we already feel like you're one of us."

"Hmmm," said Claire. "I don't know."

"SueBee and Charlotte are happy here," said Gina.

"If you'd rather I stayed, I will."

"No, no, no," said Gina. "I want you to do what you want to do. I just mentioned it to make sure you'd considered it. That's all. No, it's going to be great having you at the condo. It's going to be great."

"It won't be for long. Just until I catch my breath."

"Right. Well, I better get to work. Blake's going to take Sammy to school and if we get the okay, I'll try to take off a little early and come pick you up. That way you'll have the whole day to say good-bye. How does that sound?"

"That's fine," said her mother. "I can order us some dinners to-go. Are you sure you don't want me to go with Blake and then I can get the house cleaned up? It probably smells like the dog."

Gina assured her Blake would enjoy one final day without any interruptions."

"Well, alright. I'll wait for you to come get me."

As they had done all week, an unmarked car followed Gina to work and Blake took a cab to the condo after first dropping off Sammy at her pre-school.

Back at work, Gina was swamped. It was after two when she couldn't ignore her growling stomach and decided to run out and get a quick bite. After checking with the Captain, Gina took the elevator down and walked outside. The late afternoon sun had warmed the air but she occasionally felt a gust of wind and wrapped her long wool coat tighter. She bought a hot dog from a vendor on the corner and ate quickly, then decided to stretch her legs. The street was crowded, she wouldn't go far, just a block and back. Gina turned up her collar and circled her scarf around her neck.

As she walked along Main Street, Gina looked into the windows of the small stores. She passed a jewelry repair shop, a place with orthopedic supplies, and a ladies' wear store that looked more like a resale shop. Gina remembered there used to be an old Woolworth's on the corner and an Evert's Jewelers on the other side, but both were long gone.

At least Neiman-Marcus was still there. Gina stopped to look in their windows. It was a Thanksgiving theme with elegantly dressed mannequins in suede jackets and children playing in piles of leaves. The window did its job and Gina smiled.

There'd been so much happening, she'd almost forgotten about the holiday. She thought about the boxes of holiday decorations still in her storage space in the basement of her building. Thanksgiving was only a few days away.

Staying alert was beginning to wear on her. Gina had spoken almost every day to the officer watching the condo and every day he had nothing to report. There were no leads and the only person coming and going had been her husband. Even when Blake was there, the officer assured her, he'd done his duty and made trips up the elevator three times a day to check on the condo. At least it gave him something to do.

"But you shouldn't have anything to worry about, even if Frank did decide to show up," the officer said. "Every time I knock on your door, that dog sounds like he's gonna' kill me! No way Frank could get past him."

Gina liked that thought and decided she would take the officer a goodbye gift in honor of his service. Maybe a really good burger.

She took one more look at the detail in the Neiman's window as a wintery cloud passed overhead. In the darkening shadow, she saw a reflection in the glass. Someone that looked exactly like Frank was standing across the street looking at her. While everyone else was bundled up, ducked against the wind, this person stood upright, bareheaded and stiff. He wore a short jacket and his shoulders were scrunched up, trying to protect his ears. Gina whirled around. Her eyes frantically scanned the people but there were so many of them and the cars and buses kept getting in her line of sight. He'd disappeared, if he'd, in fact, been there at all.

As soon as she got back to headquarters, Gina hurried into the Captain's office.

"I think I saw him!" It took the Captain a second, then he picked up the phone. Gina looked out the window at the street below. He hadn't left town. He was still looking for her.

"Are you sure?" the Captain asked, waiting for someone to answer the phone.

"I'm almost 100% sure," said Gina. "It was a reflection in the glass in front of Neiman's, but his body, those eyes. That creepy look. I've still got the shivers going up my spine."

The Captain studied her, talked to someone on the phone, then hung up.

"Okay. The word's out. I've got the guys on patrol looking for him and we've got some undercover officers in the area. We're going to catch him."

Gina couldn't stop looking at the street.

"Obviously, you can't go home today."

Gina nodded. Back at her desk, she called her mother's room at The Village. The phone rang and rang. When no one answered, she called the front desk.

"Hi, Gina. No, your mother left a couple of hours ago. She was all packed up by noon and said she couldn't stand just waiting around so she asked to use our car service, said she was going to pick up the little girl from school and then run some errands. She said they wouldn't be back. We're really sad to see you all go. You better promise to come visit us. We…"

Gina interrupted him. "We're not moving out," she snapped into the phone. "I'll explain later." She hung up and dialed the condo. Blake answered.

"Hey, honey. Yeah, they're here. Your mother offered to pick up Sammy from school so they could go do girl stuff. They just got here. They're unpacking their stuff."

Gina breathed for the first time. "Oh gosh, thank God," she said, the relief pouring from her voice. "Blake, something's happened. We can't move home tonight. I'm sorry, but it's not safe yet. I'll explain later. Is the officer downstairs?"

"I don't know. I didn't tell him anything. I'm not sure if he was planning on leaving. Don't worry, Gina, we're fine."

"No, you should be worried. I don't like you all being there without me."

"It's okay, Gina, calm down. We're fine. We'll leave right now if that's what you want."

"No, don't! I'm coming there. I'll be there in five minutes."

Gina heard the dog barking in the background.

"What's Sarge barking at?"

"He wants to go for his walk. He's dragging me that way now so I'll see you in a few minutes."

"Wait!" Gina said, but Blake had already hung up the phone.

As she drove, droplets appeared on her windshield. In front of her building, Gina slowed down, looking for the police officer. She couldn't spot him and she pulled into the underground garage, just as a hard rain started.

Gina barely said hello to the concierge and took the elevator up. When the doors opened, she heard Sarge still barking. She ignored a puddle at the door and pushed her key into the lock. Her heart and mind were racing and before she could turn the knob, the door swung open and she caught a brief glimpse of her mother walking away.

"Oh it's you, why didn't you just use your key?" she said, "I've unpacked and now I'm almost packed again. This is crazy."

"I did," Gina called after her. "Use my key, that is."

"Then why did you ring the bell? It doesn't matter. Blake says we aren't staying here tonight. What happened?" she called from Sammy's room.

"I didn't ring the bell," said Gina.

"Well, somebody did," said Blake.

"Mommy!" Sammy ran into the room and grabbed her mother's legs.

"Hi, Honey. What's wrong with Sarge?" He was still barking at the patio doors.

Sammy held out her fingertips. "Look! Mimi and I got a manicure."

Gina sank to her knees so that they were eye to eye. "Beautiful."

Blake helped her up, kissing her as he did.

"I didn't see the officer downstairs. And what's wrong with Sarge?" Gina asked again.

"You know him, he's getting old. He hears something and barks. That's a pretty hard rain. It cut our walk short."

Claire walked through with a stack of magazines she was trying to decide which ones to take back with her to The Village. "I really wish we'd known we weren't coming back a little sooner. We're missing the happy hour."

"You don't drink."

"But I like their hors d'oeuvres."

"I'm ready to go," said Blake, coming back in with a couple of bags of clothes.

"Do we have to go back there?" asked Sammy.

"Why?"

"Mimi snores."

"Well, so does Daddy. Maybe we should let them share a room." Sammy laughed. "It's just for a little while longer, honey. We'll stop and get ice cream."

Rain was now hitting the glass like small pellets. A crack of thunder made them all stop and look outside. Gina shivered, then hurried to her room to get some things. When they were ready to go, Gina remembered something and went into the kitchen.

"Come on, babe," called Blake. "Let's go."

"I was hoping I'd find those flower show invitations. I know I left them here."

"Oh, I almost forgot," said Claire, finding a paper sack and disappearing in the pantry.

Blake called from the front door. "Let's go."

Claire reappeared and took Sammy's hand. "Load 'em up, move 'em out."

Sarge had finally stopped barking and somehow knew he was about to be left. He stood at the door, his tail wagging dangerously fast.

"Awww, Boy, we'll be back," said Gina, rubbing his head thoroughly.

"It smells like dog, don't you think?" said her mother. Gina locked the door behind them.

The Downing family emerged from the elevator with an odd assortment of bags, suitcases and magazines.

"Mommy," said Sammy, looking at the back cargo door of the SUV. "You need to wash your car. Someone drew a cartoon on it."

"That's okay, Honey, the rain will give it a bath," Gina said, helping her mother into the back seat, then it was Sammy's turn. Blake got behind the wheel and the engine roared to life. Gina started around the back, then stopped.

"Come on, Gina, let's go," Blake called, looking at her in the rear view mirror. Something about her frozen stare made him get out and walk to the back of the car.

"What is it?"

Gina didn't answer. They both stared at the car.

Sammy jumped out. "I told you," said Sammy, "it's a cartoon."

Someone had drawn a stick figure in the dust on the back panel of the SUV. It had a square head with two little handles sticking out from the neck. It looked like a miniature Frankenstein.

"Get in the car," said Gina. "Everyone, get in the car."

Blake had to dodge the quickly flooding streets. Gina called the Captain and told him about the drawing.

"Where's my guard?" she asked. "He wasn't here."

"Well, he should be. I didn't tell him to stop. Maybe you just didn't see him."

Not until they'd arrived back at The Village and she spotted the surveillance did she feel slightly safe. Even seeing the disturbed and confused face of Mr. Crawley gave her comfort, as did all the other faces that lit up as they walked into the open dining room where dinner was being served. SueBee and Charlotte, Minnie and Mr. Jones had already heard they were coming back and waved them toward an empty table.

Gina explained the change of plans, but left out the drawing. Staying longer was purely precautionary, she told them, but the possible sighting of Frank stimulated the minds of the greatest generation and the fervor of the crowd grew as they determined it was now up to them to protect Claire and her family.

"Just try to get past me," said a particularly wizened gentleman in a wheelchair. His cap was covered in war memorabilia and he pulled out a grabber, a long stick that allowed him to pick up things without bending over, and waved the pointed end at the enemy.

"Just try me. We need to get organized."

More veterans surfaced and men were shouting 'who-raw!', the language of soldiers. They talked about what they'd done in past wars and what could they do to fortify The Village.

At the word 'organized,' Claire had looked at SueBee who looked to Charlotte. Gina suddenly stood up and waited until she had everyone's attention.

"Hold on, everybody, we don't need an army. We're okay. Really. The Village isn't under attack. The police are doing everything they can to protect us and none of you are in any danger. I appreciate your concern, but it's just one sad little man who got lucky and got out of prison. He's obsessed with me, I understand, but I'm not afraid. Heck, we have Robert at the front desk."

Everyone chuckled over that.

"The best thing you can do is to let me know if you see anyone you don't recognize. Something like 'stranger danger.' That would be a huge help." Gina wondered if they were listening at all because as soon as she sat back down, they went back to discussing strategy.

After dinner, Gina helped Sammy get ready for bed. Her cloud nightlight glowed from a corner. Sammy flipped over on her stomach and wiggled so that her pajama top scooted up, revealing her bare back.

"Tell me a story," she said into the pillow.

Gina sat next to her and trailed her fingernails up the small of her back, then back down with the pads of her fingertips.

"Which one?"

"Paintbrush."

"Once upon a time, there was a little girl who loved to play outside. She had long blond hair that she liked to wear in messy braids and almost every day but Sundays she got to wear blue jeans and checkered shirts that were every color of the rainbow. This little girl lived on a very pretty farm out in the country. There were chickens and goats, and a big red barn that had a great big yard with a nice tall fence all the way around it.

"One day, the little girl came home from school and standing there, in the middle of the ring outside the barn was the most beautiful horse she'd ever seen. And you know what? He was hers. He was exactly the right size for a little girl and he was mostly black but there were splashes of white all over him. It looked like someone had thrown a bucket of white paint over him. And that's why she named him Paintbrush.

"On most days, the little girl would take Paintbrush on a long ride into the woods, where the horse had to walk across a stream and up a hill, and one time along the way there was a snake, but Paintbrush stomped his hooves and the snake slithered away.

"Afterward, the little girl would lead Paintbrush back to the barn. She had to feed him and brush him. It was her responsibility to make sure he was all taken care of before she could go inside to have her own dinner. The little girl was so happy because Paintbrush was her very own and she couldn't wait to go to sleep so she could wake up and do it all over again tomorrow. The End."

Sammy was quiet.

"Goodnight, sweet girl," Gina whispered, pulling the pajama top down and the covers up. "I love you."

"I love you, too."

Gina closed the bedroom door behind her and went to sit on the couch where her mother was watching TV and working a crossword puzzle. She looked very content.

"Gina, be honest with me. Are we in danger?"

She hesitated. "I'm pretty sure Frank was at the condo. He wants me to know he knows where I live. I think he was upstairs, sometime before I got home. There was water at the front door, and I know Blake and Sarge got back before the rain. He was there."

Her mother's pencil hovered over a square.

"Are we safe here?"

"Yes. He's not like a serial killer. And he's probably getting his kicks out of making me 'go into hiding'. I think he's all talk. He wants to get under my skin and I'm not going to let him do that. Everyone's looking for him so we just need to stay put. We'll be fine."

Her mother's face was a mask. "Well, alright. You're in charge."

"Thank you. Now tomorrow's Saturday, so let's all stay put."

"Do you think you could go get more invitations? I could be working on them here. Oh, and I saw on the menu they're fixing my recipe for beef stroganoff tomorrow night. Let me know what you think."

"Good night, Mom," said Gina.

CHAPTER 22

The Frankenstein sighting gave the investigation a shot of adrenaline. The department made sure there were officers watching the condo and The Village, despite the residents' protests that they were more than capable of guarding the family. They also began the painstaking process of re-interviewing anyone who'd known Frank before he went to jail. Even Gina was interviewed again. It still seemed impossible that Frank could elude them all.

The weekend passed uneventfully and Gina was starting to wonder how much longer this could go on. And poor Sargent. Blake thought the dog might be depressed.

As sometimes happens when nothing seems to go your way, suddenly it does. Monday morning, after Blake's charcoals had been rejected from almost every major gallery and even the smaller independent ones who said they thought his work was appealing but couldn't offer him space because he was still too unknown, too new, there came a call from The Spring Creek Gallery. It took him completely by surprise.

The gallery's owner Roxanne Rawlins said she would love to have Blake's work in her next show. Yes, she'd seen enough and she wanted him join with another new artist. There'd been a last minute cancellation and she was willing to put him in. When? Why, today, of course.

The Spring Creek Gallery was a small but highly respected venue in North Dallas. It was also somewhat exclusive. The patriarch of the family, who had been both artist and architect, had built a house to fit perfectly between a creek and some woods that kept it hidden from a busy street.

When Mr. Rawlins, Sr. died, the family decided to create a place for new artists to show their work. Also, the grounds were meant to inspire others. Even though it was small, it was known to collectors all over the country. Artists were selected by Roxanne personally and when given the opportunity, almost everything would sell. Only the sculptures that dotted the landscape, done by local artists, were not for sale.

When Gina told the Captain she wanted to go with Blake, the Captain made her promise not to lose her tail.

The black car pulled in to an out of the way spot while Blake navigated the rear end of the SUV to line up with the gallery door. A small woman with a long braid came out. She was dressed in high-waisted Levis and a straw hat with a wide brim. There was no make-up but her lightly tanned skin was smooth and clear.

She held out her hand to Blake.

"Thank you so much, Roxanne," he said. He introduced Gina and showed her the charcoals stacked side by side in the back of the truck.

"Oh no, Blake, thank you. We are very excited to have your work. Come on, follow me. Just leave the paintings in the truck. I'll have my guys unload them. Did you find us okay? Not many people know we're here."

"I was a little surprised when I pulled in. I've only heard about the gallery," said Blake.

"We kind of like that. But we've never had to advertize. I have a long contact list and they always show up when we change out our artists. My father designed the house, which you'll see if you have a moment to walk around, and it's where my brother and I grew up. I live here now with my husband. You'll see a few ponds. I used to swim in them. When he died, it was all in pretty bad shape and my brother and I decided that we had something special here. I'm so glad you accepted my invitation." She'd hardly taken a breath.

"You do not know... I was just about to give up," said Blake.

"Really? I think your work is some of the best new illustration with charcoal I've ever seen. I'm glad I called. And you'll see, we gallery owners are a tight community. When I heard you'd been rejected by certain others, I won't mention names, naturally, I became interested. I asked my artist friends and they recommended you. They know who the rising stars are and that's what I try to look for. Here we are."

Roxanne had led them down a short path cut between a bamboo wall, across a secluded patio area, then through an open door. They were now in a bright and open space that was filled with natural light. It had clean white walls and cinderblock benches were spaced evenly in the center.

Gina squeezed Blake's hand as they looked around the room.

"This room is for you. I think there's enough space." She disappeared around a corner, Gina and Blake followed. The adjacent room was identical to the first except that the walls were already covered with three-dimensional pieces painted in brilliant colors. An enormous piece that looked like it was made of feathers and jewelry hung in the center of the room and another in the corner was like the night sky made with light bulbs. There was also a large screen that played images of people moving as music played in the background.

"This is a fairly new artist we brought from North Carolina."

"I love this," said Blake, standing in front of a sculpture of a winged child.

"The artist is seventeen," said Roxanne. "He's a genius. We just sold that piece you're looking at for a very nice price. I can't say exactly but it was more than $100,000."

"Amazing," Blake managed to say.

Roxanne handed a brochure to Blake. One of his charcoals was on the front cover with his name beneath it.

"This is something we put together for you. I hope you like it. I used some of the pictures you sent me. We'll have them out when tour groups come through, and we have another cocktail party planned for next Wednesday. You can be here can't you?"

"I'll be here. You just tell me whatever you need," said Blake.

"Why don't you and your wife take a walk around the property. It's very relaxing and I can get the boys to bring in the work. When you get back, you can help us place things."

Gina felt like she was dreaming as she followed Blake along a different path that led them away from the gallery toward the back of the property. The exterior of the very mid-century family home was dark wood. It had a flat roof and tall windows on three sides. As they walked, Gina noticed the land was manicured but also very natural. There were settings for the sculptures – shapes and people that were either whimsical or just beautiful in their smooth curves. There were also benches off the path for one to rest and they also found the ponds, rimmed in buffalo grass and floating lily pads.

"I feel like I'm at Walden Pond," said Blake, taking her hand.

"I want one," said Gina, leaning into his side, watching small dragonflies touch the murky water, then dart into the early evening sunlight. "Can you imagine, being in the center of Dallas but inside this peaceful world? Do you think we'll ever have a house?"

"Someday," he said, holding her close. Eventually, the path led them back to the museum where Roxanne was waiting. They spent a few hours placing everything and agreed to be back for the reception at 7:00. Now they just needed a babysitter.

Claire said she'd be happy to watch Sammy.

"We're going to have pigs in a blanket."

"What's that?" asked Sammy.

"I can't believe it. You don't know what pigs in a blanket are? What else have you not been teaching my granddaughter?"

"Evidently not about pigs and blankets," said Gina.

"It's a little Vienna sausage wrapped in a biscuit."

"I don't think they make Vienna sausages anymore, Mom."

"Oh yes they do. I talked to the chef and he promised he'd make them for dinner."

"Fine, but Sammy, if you don't like them, you have my permission to not eat them."

"You're going to love them," said her mother.

Gina gave up and left to get dressed. She slipped into a black cocktail dress and heels. She had to admit she was happy her mother was teaching Sammy about things she still remembered. Not because there was anything redeeming about pigs-in-a-blanket, but because they were part of her own childhood, and maybe that was what made the memory special, having something that could be stored away for however many years so that it could be pulled out and shared as a 'I remember when'. Vienna sausages were the perfect raw material for a memory, even if they were full of chemicals.

The phone's loud jingling surprised her. Blake answered it.

"Hi Helen, no, she's here, right here. It's for you." He handed over the phone.

Gina listened. "Okay. It's okay, Helen, don't worry, I'll be right there."

She looked at Blake as he fixed his tie.

"I really want to go to the gallery with you tonight..."

"But..." he said.

"I was really looking forward to a real date, and making love quietly so that Mom couldn't hear after we got home..."

"But..."

"And you look so handsome in that sport coat and it matches the color of your eyes..."

"Stop, Gina. What is it?"

"That was Helen."

"I know that was Helen. I answered the phone. What happened?"

"Craig's been arrested. She doesn't know if it's a mistake or if he's in real trouble, but she and Richard are down at the jail now and she's really freaked out. I told her I'd stop by and see what I could do. I promise, I'll come to the gallery as soon as I can."

Blake finished tightening his own tie.

Gina put her arms around him, then tilted her head back to look up into his face.

"I'm sorry. I'll be there as soon as I can. Anyway, this is your night and you're going to be the star of the show. You won't even notice I'm not there. People are going to be fighting over your pieces. You're going to be so famous."

"Yeah and you're going to miss it."

"You wouldn't even know I was there."

"Yes, I would."

"Helen needs me more."

"You think?"

She nodded. "And if I don't get there, when I get home, you're going to tell me all about it. In detail."

He liked the look in her eye and leaned down to kiss her. "In detail," he said with a growl. Gina kissed him back, hard.

Quickly, she changed into some plain slacks and a shirt and grabbed her coat. She made sure her badge was in her purse, along with her revolver and with a second thought, grabbed an old sweatshirt.

"Thanks, Mom," she said, poking her head in her mother's room. She told her about Helen's son.

"Blake will probably make it home before me. Just make sure she brushes her teeth."

"Alright."

"Sammy, you're going to love those pigs."

"Tell Helen I'm praying for her. I'll get the details later from SueBee."

"Don't say anything to SueBee, Mom! I don't know if Helen's told her. Wait until I tell you it's okay. Okay?"

Her mother looked disappointed. "Of course."

On her way out, Gina saw the beginnings of the volunteer army. There were two men patrolling the hall and entrances. Another was stationed at the front door. It must have been the changing of the guard as they rolled past each other giving mini-salutes, their craggy faces serious.

It was dark when Gina arrived downtown. The Justice Center housed the courtrooms and the city's juvenile jail. Helen and Richard were sitting on a bench in the lobby.

Helen hugged her hard. Her face was lined with worry. Richard didn't look much better.

"It's going to be okay," said Gina. "What happened?"

"It's such a mistake. Craig's only fourteen! They haven't let us see him but Richard's called an attorney. I had no idea so many of our friends have had kids get arrested! But never mind, let's just say we got a lot of references. Anyway, we called a lawyer who goes to our church. He should be here soon. I just want to get him out of here."

"Are you sure?"

"What do you mean?"

"That's my cue," said Richard. "I'm going to go find some coffee."

Helen watched him go.

"He thinks we should let Craig stay overnight. I don't agree. He doesn't belong here."

"Tell me what happened," said Gina.

"Craig said he was hanging out with friends. I know some of them, but not all of them. After school, they decided to go for a walk. They weren't doing anything, just killing time, walking in the neighborhood." Helen twisted her hands in her lap.

"Craig's always been my good kid and he has the biggest heart. He wouldn't hurt anybody, but he loves his friends. Benji was the one that pushed all my hot buttons, not Craig. If there was a rule, Benji will find a way to break it."

"Wonder where he got that," said Gina, remembering the night she found Helen and Benji in the alley, clipping other people's flowers for their first flower show.

"But Craig doesn't mean to break the rules. He just doesn't think sometimes."

"What did he do?"

"He said they took someone's laundry that was hanging in their backyard. Can you believe it? They called the police because they stole some laundry."

"How'd they catch them?"

"They were walking down the middle of the street wearing ladies' lingerie. They weren't even hiding when the cops pulled up. They just thought it was so funny. It was probably pretty funny looking. Can you imagine Craig in a ladies' nightgown?"

"Are the other kids here?"

"Their parents came and got them hours ago. Richard and I were at a movie so we didn't get the call until just now. He's so scared, Gina. Can you do anything?"

"Probably not. I mean, you can bail him out and then bring him back with your lawyer. The judge will probably let him off. Or you could let him stay in there for a while. Nothing bad's going to happen to him back there. If anything, it'll make him think twice before he breaks the law again."

"I don't want this to go on his record. I just want to take him home."

Gina stood up. "The attorney will help with that. I'll go back and check on him. I know this wasn't murder, but if I were you, I'd take advantage of the situation and leave him in there until the morning."

"For wearing a lady's nightgown? Really?"

Gina shrugged. "Hey, he stole something. This time it was just for fun, but if he gets away with it, without suffering just a little, he might do it again. Next time he's out with his friends, looking for some fun, he's got to learn how to think for himself. He's getting close to being an adult. I'd take advantage of it."

"Downing!" a burly Sergeant Gina recognized yelled at her from behind a desk.

"Your Mom called. She wants to know if you need her."

"Tell her thank you, but no," said Gina.

Helen's husband came back with coffee.

"Y'all need to decide what you want to do."

Helen looked up at Richard. His eyes were hopeful and they talked to each other without saying a word, then Helen turned to her friend.

"Okay, we'll let him stay the night, and Honey," she said to her husband, "call the attorney and ask him to meet us here at nine tomorrow morning. We can rescue Craig then."

"Brilliant," said Richard.

Gina had to wait an hour before they'd let her back there. She walked down a long hallway that led to the holding cells for juvenile boys. Her first impression was how cold it was. Not just a little cold. It was freezing cold. There were bright lights and a lot of benches. The young men sat huddled on the benches. No one was talking, probably because it was late and they were all thinking about their misery. Gina checked with the officer on duty and got permission to talk with Craig.

The young man was shivering as he came closer. He recognized her and his face was respectful but hopeful. Craig was tall for his age, but still had the round features of a child. His face was pale and his acne had flared up in bright red pimples across his forehead.

"How are you doing?" Gina asked. She could tell he was expecting to come out to talk to her, and when that didn't happen, the disappointment showed. She was afraid he might start crying.

"Where's my mom? Why am I still in here? All the other guys got to go home. When are they going to get me out?"

"I don't know, Craig. Your parents are pretty tired. I think they want to get a good night's sleep so they don't kill you whenever they do decide to get you out."

"Really?"

Gina almost changed her mind. "Yeah, it's pretty nasty in there."

"Uh, yeah, it stinks, too. I hate it in here. I want to go home."

"I'm sorry, I wish I could help."

"What's going to happen to me?"

"Well, eventually you'll get to appear before a judge. Your parents will probably hire an attorney to represent you and he'll tell the judge the facts and then the judge will ask you some questions. What happens after that all depends on the judge."

"I could go to jail for taking a lady's nightgown?"

"Stealing is a crime, Craig. You know, if you were in college, on a football team, you might get kicked off. If you worked for a company, they could fire you if it was in their policy. Bad things happen when you break the law."

"We were just having fun."

"Well, the good news is, you're fourteen and I know you're a good kid. Your lawyer will help the judge see that. And maybe, because of this, you can tell someone else what jail's like and maybe keep them from getting in trouble." He was listening. Gina handed him the sweatshirt she'd brought and a wave of gratitude transformed his face. Gina knew she would have hugged him if she could.

"I want that back," she said instead. "Hang in there. Your folks love you and they'll see you in the morning."

Craig shuffled back to the bench, huddled inside the sweatshirt. The experience would count for something. Gina was proud of Helen and Richard, but she was even prouder of Craig. She knew she'd never see him in that room again.

By the time she left, Gina knew Blake's show would be over. She hurried back to The Village with the police escort dutifully following. The front desk was dark now, but before she could round the corner, a voice rang out,

"Who goes there?!"

One of the sentries came rolling into the light. He had on his pajamas and a dark robe and she recognized the slippers. Blake had a pair just like them.

"Hi, Mr. Franklin. It's me, Gina. What are you doing up so late?"

"Couldn't sleep. Everything okay?"

"Yes sir. I'm just getting home late."

"Alright. We're watching out for you."

"Thank you, Mr. Franklin."

Gina returned his salute and wondered what he would have done if she were one of the bad guys. It was almost eleven and Blake had left the door unlocked. The apartment was dark but a light was on in the kitchen where she dropped her keys, then threw her coat over a chair. There was a glow coming from beneath the bathroom door.

"Blake?"

The twin beds were empty, the covers turned down, the way Blake knew she liked it.

Gina opened the bathroom door. The bathtub was already drawn and filled with bubbles. Candles glowed at the corners and there was a glass of wine on the rim of the tub and a bowl of chocolate covered strawberries in the corner. Blake looked up from her dressing table. He was concentrating on something. Seeing her, he smiled."

"What's all this," she said.

"I thought you might need to debrief."

"Strawberries, wine? I like your idea of debriefing."

"The strawberries are from the show. Roxanne sent me home with them. The wine, too."

"How did the show go?"

"Well," he began, looking at her with a gleam in his eyes.

"What?"

"They loved them, Gina. I sold every piece."

Gina screamed and leapt at him, hugging him so that they almost fell over together. "I knew it, I knew it! I'm so happy for you, Blake. Finally! I knew it would happen. I'm so happy for you!"

He held out what he was working on. It was a handmade card with an ink drawing of the Valley house.

Her heart swelled in her chest.

"The house?"

"Maybe it's time we start looking."

She kissed him. His talent always took her breath away.

"I did love that house," she said, looking at the sketch.

"So what did Roxanne say?"

"She wants me to bring her five new paintings by the first of the year. I also made some contacts with some dealers that want me to eventually come show."

"That's wonderful, Blake. Finally!"

"I'm not there yet, but it's a start."

Gina looked at the tub.

"So this is sort of like a celebration, isn't it?"

"Kinda' feels like that."

"Well, let's celebrate," said Gina.

Before the wine had gotten warm, Blake was sitting behind Gina, sponging the bubbles from her shoulders. She took a slow sip.

"I have a question for you."

"Shoot."

"You don't have to give me an answer now, there's no rush."

"My God, woman, just spit it out."

"Well, now that you're a famous artist, do you think it's time for me to go out on my own?"

He continued to rub the sponge back and forth across her shoulders, letting the warm watered bubbles glide down over her arms. She smiled to herself, waiting.

"No, not yet," he said.

It caught her off guard.

"Why not?"

"I think it's too soon. Let's get some more savings under our belts. I don't want to completely lose your income just because I had one good show."

Gina stood up, got out of the tub and, without turning around, she wrapped herself in a towel and walked out of the bathroom.

"Where are you going?" Blake called after her.

"I'm going to bed."

CHAPTER 23

Perched on the edge of her chair, Gina turned down her mother's recommendation to get the scrambled eggs, biscuits and gravy and ate a bowl of Cheerios. She'd come in from her run and sat at the table with the usual group – her mother, Minnie, SueBee, Mr. Jones and a few other early risers. They greeted her with a cheery hello, then continued in their conversations. This had become their routine.

"You going to catch criminals today?" Minnie asked as she did every morning, her fork shaking slightly, to which Gina replied, "I sure hope so."

"Good for you," said a kindly Mr. Kensington, a British gentleman who dressed in a suit for breakfast. "Hope you got your running shoes on," his favorite phrase and to which she showed him her tennis shoes.

After almost three weeks, the Downings had become accustomed to living at The Village and The Village with them being there. Gina had found that grocery sacks were perfect to transport laundry and retrieve necessities from the condo. Evenings were spent playing games and chatting with the residents and there was a constant flow of lectures, choir performances, nursing organizations bringing puppies, Bible studies and sing-a-longs to keep them busy.

Claire had already finished her breakfast and was carefully sorting pieces of paper in small piles. A thick green ledger sat open, along with unopened boxes of invitations and envelopes.

"What are you doing, Mom?"

"I'm trying to catch up on the bookkeeping. My mail's been late ever since I sold the house. It's all those change of address cards. First, there was Mona's, then your address, and then I changed it to The Village and eventually I'll need to change it back to the condominium. The post office thinks I'm making this up and I certainly understand why but now the boys are getting worried. They think I should hire someone to help. I think they want me to retire."

The 'boys', in their fifties now, lived in Colorado. They'd purchased the Garden Club's closet marijuana business several years ago and were happy to let Claire continue on as bookkeeper. At the time, she'd needed the job.

"I'm sure they don't want you to retire, Mom, but since you sold your house, you know you don't have to keep working."

"I guess I could," she said, looking at the growing mess of receipts and printouts.

"Are you done with the invitations for the flower show?" asked Gina, referring to the boxes.

"Yes, and they really should go out today."

"Let me call the boys, Mom. We can send them all this stuff and you can get started on the invitations."

She'd struck a note.

"I should probably train someone to take my place," Claire said, looking hopefully at Gina. "The pay's pretty good."

"I don't think so."

Her mother shrugged. "Okay, well, let me know if you change your mind."

Gina finished the last of her cereal and felt her mother's fingers fixing stray hairs in her runner's pony tail. A police siren pierced the air and she shot a look toward the only escape route.

"Don't worry about that," her mother said, continuing to reposition her hair, "it's just an ambulance. They come about twice a day."

"Mom, stop," she said, pulling her head out of reach.

"I'm afraid we're going to lose some of the guard today," Minnie informed the table. "They're a little worn out."

"Really?" Gina pretended to be worried. "They've been so diligent."

"Yes, and I'm very disappointed, but what can you do? They're volunteers."

"I'm surprised they lasted this long. Don't worry, Minnie, I'll be on my guard. It's been two weeks since anyone's seen or heard from Frank. I'm getting a little bored myself not to mention the colder it gets, the harder it is to keep going back and forth to the condo for clothes. Honestly? I want to be in my own home for Thanksgiving. I haven't even decorated."

The lunchroom was slowly emptying of the breakfast crowd. "You know what? I'm going to talk to the Captain today."

"Today? You think we can move home today? What time? I need to start packing," mumbled Claire, her pencil between her lips.

"Claire, are you sure you don't want to stay? Gina's condo isn't big enough for all of you," said SueBee.

"It's bigger than my room here."

"But for all four of you?" she said, looking at Gina.

"Whatever you want to do, Mom. Please just focus on the invitations today. Even if we move home tonight, it won't take you thirty minutes to pack. Where is Sammy, by the way?"

"Charlotte came and got her. She wanted to teach her to knit."

"This place is better than camp," said Gina, getting up. "I'll see everyone tonight."

Knocking lightly on Charlotte's door, Gina let herself in. Charlotte was sitting in a chair across the room, knitting. When she saw Gina, she held up a four-inch square. "Look what your daughter did. She's a natural."

"Amazing. Is she here?"

"No. Someone came and got her and took her to the card room. They needed a fourth."

Gina looked at the time. She hurried down a different hall until she'd found the players.

"Sammy, what are you doing? You need to get ready for schoo...'

"Shhh," interrupted the three women.

Gina stood quietly behind her daughter.

"I say three," said Sammy.

"*Bid* three, dear," corrected the woman seated across the table. Evidently her partner.

The woman on her left said, "I'm going to pass."

"You sure about that?"

Sammy shifted away from her mother's hand messing with her hair.

"Then I guess that makes me the dummy," said another player.

"My daughter's a genius," said Gina. "Two weeks and now they've taught you how to play bridge."

"They taught me how to play poker, too."

"Thank you, ladies. I'm amazed and proud but you, little girl, you need to get to pre-school. Where's Daddy?"

"There's no school today. It's a teacher day. Daddy's reading the paper."

"Of course." No one at the table had any interest in Gina's day, so she kissed her daughter good-bye, knowing she was in good hands.

Gina got to work but it was hard to concentrate. She couldn't help but think about what it would be like to be on her own. The urge to become a private investigator had gotten worse. She understood and agreed, in a way, with Blake. But it had been hard. It didn't help that there was still the cloud of Frank hanging over them. The Captain noticed something was wrong and called her in.

"Well? You've been sitting over there looking out your window all morning."

"Nothing, Sir. Actually, there is something. Nothing's happened for two weeks. The FBI hasn't found him and I'm not so sure staying at The Village any longer is going to make any difference."

He thought about it until the computer screen behind him went blank. He rubbed his forehead like he was trying to work something out. Or had a bad headache, she wasn't sure.

"Aww, heck, I guess you might as well move back home. FBI hasn't seen him in New Mexico. We can't find him here. No use you staying at that old folks' home any longer. You might as well go home and I guess we keep someone there. At least we only got one guy wanting to kill himself he's so bored."

"Thanks," Gina beamed. She started to leave but changed her mind.

"One more thing, Chief. I really appreciate all that you're doing to protect my family. I just wanted you to know that."

"Sure. Anything else?"

"That's it."

Later that day, Gina arrived at Helen's for one last meeting before the Club's flower show now just two weeks away. With everything that had been going on, there was a different feel to the meeting. It was as though they'd spent all their anxiety on taking care of Sheralyn and knowing Gina's life was in danger. A flower show would be a walk in the park.

Helen's crowded living room was a dramatic difference over last month's attendance, a sign that the pilgrimage to San Antonio had worked. As President, Brooke opened the meeting then quickly turned it over to Gina.

"Does everyone have a copy of the Schedule?"

It was obvious some had hoped the schedule would not be as important. There was the look of dread in their eyes as they flipped through the thick ream of pages explaining the rules and requirements for all standard flower shows.

"Don't worry, just do your best. Two of the mothers are judging so let's pretend we know what we're doing." Gina reminded everyone to get their silver polished and to drop it off at Brooke's house no later than the Friday before the show.

"The mothers want to help," said Brooke.

It came as no surprise.

"I think we should let them," said Sheralyn who'd been sitting quietly on the couch. There was new life in her eyes and the color was back in her face. She looked like royalty in a teal turtleneck that acted as a pedestal around her long neck.

"I'm so glad you said that because I think they've already planned on bringing lunch."

"And what are we having?" asked Helen.

Gina searched and found a folded piece of paper. "Pumpkin soup, a crabmeat mousse, orange and cashew chicken, shrimp torte, an oriental chicken salad, and strawberry melba."

"Wow," said Helen.

"Any questions?" Gina asked. No one did. "Alright, I need to get back to work. I'll see everyone no later than 8 am at Brooke's on December 4th. Don't be late or you'll be disqualified and have a very Happy Thanksgiving."

That evening, Gina arrived back at The Village expecting her mother to be waiting on the curb with her suitcases. Instead, it was eerily quiet in the lobby and the familiar hall strangely dark. Gina looked left and right into the rooms, naturally their doors were open but all the rooms were empty. She started walking faster, and as she turned the corner to the lunchroom she was about to find her gun when a hundred voices screamed, "Surprise!"

She screamed. Blake, Samantha and her mother were already dressed in honoree regalia of paper hats, surrounded by balloons. They laughed and clapped with the others at Gina's surprise.

Minnie rolled up, looking like the conquering army.

"Did we scare you?"

"Of course you scared me. You're lucky I didn't shoot you."

"We heard you got the green light to move home but we couldn't let you go without a good-bye party."

Surrounded by residents, they showered the family with hugs and kisses. There was going to be a program. As soon as she could, Gina pulled Blake aside.

"I thought we were going to get to go home tonight," she said, talking between smiling teeth.

He did the same, taking a bite of cake. "I did, too, but I'm not going to spoil their fun."

Mr. Crawley called for everyone's attention as he stood in the center of the room.

"Detective Downing, we've enjoyed having you and your family very much and we're all sad to see you go but we're happy for you as well. I'm sure getting back to your own home will be nice. But now you know what I've been dealing with all these years."

Gina laughed and saluted him. "Thank you."

"Do you think your mother is planning on joining us one of these days?" Gina shrugged and the expression on his face was slightly fearful which made everyone laugh.

"I wish she would. You have a great place here."

"Then I will try to prepare myself. We hope you'll come visit us often and now I better get back to the front desk."

There were some musical numbers and a short play. Much of the attention was on Sammy and suddenly, she started to cry. It was all too much. Gina rescued her and excused themselves from the party. Sammy needed to go to bed and it looked like they'd be staying one more night.

Later, as Gina and Blake shared her small bed, she asked him, "How much longer before we can start looking for a house?"

"A house is a lot of work," he said.

"I know." She turned on her side so that Blake could rub her back.

"Maybe we can start looking after the holidays," he said.

Peace settled over the room. The moonlight outlined the drapes and the heater made its soothing purr-like sounds.

She knew what he was thinking by the way his strong fingers kneaded her back.

"It's all going to work out. We just need to be patient."

"When we have a house," she mused, "we'll decorate the front door with pumpkins and scarecrows and I'll have a really long dining room table so that I can invite gobs of people over and even your relatives that I've never met could come down."

"They would never come," he said.

"Then I'll invite the homeless people that live on the street outside our condo."

"Yeah, you would."

"I'll put the PI thing on hold. It's just too risky."

She held her breath, wishing he would disagree which he did do, in a way.

"It's just the timing, that's all. I think it would be great, someday," he said, now tracing her spin with his fingers.

Suddenly, he flipped over on his back, taking up almost the whole mattress. "Our last night in this place."

He pushed against her. "You're taking up too much room." It was a familiar complaint.

"Hey," Gina said, nearly falling out of the bed. "Then get in your own bed."

"Move over."

"Stop!" Gina said again, only this time laughing. He was doing it again.

"Do I need to get my wrist guard," she said, trying to push him back on his side of the bed.

Blake caught her wrist and pulled her over on top of him. There was just enough light that let her look into his eyes. She was smiling and his face mirrored hers. She bent down to kiss him.

There was a loud tapping on the wall above their heads.

"Gina?"

"Yes?"

"I hope I didn't wake you but I thought I heard the TV."

"Yes, you did," Gina called back.

"Well, can you please turn it down? Samantha and I are almost asleep. I'll have everything packed in the morning to move back to the apartment."

"It's a condominium, Mom, it's not an apartment."

Blake whispered in her ear, "I'm glad we're going home tomorrow."

"Me too," she said, giggling again.

CHAPTER 24

There were unexpected consequences to spending the night at The Village, things no one could have foreseen. Between midnight and four am, the temperature plummeted. Even though it had been getting colder every day, this sudden blast of winter caught everyone by surprise. If newspapers got delivered they were late and dogs left outside crept against open vents or dug themselves into deep holes beneath shrubs or against barriers. Gina woke up at five shivering and hurried to find extra blankets. She turned up the thermostat in both rooms, took blankets into her mother and Sammy, then crawled into bed with Blake and tried to go back to sleep.

Gina eventually wrapped herself in a blanket and sat in front of the TV, her hands holding a mug of hot water as she watched images of storm fronts and icicles hovering over North Texas.

"This is crazy," Gina said to Blake when he came out of the bedroom. Outside, she could see the pecan trees swaying like they were made of wire and leaves circled in gusts as if they'd been shot out of a canon. Buried in her blanket, Gina followed them with her eyes across the lawn and parking lot until they ended up in piles against fences and curbs. She thought she saw small patches of standing water that had iced over. Dead branches brought down by the heavy winds littered the street.

Blake huddled off to the bathroom, shivering, half-naked. "Crazy," she said again. "It's never this cold in November."

Thanksgiving was typically a great disappointment to Dallasites who had been toiling in the lingering heat of summer while longing for Fall. The cool days of October would arrive, lulling everyone into putting away their shorts and T-shirts, but suddenly, in the midst of making homemade pilgrim hats and 'What I'm most thankful for' projects, the thermometer would climb again. Thanksgiving was usually warm.

Gina showered, then found Blake and Sammy sitting at one of the big round tables in the lunchroom with the usuals. Father and daughter each had a plate of pancakes and there was a waiting pile in the center of the table.

"Hi Mommy," said Sammy, her right hand resting in her lap with a napkin while she held a fork properly with her left. She was also sitting up very straight. Blake sat in an identical way.

"Good morning," Gina said as she went to kiss Blake. "How are the pancakes?"

"So yummy," he said. "Your Mom put my syrup on for me."

"Where's the paper?" asked Gina, looking around for the news. The Village always got several copies.

"Mimi says it's not polite to read at the table. We're making conversation." Her mother looked innocent.

"You both look like you're strapped to a backboard."

"We're keeping our shoulders back," said Blake.

"Mimi said Daddy's going to be a hunchback," said Sammy.

"Pancakes?" Claire asked.

"No, thank you. Okay, here's the plan. Breakfast, bath, then pack. I don't know about y'all but I'm ready to go home."

"Yeah!" yelled Sammy."

"It's freezing out there," said Minnie. "You're welcome to borrow some hats and coats."

"Thank you."

"Can we stop by my storage unit?" asked Claire.

Gina knew better than to ask why.

Once they were packed, Blake and Gina were unrecognizable in borrowed coats, scarves and mittens that smelled of mothballs as they ferried suitcases back and forth to the car. The wind beat them like they were running a gauntlet and the residents watched from the windows until it was time to say good-bye.

"Y'all better come back soon," Richard made them promise from his spot behind the front desk. The TV was on in the background, still covering the weather.

"Please say you'll come for tea, Samantha, any time your mommy can bring you," SueBee and Charlotte begged.

"I'll bring back the clothes as soon as I can," Gina said, trying to give Minnie a hug despite the heavy clothes. She would never forget their generosity and love and she began to get teary eyed. She was grateful that most of her face was wrapped in a scarf.

Their police escort followed them first to the storage unit where everyone froze to death while Claire looked for the box containing her cast iron skillet and turkey pan, then home. There, another officer met them in the underground garage, travelled up the elevator and after a resounding 'Welcome Back!' from the concierge, they took the second elevator to their floor. The officer insisted on being first inside.

Sarge barked ferociously on the other side of the door and when they opened it, he backed up, but continued to roar at the stranger. He wouldn't stop even though Blake and Gina tried explaining this was a friend. The man looked like he might pull his gun when Sammy ran and put her arms around his furry neck. Only then did the dog calm down but the officer never took his eyes of the dog and quickly checked the condo.

Once he'd left, Gina turned up the heat, ruffled Sarge's head, looking into his deep brown eyes. Sarge suddenly became a puppy and tried to wriggle between their legs, his tail swishing back and forth like a metronome on high. He even tried nuzzling Claire but she pushed him away with her leg. Between the Downings and the dog, it was hard to tell who was happier to be home.

Blake had obviously not been the best housekeeper. He'd come and gone almost daily, occasionally eating, watching TV, playing with Sarge. There were dirty dishes piled in the sink and except for a papier-mâché turkey on the kitchen table, there were no other signs of Thanksgiving. If she hadn't been so happy to be home, Gina would have lit into Blake for being such a slob. Instead, she put her suitcases in the bedroom and rolled up her sleeves. She might as well get started.

Claire took hold of her own suitcase handle.

"I know you've got a lot to do and I'll help you clean up in a bit. First I want to unpack in my new room." She snapped up the silver handle and rolled away into the spare bedroom, shutting the door behind her.

"Okay, that's strange," said Gina to Blake. "Never in my life have I known my mother to walk past a sink full of dirty dishes."

Gina put her ear against her mother's door.

"She's calling someone."

"Gina, that's her room now. Give her some privacy."

Gina listened.

"She's laughing."

"Gina!"

Reluctantly, she abandoned the door to pull out recipes and started making a list. When her mother came out of her room looking refreshed, flushed and full of energy, Gina knew something was going on.

"Everything okay?"

"Wonderful. What can I do to help?" she asked.

Gina decided she'd wait until later to find out what her mother was up to.

The days leading up to Thanksgiving went by quietly and without any sighting of Frank. On the outside, Gina was grateful, but inside, she worried that his goal was to lull them once again into complacency. Or was it possible he'd truly disappeared? Despite her worries, they settled back into a routine. Since Gina was on vacation and Sammy had no pre-school, she and Blake slept late, letting Claire take care of Sammy. They drank coffee and ate big breakfasts, read the paper, and took turns walking Sarge. Afternoons, Blake painted in his studio while Claire and her mother went through boxes of old pictures and watched movies on TV. It was still too cold to go outside unless they had to. The invitations for the flower show had already gone out and there were only minor details to manage. Gina was surprised how smoothly the days passed.

The night before Thanksgiving, as the wind beat against the patio windows, they watched a movie and ate hotdogs. The weatherman kept interrupting programming to tell them it was going to get worse. Sarge lay heavily over Gina's feet.

"I'm so glad we're home," said Gina, nestling against Blake with Sammy on top of her.

"Me, too," he said.

"Mom, you need anything?"

"No, thank you." But Gina noticed her fidgeting. Finally, as though she couldn't sit still any longer, Claire got up and began taking things into the kitchen and when she came back, she gathered up her puzzle book and sweater and was already half-way to her room when she said, "I think I'm going to turn in early. Goodnight."

"Who could she be calling?" asked Gina.

"Mimi has a boyfriend," said Sammy.

Gina jerked around and looked at Blake. He acted as though he didn't know anything.

"Why do you say that, Sammy?"

The little girl shrugged, brushing the hair on her Strawberry Patch doll.

"I don't know. Mimi giggles when she's talking on the phone."

Blake tried to catch Gina's hand but she'd already gone to listen at the door. A moment later she came back.

"It's quiet."

"Gina, just ask her."

"She'd tell me if she wanted me to know, right?"

"Exactly. So don't ask her."

"You're no help," Gina said, slumping back on the couch but soon she was caught up in the movie again and Sammy fell asleep between them.

At midnight, Gina put the turkey on, then got up to baste it at three. At six am, she woke, buried beneath two blankets and a comforter. Exposing only her nose, she sniffed. The air was ice cold but she could smell the turkey. She elbowed Blake.

"Blake, wake up. It's freezing." He was wrapped in his cocoon.

"Please..." he growled.

Gina exposed her arm and found the phone. She dialed the maintenance number for the building, discussed the issue with someone, then pulled her arm back in. "The heat is broken again. He says they're working on it. At least it's not the electricity."

"Gina?" Claire poked her head in their room.

"Hi, Mom."

"I think the heater's broken."

"It is. I just called downstairs. They're working on it."

"Okeedokee. The weatherman is still saying it's going to get worse."

Gina heard noises from the kitchen and pulled the covers over her head. An hour later, she woke again, found daylight and was relieved to find the air was toasty warm. The dog started giving himself a bath. Gina yelled and threw a pillow at him. Finally, she got up, pulling on her big sweater. Sarge stopped bathing and followed her into the kitchen where she saw her mother bent over the dishwasher.

"Morning. What are you doing, Mom?"

"I'm organizing your dishes. You could get a lot more in here if you did it right."

Gina was about to argue when she looked around the kitchen. It was spotless. The table was set for four with her china and silver. The stove and sink shone. Even the counters were cleared and the floor had been swept. The placemats looked vaguely familiar.

"Happy Thanksgiving. How'd you sleep?"

"Happy Thanksgiving, I slept great." Gina opened the oven door to check the turkey. The skin had turned a light shade of golden brown and the juices were starting to push through and were bubbling in the bottom of the huge pan her mother had brought from the storage unit. Gina did a couple of spoonfuls of juice over the top. She already knew the refrigerator had been crammed full of dishes that would be ready to go in the oven when the time came. A large bowl with a towel over it told her her mother's dough for the rolls was rising nicely. She could smell the yeast and it made her nose hairs tingle.

Claire poured her a cup of coffee and set it on the table.

"Coffee?"

"Thank you."

"I was just about to fix everyone a big breakfast. Can I make you some eggs?"

"Sure."

"I've already made the cornbread in my cast iron but do you also want me to make the beans? And you're out of milk," she added. "I'll go to the store later."

"Thank you."

"What?"

"Thank you. I really appreciate you doing all this."

"Reminds me of Thanksgiving when you were little. My pleasure."

The phone rang and they both jumped. Something about phone calls on Thanksgiving wasn't natural.

"Everything okay?" asked the Captain.

"Fine, why?"

"I just heard from the FBI. Frank set fire to his ex-wife's house in New Mexico. She survived but they didn't catch him."

Gina sat down still holding the basting spoon. Hot grease dripped on her knee.

"What do you mean they missed him? How is that possible? How can he be so lucky?"

There was something else in the Captain's voice.

"What?"

"He's coming back to Dallas."

"Whatever. We don't know what that guy is going to do. I'm getting sick and tired of waiting. He's probably headed to Canada but if he comes back here, I've got my gun and I'll shoot him."

"Gina, I mean it. This is serious. He did another cartoon. He drew a picture of the Frankenstein."

"So?"

"He also drew a picture of a man with a paintbrush, a woman holding a gun, a girl child, and a little old lady with a cane."

"Oh. That's not good."

Her mother stopped what she was doing and came to stand beside her.

"I want you and your family to stay put but starting tomorrow, I think you and I need to get creative. We've got to figure out a way that makes him think he has a chance to get to you. Away from your family."

"I agree. I want my family to stay completely out of this and you better protect them for me. No one gets in or out of this building without you knowing about it. Okay?"

"Okay. Don't worry. But you'll have to pretend to look vulnerable. I know you love that," added the Captain.

"Not funny. I'll start working on it tomorrow."

Gina relayed everything to her mother and Blake. The phone rang again.

"Okay Captain, you know it's Thanksgiving, right?"

"Gina? Hello, this is Andrew."

"I'm sorry, who?"

"Andrew, your mother's friend. Heavin's father?"

Gina eyed her mother who was pretending to dry a dish.

"Sure, Andrew. I remember, I'm sorry. How is Heavin? How's the riding these days?"

"It's been a little too cold for me. How are you?"

"Fine. Everything okay?" Gina gestured to her mother, who looked worried. *What*? she asked with her eyes.

Andrew continued, "Actually, I'm calling because Claire invited me to Thanksgiving dinner and I thought I should ask if it was alright with you. I told her I wanted to make sure it wouldn't be an imposition."

Gina didn't need to think about it.

"Well sure, of course! We'd love to have you." Her mother began to smile while Gina finished the conversation and hung up.

"Well isn't this interesting. Andrew's coming for lunch."

"That's nice," her mother shrugged, still drying the same dish.

"Okay, Mom, what's going on?"

"Nothing. I think there's plenty of food."

"I mean Andrew. How did this happen?"

"He asked if he could call when we were in San Antonio. I must have said okay because he's been calling ever since and Heavin is going to his wife's family for Thanksgiving so I invited him to join us. You're always talking about having lots of people around the table."

"Of course! I love it, Mom. I'm happy for you."

"Gina, please don't make a fuss. I've just enjoyed talking to him. Anyway, you have enough on your mind and now I need to get started on breakfast. You go watch the Macy's parade and relax."

Gina didn't need to be told twice. She loved the parade and with the interesting developments with Andrew, she couldn't wait to tell Blake. When he finally emerged, sleepy-eyed and slow, Gina pounced on him with the news. He was not as excited as she was, but that didn't matter and she danced around him with the idea of her mother finding someone at her age.

Shortly after noon, the doorbell rang and the white-haired man, slightly shorter than everyone but Sammy, stood at the door with a bouquet of roses.

After everyone's plate was loaded high with turkey and dressing and all the other dishes, enough to feed twice their number, they bowed their heads and closed their eyes. Just as Blake was about to give thanks, Gina felt Andrew putting his hands quietly on the table toward she and her mother. Instinctively, she took it, as did her mother, and then they did the same thing, until everyone was connected. Then Blake prayed and Gina thought she'd never heard him give such a heartfelt thanks to God for His blessing and provision. He thanked God for their guest at the table and for their friends at The Village. He asked God to continue to protect them, and for Gina's career and Sammy and Sarge. In those few moments, the love of God travelled between them and they were knit together in a spiritual way which was always so much more meaningful than anything they could have planned.

After the prayer, Gina didn't waste time bombarding Andrew with questions. He answered most with a chuckle, but he especially relished the starry-eyed questions from Sammy who wanted to know all about the North Pole which was understandable considering he'd worn a red sweater vest and tie.

When everyone was stuffed, Gina picked up some plates and carried them into the kitchen. Like a bad penny, the phone rang again.

"What?" she answered, assuming it was the Captain. She hadn't meant to sound so harsh but after all, it was Thanksgiving!

"Hi, Officer Sessions."

"Frank?" Gina turned away from the family.

"How are you? Did you hear about New Mexico yet?"

"What are you talking about? Where are you?"

"Oh, come on, Gina. I know you know all about it."

The sound of his voice was enough to make her heart start pounding. She forced herself to take a deep breath.

"Get over yourself, Frank. It's Thanksgiving. I'm eating turkey and dressing."

"Well, it was really great. Did you get my message?"

She knew he meant the cartoons. "I did. So when are we going to get this over with?"

"Tonight. Come to the motel across Industrial near the bridge at five o'clock. There's a pay phone on the corner. And I've seen all those movies where the cop brings more cops, or they send them in early, or whatever so don't try it. When you get there, I'm going to call you on the phone and tell you where to go next. So come by yourself."

"That sounds awfully complicated, Frank, and I don't want to do it today."

"What?" She'd definitely caught him off guard. She thought fast.

"Have you looked outside? They say it's going to get worse. And it's Thanksgiving. Why don't we do this tomorrow?"

"I didn't ask you, I'm telling you to come to the motel at five o'clock!"

"And I don't think I can make it."

"What do you mean you don't think you can make it! What kind of police officer are you?"

"Not today, Frank." She wasn't prepared. She wasn't ready. "I'll meet with you, just not today. And you can come to my new office. I'm leaving the force, going out on my own."

There was silence on the other end.

"So call me tomorrow? We'll set something up."

His voice was like ice. "Sure. Wouldn't want to interrupt your family plans. Or maybe I'll just stop by your condo," and then the line went dead.

"He'll call back," Gina told her mother who was standing watch.

"Who was that?" asked Blake, still holding dirty dishes. Andrew stood next to him. "Everything okay?"

"There's something I need to tell you, but the Captain and I have talked about it and there's nothing to worry about. Now, who wants pie?"

CHAPTER 25

The idea for an office had popped into her head and the Captain agreed. They'd say that after San Antonio, she'd decided to leave the department and start her own Private Investigation company. Even if it wasn't for real, it was the best she could come up with on her own.

When she woke up Friday, the clouds had moved on and the wind had died down enough to remind everyone once again that the weatherman wasn't God. Gina went looking for office space and she already had a good idea of where to start.

Rusty, a muscle bound wise guy, owned a small pawn shop and several other small spaces along the same shady strip of real estate near Downtown. He was a good one to know when she was looking for certain information.

Rusty sent her to some office space about the size of a UPS store. It was small, had a back office and a long counter that would act as a nice barrier if an unhappy client happened to walk in with a grudge. Even better, the former tenants had left two desks and a couple of filing cabinets.

Since it only had to 'look' like an office, it didn't take Gina long to set the stage. In case Frank was watching, she visited a Kinko's and had a big banner made to hang in the window announcing she was ready for business.

She was surprised and a little disappointed that Frank didn't call.

CHAPTER 26

Gina straightened the candlesticks, then dropped her keys in a bowl. Sammy went straight for the kitchen. It was Monday and Frank still hadn't called.

"Hi Mimi," she heard Sammy say.

"Hi, darling. Can I fix you a snack?"

Claire's accounting books were spread out over the counter along with an antiquated calculator with a tape.

"Are you still doing that?" asked Gina.

"I'm checking one more thing. The boys said I might have made a mistake."

Gina poured a glass of water and sat down.

"A big one?"

"I don't know yet," she answered.

Gina noticed a slight tremor as she made marks inside the tiny boxes.

"Everything okay, Mom?"

"Why?"

"You look a little worried."

Her mother warned her with a look. "Well, I'm not worried. Actually, they offered me a retirement package. I must not be doing a very good job."

"I'm sure you're doing a good job, but maybe they've decided it would be better to keep things in Colorado. And you know how much they like their computers and you hate computers."

"I guess."

"What did they offer you?"

"A million dollars."

"What?!" Gina nearly jumped out of her chair.

"They invested some of the profits. I know, it's a lot, isn't it. And they said that they always considered me as a part owner. They said 5%. I think I could live on that."

"Mom!"

Claire smiled sheepishly. "Pretty good, huh?"

Gina hugged her. "I'm so happy for you! When's your last day?"

Her mother looked at the tattered books and antiquated adding machine. "This is it. I'm done. I'm going to mail them everything."

Later that night, Gina threw back the covers and climbed into bed.

"That was smooth," said Blake, reaching for a book.

"I know. They called me a few weeks ago because she refused to use the computer. She said it kept making mistakes. They've been using someone else locally for months, they just didn't know how to tell her. Thank goodness it all worked out."

"So do you think she'll move out anytime soon?"

"That I don't know."

CHAPTER 27

"Did you feel that?" Brooke asked her friends before sitting down with a coffee and muffin at the coffee shop. It was Tuesday, just two days before the flower show and they'd decided to meet one last time to make sure everything was ready. Every time the door opened, a gust of wind made them huddle closer around the table.

"It's freezing out there," said Sheralyn, wrapped in a fur coat. "I think it's supposed to get worse."

"That's what they said last week," said Gina. "Anyway, there's nothing we can do about it, so think happy thoughts. Brooke, has everyone dropped off their silver?"

She nodded. "Most of it looks pretty good. I may have to polish a few pieces."

"Okay," said Gina. "I know Mom and the mothers are hard at work on the food. Mom's making her homemade rolls tomorrow night and she's been over at SueBee's every day. I think we've got about fifty RSVPs."

"What if we get ice?" said Helen.

"Still no word from Frank?" asked Sheralyn.

"No. I'm afraid I scared him off. The Captain's furious I didn't meet him when he called."

"But the police are still guarding you, right?"

"Right."

CHAPTER 28

  A sense of gloom hung over the condo. Frank still hadn't called. There was always someone from the police force watching, and soon it became embarrassing for the days that dragged on with nothing but cold and wet to account for their whereabouts. By Wednesday, they'd begun to look at Gina with downcast eyes. No one had any answers and while Gina obediently travelled to and from her pretend office in case Frank was watching, Blake ran errands, or at least that's what he said he was doing. It seemed he was gone most of several days in the early part of the week and got very little painting done. At least Claire was content to bring the condo up to her standards and Sammy became her helper and when Wednesday arrived, the urgency of the flower show was apparent.
  The weather was no longer discussed. Thursday would be cold and wet and even though it was only rain, the threat of ice remained. They tried not to stay glued to the TV but it was hard because the stations remained on topic. By late afternoon, the rain was beating relentlessly against the glass doors to the balcony and even Sarge had grown tired of barking.
  After dinner, Gina unloaded the refrigerator of three large buckets of flowers that were stuffed to overflowing. She looked at the clock, then turned the heat up again on the thermostat. They could feel the cold coming through the thin glass windows. Gina prayed the heating system wouldn't choose this night to break again as she listened to the old system knocking loudly through the vents. The weatherman warned her to stay inside and to avoid travel at all costs. As the hours passed, there was little doubt that once the rain stopped, it would all turn to ice.
  Gina compared the sketch she'd made for her flower arrangement to the display of colors on the counter.
  It had already been agreed that Brooke would make the call on whether or not to cancel the flower show. Unlike their mothers, the daughters had decided not to risk life and limb for the flower show. They'd cry UNCLE if the weather got that bad.

The windows rattled behind her as her mother dropped a five pound bag of flour on the counter.

Gina jumped. "Mom!"

"Sorry," Claire said, disappearing into the pantry, singing as she searched for something. She emerged with the sugar. "I've got to make the rolls for tomorrow."

Standing at the other end of the counter, Gina centered the container she was going to use in front of her. She'd found it at a craft store. It was a large discolored porcelain square, fifteen inches long, eight inches wide, and ten inches tall. She plugged in the drill.

Without measuring, Claire poured out a pile of flour on the countertop. She opened a can of Crisco and with a wooden spoon, threw on a few large mounds of the white grease. Pinching the grease and flour between her fingertips, it was soon mixed in enough so that she could start kneading it.

Supporting the house with one hand, Gina pressed the diamond tip drill bit into the fragile sides of the box over and over again until she had a few dozen clean, tiny holes. The porcelain was now polka-dotted with holes.

"Mom, can you hand me the oasis?"

Claire wiped her hands off on her apron and brought over a deep Tupperware bowl that Gina had packed with oasis and water earlier that morning. By now, the oasis had soaked up all the water. Now it was like wet concrete.

Using a long flat blade, she cut the green stuff into tall bricks and put them side by side into the porcelain house. She made sure all the drilled holes were covered.

"Can I watch?" asked Sammy, clamoring up on a stool next to the counter.

"I thought you were asleep."

"The rain woke me up. And I heard you and Mimi playing. Daddy's painting. Can I watch?"

"I guess so, but just for a few minutes."

"I'll teach you how to make rolls," said Claire. She dipped her fingers in a glass of water and shook them over the dough, then sprinkled over a pinch of sugar.

"My secret ingredient."

Next, she rubbed the rolling pin with flour, then threw another handful of flour onto the counter before slapping down the mound of dough, once, then twice. Flour dust flew in every direction. With deep long strokes, she began rolling out the dough across the countertop. With each push then pull, the shape grew larger and larger.

"Once I have this big enough, we'll cut out all the rolls. You can help."

Gina watched her daughter's eager face. Hair stuck out from a ponytail at her crown and there was toothpaste at the corners of her mouth.

While Sammy was happily focused on the roll-making, Gina chose five pink peonies from one of the buckets. She took the first one and measured it against the house, then made a sharp cut before pressing it down into the thick oasis. She repeated the process until there was a distinct roof line. Next, she picked out flowers at random. These would fill the rest of the spaces and while it didn't matter so much which flower she chose, she needed to make sure to cut it at just the right length so that the end result looked like a smooth blanket of color.

Armed with a small glass jar, Claire and Sammy cut out circles of dough, then swiped each roll with a strip of melted butter down the middle. Then with three fingers, her thumb in the middle, Claire showed Sammy how to stretch the dough and fold it into an oval shape before placing it on the cookie sheet. Sammy's fingers were small, but nimble. The rolls were slightly misshapen. She looked up proudly.

With the roof finished, Gina started on the walls. For this part, the colors and textures were more important. She wanted each flower to have a presence, but not stand out too much. And there couldn't be any empty space between them.

Sammy hovered over the top of the house. She squirmed on her stool.

"Can I help?" she asked her mother.

Gina dragged the stool closer and handed her daughter the knife and a daisy. She watched Sammy trim the flower then search for an empty hole. She pushed the flower through.

"Good job," said Gina.

Claire laid some thin kitchen towels over the two large trays of dinner rolls and put them in the cold oven.

"We'll let these rise overnight, then pop them in the oven right before the girls' luncheon."

"Do you think this looks like a candy house?" Gina asked.

Claire stood back and tilted her head left and right. Flour covered her checks and forehead. Sammy's too.

"I don't know."

"Mom, you aren't a judge. Just tell me."

Claire wiped her hands against her apron and looked more closely at the arrangement.

"I forgot, what is it?"

"It's the witch's house from Hansel and Gretel."

Claire walked her way around it, humming a few notes. "I think it's charming," she said.

"Thank you. I wish I had a few more small pink flowers, though. I'd make windows with them."

Claire immediately reached for her coat and began looking for her purse.

"Where are you going?"

"I'll go get you some flowers. I know just what you need and I saw them in that downstairs drugstore. I think they're open until nine."

"Oh no, Mom. It's too late."

"I'll be right back."

Before Gina could protest again, Claire was gone.

"Okay, little girl, time for you to go back to bed." Gina ushered Sammy to her room. There was no argument and without any prompting, she went straight to her bed and climbed in, settling under the covers. Her eyelids were heavy as Gina smoothed her hair around her face.

"I hope you win, Mommy," Sammy said, closing her eyes. "It's a pretty house."

"Thank you, Honey. But there are going to be a lot of pretty arrangements. Even if I don't win, I'll be happy I finished something."

"What will you win?"

"Well," said Gina, "I might bring home a big beautiful tray, or a silver pitcher."

"Do you like making flower arrangements?"

"I do."

"I'm glad that you're home more."

"Me too," said Gina.

"Please tell me a story."

"I think you're going to fall asleep. And Mommy's got to finish her flower arrangement."

She opened her eyes. "No I won't. Just until Mimi gets home? Please?"

The kid would make a great lawyer.

"Alright. If you'll close your eyes and try to go to sleep." Claire tucked the covers in over her shoulders and waited for her to close her eyes.

"Imagine a beautiful big meadow and there are mountains all around. The grass is a golden brown, and parts of it are tall with wheat and it's waving in the wind. The sun is shining. Another part of the land has short green grass and it's cleared because there's a big old barn and there's a pasture and a white fence all around it."

"Got it?" said Gina.

"Got it," her child said, smiling.

"Okeedokee," Gina said in a slightly Russian accent, "I vill begin. Once upon a time, there was a little girl who was strong and smart and she had her very own horse. His name was Paintbrush because he had black and white messy spots, as if someone had thrown a can of paint at him."

"The little girl took very good care of Paintbrush because he was her responsibility and it was a lot of work, but the little girl didn't mind because she loved Paintbrush very much.

"Every day when the little girl got home from school, before she did her homework or had a snack, she had to take care of Paintbrush. She would give him fresh oats and then water and then she turned over all the hay inside his stall so that it was clean and fresh. And then, if she didn't have too much homework, the little girl would put her saddle on Paintbrush and off they'd go, to have an adventure somewhere on the farm."

"On other days, the little girl taught her horse how to walk forward and backward. She taught him to turn left and right, all by the way she held the reins. Paintbrush was very smart and he knew how much the little girl loved him because she took such good care of him. At the end of the day, after she'd brushed him and made sure he was all tucked into bed, she would hug his neck and say goodnight. The End."

It was virtually the same Paintbrush story she always told.

Sammy rolled over.

"You don't tuck horses into bed."

Gina leaned over and pressed the covers up around Sammy's chin."

"How do you know? Anyway, it's my imagination."

Sammy turned back over. "Goodnight."

Gina closed Sammy's bedroom door behind her. She walked by the front door and straightened the candle. Back in the kitchen, she decided the arrangement was good. She looked at her watch.

"Blake, would you mind going downstairs to look for Mom? She's been gone almost twenty minutes."

Blake stopped what he was doing. "Sure."

The phone rang.

"Hello?"

"Gina?"

"Mom? Wait up, Blake, Mom's on the phone. Where are you?"

"Don't worry, I'm fine. Frank is here."

"Frank who?"

"Frank. You know, that Frank."

Gina's heart stopped. She waved at Blake wildly to come closer.

"Mom? Are you alright"

"She's fine," said Frank's voice.

"Frank! What are you doing?"

"Hi, Gina. Are you surprised? There wasn't one cop downstairs. I just walked right up to your mother."

"What do you want?"

"I wanted you but she came out and I thought, why not?"

Gina grabbed a piece of paper and wrote a note to Blake to call the police. She tried to slow her breathing, to think clearly.

"Where are you, Frank? I'll be right there."

"No need. But, listen, do not call the police. I have a police scanner in my back pocket and if I see or hear anything that sounds like the police, I'll take your mom with me and you'll never see her again."

Gina got Blake's attention, telling him to stop.

"Now open the front door," he said.

"What front door?"

"Your front door, stupid."

Still holding the phone to her ear, Gina did as she was told.

Frank and her mother were standing in her doorway. Water dripped from his hair and his shoulders. He held a gun to her mother's head, smiling. She gave a little wave.

"Hi, Honey."

"Are you okay?"

"I'm fine."

Frank lowered the cell phone and pushed Claire ahead of him until they were inside.

"Frank, really. She's eighty-something years old."

"Gina!"

"Like I said, I was hoping for you." He looked at Blake who was still standing by the phone. "Step away from the phone. Everyone, sit on the couch."

"I'm sorry, honey, he got me before I could get the flowers."

"That's okay, Mom."

Frank waved his gun at Gina again.

"Before you sit down, give me your gun. I know you always carry it." Gina obeyed.

The three of them were now lined up on the couch.

"So how's the flower show going?"

Gina didn't answer.

"Oh, I know all about that. I grabbed all your stuff off the table a few weeks ago. I knew I could find you there if this didn't work out."

Frank swept the room with his eyes and saw the arrangement. "Is that it? It looks pretty. Fairy Tales, right?"

She nodded.

"Nice."

"Frank, what do you want?"

His face soured. Blake saw it too and took Gina's hand.

"I want you to come with me, but I'm still working on what to do with them," he waved his gun at Blake and Claire. "Can't take everyone with us. My car's not big enough."

A scratching noise came from down the hall. They all heard it.

"What was that?" asked Frank. "Is someone back there?"

"My daughter's room. She must be playing."

"Oh yeah, the daughter. You know I have a daughter, but she hates me because of what you did. You can't imagine what it's like for your own child to want to run when they see you."

"It's your fault," said Gina. Blake pinched her.

"No it's not. It's your fault. If you hadn't kept talking to my wife, she never would have filed charges.

"You nearly killed her, Frank. Don't you think you should be held responsible for that?"

"Don't worry, I've taken care of her."

Gina knew about the fire, and wondered what else Frank was thinking. There were more sounds from the bedroom.

"What's she doing?"

"Don't worry, she won't come out here. She's supposed to be in bed. She's probably just playing. She won't come out."

Evidently, Frank believed her. He walked nervously around the room, taking in the furniture and pictures on the walls. He was taking his time.

When Gina was sure Frank wasn't looking, she mouthed to Blake 'Sargent'. Blake nodded. The dog must have followed her into Sammy's bedroom when she went to put her back to bed.

"What did Gina do to you, Frank, that you didn't do to yourself?" her mother asked.

"Well, Mrs. Sessions, basically, she ruined my life. Just like my wife. If it weren't for women, I would have been a great man."

Gina held her breath. She warned her mother with her eyes.

"That's ridiculous," said Claire. Gina's head dropped.

"You need to take responsibility for your own actions, Frank."

Frank's goofy smile disappeared.

"Gina said she was trying to protect your wife and daughter."

"They didn't need protecting," he shouted. "They put me in prison. I did not belong there. I'm not a criminal. And those people in there, they are animals. They beat me and stole from me. And she put me there. You told my wife what to say on that stand. Those were lies. I did not do those things. I just hit her a few times. I was doing the best I could."

Gina wanted to yell, "and you gambled all her money away and then sold everything she had and you burned your wife and daughter for fun," but she didn't.

Frank waved his gun and stomped in front of them.

"Give me your phones," he barked, then closed all the drapes. He sat down across from them.

"Okay, now, here's what we're going to do. It's getting late," then he laughed, "I really didn't think I could pull this off, but hey, look at me."

"Congratulations," said Claire.

The scratching got louder.

"Are you sure your daughter's asleep? Maybe we should bring her out here?"

"Yes, maybe we should," said Blake.

"Blake!" Gina said, but he avoided her stare. "Or let me go check on her?"

"How old is she?"

"Four."

He relaxed. "Cute. I remember my daughter at that age. Really sweet. Not a mean bone in her body."

Blake attempted a smile. He took Gina's hand and squeezed it. She suddenly understood.

The scratching was more frequent now.

"That's really annoying," said Frank.

"Are we going to sit here all night? I'd really like to finish my arrangement," said Gina.

"And my rolls," said Claire. "I'm making rolls."

The sound of clay pots crashing came from the patio and the windows rattled in their frames. Frank hurried back to the doors and looked out. They could all hear that it was sleeting outside, and sleeting hard by the sound of the ice hitting the glass.

"Great," said Frank.

"Do you mind if I turn up the heat?" Blake said.

Frank didn't answer.

"I gotta get you out of here but what to do with the others. Think! Think!"

"It's bad out there, Frank. It's too icy to go anywhere," said Gina. "And if you take me, you know how cops feel about other cops. They're going to go ballistic. You don't want that coming down on you."

"Shut up, Gina. I told you, I'm not going back to prison. I can't."

"Frank, listen to me, you're not a bad guy. You've just got a bad temper and there's medicine for that. I'm sure we can get you some help. Even if you did go back to prison, they'd put you in the hospital part."

"Gee, thanks, Gina. Help me go back to prison. Again. No thanks."

Frank paced back and forth in front of them. He pointed the gun at Blake who raised his hands.

"What are you doing?" asked Frank.

"I don't know. You're the one with the gun."

"I thought you were going to turn up the heat. It's freezing in here."

Blake edged around the gun and headed for Sammy's room.

"Hey! Where are you going?"

"I'm going to go turn up the heat."

"I'm looking at a controller right there." Frank pointed the gun toward the small box across the room.

"That one's broken. There's another one back here that works better."

"Really?" Frank walked the few feet to the box on the wall. "This looks fine to me." He adjusted it and everyone heard the furnace crank on. "Working. Now sit back down."

Blake went back to the couch. Gina's mind raced. How could she get word to the police? How could she get the gun from Frank? Surely, she could do that. She was afraid for her mother and Sammy in the other room. Sarge's scratching continued. Claire suddenly clutched her chest.

"What's wrong, Mom?"

"I don't know. I think I'm having a heart attack."

Gina and Blake jumped up and gently lowered her on the couch.

"Where's your medicine? Take it easy, Mom. You'll be alright. Let's get your feet up." She looked into her mother's eyes and she winked. Gina turned around.

"She needs a doctor, Frank!"

The gun was down. "What's wrong with her? Just get her some water or something."

"Blake, go get the aspirin. Frank, I need to call 911!"

He shook his head. "Nobody goes anywhere. Maybe it's just acid reflux or something."

Gina rolled her eyes.

"Frank, what would you do if your mother was having a heart attack? Wouldn't you call a doctor?"

"No, I definitely would not. She ruined my life, too."

"Oh, for Heaven's sake, Frank!" said Claire.

Gina covered her mother's mouth with the wet cloth Blake had brought her from the kitchen. She told her to be quiet with her eyes.

"Okay, Mom. Just try to stay calm. I'm sure Frank is going to do the right thing. Aren't you, Frank?"

Frank began pacing.

"This is getting too complicated. I can't think. We need to leave. Gina, tie up your mother and Blake. Use that drapery cord. We're getting out of here."

"She needs a doctor. If she dies, Frank, it will be all your fault."

"We're all going to die someday. I don't want to be here anymore. So chop chop."

Sleet was slamming against the windows now. She got the drapery cords and started wrapping Blake's wrists.

"And do it tight. I'm going to check."

Gina knew she had to get Sargent out. Or somehow get Franks's gun. This was going to end here. She was not going to leave with him.

"Gina," Blake said, "it's not very tight."

"What?"

"The drapery cord. It's not working. It's too thin. You need to do what he says. He's not going to hurt us. We'll be fine."

Gina was confused. Then she remembered.

"This cord isn't working, Frank. If you want me to tie it tight, I need to go get the rope out of my daughter's room." Gina started down the hall.

"Get back here," said Frank. "We'll all go together. Except for her." He waved the gun in Claire's direction who was still lying motionless on the couch.

Gina's heart was pounding. Blake went first, then her, then Frank. She could feel him following close behind her. Sargent's scratching started and stopped and she prayed he'd be quiet for just a few minutes, until they got there and could open the door. She didn't know what was going to happen. There was no plan at all. What if Sargent did nothing? What if he lunged after Frank and the gun went off? What if Sammy was standing there? They were getting closer and closer. She didn't know what she was going to do, except that she would do whatever it took to protect her daughter. Gina's heart was pounding. He was right behind her. Blake let go of her hand and reached for the door. Sargent was miraculously silent.

CHAPTER 29

There was a loud crash and the condo went completely black.

"Hey," said Frank, "what's going on?"

Gina heard Blake open Sammy's door.

"Sargent!"

"Turn the light on," yelled Frank angrily. Then Gina felt herself being pushed from behind and she went flying into Sammy's room, falling on the floor. The dog started barking ferociously, she'd never heard the sounds he was making. The door slammed behind her and she crawled as fast as she could to Sammy's bed.

"Gina!" Blake shouted.

The gun fired.

"Mommy?"

"Shoosh, shoosh," Gina said, pulling her child off the bed and covering her with her body. "It's okay. Stay still, Sammy."

The same instant Gina had been pushed into the room, Sargent had leapt out. Frank had screamed and then the gun fired. She heard bodies slamming against the walls and the door. Frank yelled. The gun went off again and then she could hear Blake grunting as both bodies hit the wall again. Sargent was barking with sharp rapid yelps that hurt her ears. Sammy started to cry.

"Stay here, Sammy. Do not move!"

"What's wrong with Sargent? Where's Daddy?"

They were still fighting. Sargent was barking and both men were grunting and pushing. She couldn't tell who was who.

She crawled with Sammy under her farther away from the sounds. "It's okay. I'm going to hold you, baby." She tried turning on the bedside lamp but it was dead. Sammy's nightlight was out as well. The room was pitch black. Only the glitter of the hail could be seen on the windows.

There was another gun shot.

Claire screamed.

"Mom!" Gina cried. A beam of light had appeared around the corner, then suddenly gone out.

"Mom?" Gina cried again, crawling toward the noises.

Sargent was no longer barking.

"I'm okay," her mother said from somewhere in the hall.

"Sargent." It was Blake's voice.

"Blake?" Gina whispered, her heart pounding.

"I'm okay, too," he answered. She could tell by the way he was breathing there was something else, something wrong.

"Is everyone alright?" her mother called. Gina could tell she was on the floor, too.

"Frank?"

There was no answer.

Suddenly, the beam of light came back on. Her mother had brought a flashlight and was shining it at the men's bodies.

Still on all fours, Gina crawled toward Blake. Frank was slowly moving. He moaned.

"Owww," he said, his voice filled with pain. "That dog bit my arm and my leg really bad, I can't move, I think I hurt my back..."

Gina punched his face as hard as she could and Frank was quiet. She saw the glint of the gun by the door and quickly put it in her back waistband.

"Blake? Are you hurt?" Gina pleaded.

He was slouched against the wall. She ran her hands over his head and shoulders. She didn't feel any blood and he didn't flinch. Her hands travelled down his arms to his hands which were buried in Sarge's thick fur. He wasn't moving.

"He's hurt," said Blake.

"Sargent," said Gina. She rubbed the limp head, then his back. Her hand felt the warm thickness and knew it was blood.

"He's been shot," Blake's voice quivered.

"Did you get hit?"

"Just a punch in the face with the gun."

They held the dog as Sargent's breathing slowed, then stopped.

"Mommy? Daddy?" Sammy was still in the bed.

"It's okay, Sammy. We're here. Get in the bed and stay right there until I can get some candles."

"Okay."

Claire was still on the floor. Gina hurried to her.

"Some heart attack," said Gina, trying to help her mother up.

"Owww," Claire cried out when she tried to use a leg. "I think I got shot?" she said incredulously.

Gina grabbed the flashlight and shone it on her leg. Bright red blood covered her calf. Gina quickly tore off a piece of a sheet and wrapped it tightly around her calf.

She helped her back to the couch then went to Blake, who was still cradling Sarge. Silently, Blake carried him to the kitchen and placed him on a bed of towels, then together they dragged the still unconscious Frank into the den and put him in cuffs.

Gina shone the flashlight on her mother's face.

"I'd say that was an adventure," she said, squinting into the light.

Thank goodness their landline still worked. Gina called the cops, then cuffed Frank to the handle on the oven in the kitchen where several candles burned to wait for the police. Blake built a fire in the fireplace and Gina got out every blanket she could find. Even without the phone tree, she knew there would be no flower show.

Blake found their battery operated radio and they listened to the National Weather Service. A meteorologist was saying, 'this certainly ranks among the most significant winter events we've ever documented, based on the temperatures we're seeing and for the amounts of sleet and snow, particularly off to the northwest of Fort Worth.' It was not expected to get better until after the weekend.

Gina went out on the patio and watched the street below. It was deadly quiet except for a slow-moving pair of headlights that crept along beneath her. In a few minutes, the lights from an ambulance and a couple of police cars with tire chains pulled in front of the condo. A few minutes later, they were at her door.

The Captain, himself, showed up. Frank was bound tightly on a stretcher. They'd wrapped his wounds and as soon as he regained consciousness, he started yelling. Another pair of medics took care of Claire and Blake. She needed to go the hospital and Gina promised to follow soon. With the ice outside, it wasn't going to be easy.

Gina and Blake sat at the kitchen table answering questions. Since Gina was a cop, it went quickly, but without the sounds of Sargent licking or panting, or the weight of his paws covering her feet, the atmosphere was tragic.

Blake had wrapped Sargent's body in a blanket and then a waterproof sheet. With tender arms, he settled him on the porch. They would wait until morning to decide what to do.

They set up their mattresses in front of the fire where it was warm and only the excitement and drama of the last few hours could explain why they were able to sleep. When they woke, Blake built up the fire again. With Sammy between them, they told her that Sargent had been hurt badly and in too many words, he'd died saving them. He was a hero. Sammy only had one question.

"Is Sargent in heaven?"

"I think so," said Gina, "because we're all going to be so happy in Heaven and that makes me very happy to think that he's there."

Sammy nodded.

"You know, Sargent was having a rough time lately. His joints were always sore and he couldn't see very well," said Gina. "He's probably running around and playing like a puppy. And he gave his life for Daddy."

"Like Jesus. He died for us."

Gina brushed away a tear. "Yes, like Jesus. He died for us."

"I think we should have a funeral," said Sammy.

"That's a great idea, Sammy. A nice funeral and a proper reception."

Blake agreed. "The porch is like a freezer. And we can't get anywhere for a couple of days."

"What do you think, Sammy? Should we have a funeral for Sargent?"

She looked happy for a child who'd just lost her best friend.

They found more candles and arranged them on the dining room table. Blake put on his Hawaiian shirt, the one he wore when he took Sargent to the park. Gina wrote down a few thoughts and found leftover frappe and Halloween candy to serve for the party afterwards.

Sargent was covered with a dusting of snow. Using most of what was left of her flowers, Gina made a blanket over the coffin-like figure, then placed her flower house arrangement on a table by the fireplace. Though it was winter outside, it felt like spring inside.

CHAPTER 30

Claire's injury was minor. She spent two days in the hospital, then moved to The Village where they had excellent physical therapists on staff.

It didn't take long for Andrew to find her there. He became a regular visitor and soon there was talk of him possibly moving there, too. The possibility thrilled SueBee and Charlotte and the dining room became a popular place to hear the latest news of Claire's recovery. When Sammy came to visit her grandmother, there was even a crowd.

Soon the December days returned to a reliable chill because of the clear skies and sunshine and life was able to return to normal. The family still missed Sarge and they often stopped at odd moments to sigh or brush away a tear.

A week after Gina had returned to work, Blake arrived at Gina's office, unannounced.

"Can you go to lunch?"

"What are you doing here?"

"I can't take my wife to lunch? I just thought we should do this more often. So come on."

"Where are we going?"

"You'll see."

Blake drove and soon they were in her mother's old neighborhood. Gina watched curiously out the window, waiting for a clue.

Blake pulled up to the little cottage that had been her mother's house. There was a sold sign in the front yard.

"That's weird," said Gina.

She looked at Blake. He was watching her, waiting.

"What?"

He reached into his pocket and pulled out a set of keys.

"You're home."

Chills ran through her body.

"I drove by a few weeks ago and saw a For Sale in the yard. Turned out the people that bought it from your mother were transferred again. So I told them all about our family and they agreed to let us do a lease purchase. So it's ours, Gina. We're home."

About The Author

The author both writes and directs her family from her home in Dallas, Texas. There are several more books in the making, beyond the subject of gardening and flower shows, but always about faith, family and friendship because those are the things that inspire her.

Please feel free to contact her at diane-burns@att.net.

Made in the USA
Charleston, SC
08 January 2017